NO DRESS REHEARSAL

No Dress Rehearsal

Ken Newport

OTTAWA PRESS AND PUBLISHING

ottawapressandpublishing.com

Copyright © Ken Newport 2019

ISBN (pbk.) 978-1-988437-31-6
ISBN (EPUB) 978-1-988437-33-0
ISBN (MOBI) 978-1-988437-32-3

Design and composition:
Magdalene Carson at New Leaf Publication Design

This is a work of fiction. All of the characters, names, incidents, organizations,
and dialogue in this novel are either products of the author's imagination or are
used fictitiously.

I dedicate this book to family.
To my late parents, Chris and Fred,
who gave me roots and wings.
To my wife and boys,Christine, Matt and Nick,
who simultaneously keep me grounded
and encourage me to fly.

NO DRESS REHEARSAL

Prologue

AM radio was only bad in hindsight. At the time it was all we had and we loved it. Every town in Canada had their own top forty station that spoon fed the mushy hits of the day. Montreal had CKGM, Toronto had CHUM and in Ottawa we had CFRA.

We loved CFRA's ridiculously short playlist because it meant that our new favourite song would be on soon. We adored the disc jockeys with their high energy, bombastic voices, almost as much as the artists that they played. We loved tuning in on Sunday night to listen to Casey Kasem count down the week's Top 40. It was all so cool. Right until the moment that it wasn't.

I may have only been thirteen in 1978, but my musical taste was pretty mature. I loved many bands that had been with me since birth, including The Beatles, The Stones and The Who. I also loved seventies bands like Steely Dan, The Eagles and Queen. The problem was that my music wasn't being played on CFRA. Disco was king in 1978 and the first half of the year, radio play was dominated by the dreadful soundtrack of Saturday Night Fever, including musical affronts like "Stayin' Alive" and "Jive Talkin'". The Saturday Night Fever album and the summer of 1978 ruined AM radio for me and I found myself turning off my radio for the first time in my life.

I felt like a musical outcast, but still saved my paper route money for the occasional album purchase down at Treble Clef Records. During my first week of high school I heard some older kids talking about a new Springsteen album and so that Saturday afternoon I found myself at the cash register holding my copy of *Darkness on the Edge of Town*. The bearded giant behind the counter smiled and commented on my timing because "Bad-lands" from that album was playing on the radio station blast-ing in the store. The radio was playing Springsteen? What?

"It's CHEZ," offered the giant. I returned a blank stare. "CHEZ 106 FM." Until that moment I thought that FM was reserved for Bach and Beethoven but I learned that the owner of my beloved Treble Clef Records had recently started his own station playing music that AM stations wouldn't play. It was my salvation and, over the years, CHEZ would become a close friend.

I became devoted to the station in that manner that only young teenagers can comprehend. I talked about CHEZ non-stop. I listened as much as possible even keeping the radio qui-etly on in my bed for the overnight shows, and I collected every promotional item that I could find. I amassed a collection of posters, bumper-stickers and t-shirts and even created my own, now famous, CHEZ message board.

With a little help from Dad, I converted a four-by-three-foot wooden picture frame into a gaudy CHEZ promo message board. We placed a two-foot chalkboard in the middle of two cedar wood slabs and snuggly bound those into the picture frame. I then sacrificed a couple of posters to come up with a message across the top that said "Ottawa's Home of Classic Rock" and "CHEZ 106" across the bottom. The messages and logos got a coating of shellac and the art project was complete.

One would expect that the message board would have hit the trash bin before I finished high school, but this board has been my prized possession since the day it was made. I am unequivo-cally a non-believer in anything mystical, so I guess that I will call it a series of weird coincidences, but that homemade, tat-tered board has played a role in some life-changing events for me and many others.

In the era before cell phones and texting it was quite literally how I got my messages. The board hung on the outside of my bedroom door and would be where my mom would leave mes-sages like, "Your father and I are out for dinner. Leftovers in the fridge for you." It would also be the site of profound messages like the one that my emotionally stunted father wrote the day that I was moving away to university: "I am so proud, I am so happy, I am so sad."

The fame of my message board grew in university residence where it was adopted by my floormates as the place to post messages about important things like where the party was or where you could buy weed. The board followed me into a string of dingy student apartments, but always claimed a place of prominence and seemed to be the place that life events were noted. In my final year of school, the board was the place where my girlfriend (now wife) told me that she loved me for the first time. Years later, when the board hung in the garage of our starter home, she told me that we were going to have a baby by writing out "I think that it's going to be a boy" in blue. She was right.

Dad and I made that board thirty years ago and it really doesn't look like much these days. The CHEZ logo is barely visible and the wood has cracked in a couple of places, but I still love it. It has the prime location in my coffee shop and is the home of a little music game that we play every morning. I know that for many customers the game brings them a little pleasure and is one of the reasons that they are so loyal. I also know that the board is strangely important and that for a few lost souls the board will work its magic and play a role at a big moment of their lives.

Part One

Life is what happens to you while
you're busy making other plans . . .

Lee

What an asshole! I clean the office of this hotshot, banking executive. I rarely see him, but on the late nights when he is working, he treats me like I am invisible for fear that he might make eye contact with the lowly cleaner. Tonight was different—he came off the elevator with a woman at least fifteen years younger than him and they clawed each other all the way down the hallway. I was frozen behind his desk with a bulging garbage can in my hand when they noticed me. She didn't give a shit that I was there, but did I ever freak him out. He saw me and snapped into this whole act of showing her his office and getting the papers that he promised her as if I was his wife's bridge partner. He didn't speak to me but spoke to her about me and I'm pretty sure that he thinks that I don't speak English. Like fuck, dude, we were in the same ECON101 class back in Ottawa and I might be the only person in Toronto who knows what an uptight dweeb you are at heart.

Every Asian girl is supposed to get straight As and be quiet and proper. Maybe if you just got here from a Vietnamese field or a hovel in Bangkok that makes sense, but if your family has been here for fifty years and you grew up in suburban Ottawa watching music videos and smoking weed, then that image doesn't work. If my eyes and tits were a little rounder I would have been a perfectly normal, average student getting in an average amount of trouble, but because I look like this I was the shocking screw-up.

When the Grade 9 teacher first took the class attendance, he read a name and then searched out over the field of heads to see who would pop up to be identified:

"Here."

"Present."

"Yo."

"Pardon me young man?"

"I mean present, sir."

When it was my turn, he walked over to me and read, "Li-wee...La way.... Well that is a tough one. I am going to call you Lee—welcome to Canada."

I now have so many things that I wish I had said to that prick, but at the time I was fourteen and looked like a nine-year-old boy, so I said nothing.

People think that there is something special about teaching and that we should all have great respect for teachers, but truthfully, they are chumps. Almost all of them started to teach because they couldn't think of anything else to do. Honourable profession, my ass. Maybe if you are the hotshot professor at a big university, but in all of my education, including the one and a half terms of university, I have only met teachers who can't make it in the real world and need the job.

Most teachers don't even try the real world—they start teaching as soon as they finish school themselves. This chickenshit mentality comes from their wish to stay in the one environment where they find a little comfort in their frightened existence. Sometimes it comes from a complete lack of creativity.

"What would you like to do after graduation?"

"I don't know, can't I just stay here?"

I wouldn't mind so much if they would just take their place with the other meeks waiting for their inheritance, but they have to pile on the righteousness crap to create a mirage of self-importance. "We teach because we love children."

Teachers hate children and spend most of the day trying to defend against that enemy class. Sure, there a couple of kids that they can actually teach something to and feel good about themselves, but most of their days are spent worrying about the three or four little bastards that would be on higher doses of Ritalin if their damn parents would just listen. Every day is: "Three more hours. Two more hours. Just one more hour, and I will be home to my socially acceptable chardonnay."

"I could have been in business instead of teaching, but I'm just not into cutting throats for money. I could never bring myself to work for big business." No wonder every eighteen-year-old starts with the ridiculous idea that they should vote NDP.

When it comes to money, teachers split into two categories. There are those who have engaged in some form of self-hypnosis to delude their fear of failure into a nobility of not trying. These bean sprouters have convinced themselves that there is no happiness in money and that all they need to enjoy life is a great novel and a big cup of tea. See you at the bake sale, loser. The second group is the more energetic but clueless group, with teachers who sing the virtues of their short workdays and summers off so that they can have a second job or a business on the side. This group—predominantly phys-ed teachers—hasn't figured out that running their own basement renovation business isn't the key to happiness.

If the basement renovation business isn't run by a phys-ed teacher, it is probably run by a firefighter who inexplicably has found a reason to take his shirt off. Did you know that Cosmo reports that since the post 9/11 fuck-a-firefighter fad, the average no-neck, new recruit on the force joined because he lacks the brains to get laid without the uniform? Cosmo says the fireman fantasy is over. And I agree.

They all make the same money—firefighters, teachers, sanitation workers, bus drivers, tax collectors.... I like sanitation workers more than all of the others—at least they don't pretend that they have important jobs.

All of that is to say that everyone calls me Lee because I didn't stand up to that jerk-off, Grade 9 teacher. I guess it sounds less chinky than LeihWei.

By the time the big boss man and I got to ECON101, I had figured out how to survive in the system, but surviving was all that it was. I was way under everyone's radar. My parents decided that my two younger brothers must be the smart ones, so they got all the pressure of expectations heaped on them while I was permitted to cruise along. I wasn't popular, but had enough friends to make it tolerable. I learned to listen on the day that my teachers discussed what would be on the exam, so I was able to pull off solid Bs.

That was good enough to get into the decidedly mediocre B. Comm. program at Carleton University, which seemed like some kind of natural progression from an aimless high school career. Maybe I would have gotten something out of university if I had stayed long enough, but I was too cynical to see any benefit at the time. On the other hand, maybe it truly was all bullshit and I was right to get out when I did.

Nothing really grabbed my attention, which suited me just fine because I could keep cruising. And since I didn't know where I was going, I wasn't in a big hurry to get there. Little did I know that when I did get here I would have to save face for an ECON101 classmate by quickly dumping the trash can, giving a little Asian bow, and wheeling my cart past him and down the hall as if I saw nothing at all.

Terry

There is a ridiculously easy trick that accounts for the success of this place. I can't believe that so few business owners have figured this out, but I know that most of them would laugh at me if they heard this explanation—this business is a success because my staff love working here. There must be whole book-store sections of "how to" books that tell people how to whip staff into high performance and how to squeeze out the last few drops of blood and dignity from employees to maximize profit. But I am lucky enough to have never read any of those books. My job is to make my employees happy—they take care of the rest. When my staff is happy, it somehow makes my customers happy. When my customers are happy, they come back and that makes my staff happy. Every time this cycle turns, a little bell goes off that means that I just made another thousand bucks.

Now you can't be stupid about this and confuse money with happiness. I can't pay a soup cook or a barista forty bucks an hour. They know that and don't expect it. I can, however, pay them a little more than Starbucks and give them a little more dignity than Tim Hortons. The trick is to find out what button needs to be pushed to make someone happy. There is no short-cut for this because each person has unique buttons, so you have to take an active interest in each staff member. I suspect that most business types wouldn't want to do that or that they would put on rubber gloves before actually interacting with the "great unwashed."

Cory was working for a coffee shop a block away and hated it because he had to wear a uniform and listen to a soft-rock station. He loved everything else about the job and was great with customers. When he joined us at Beanfest, he didn't have to wear a uniform and I gave him the additional responsibility of programming all of the music each day. He went crazy with that role and he profiles all kinds of classics plus lesser-known bands, indie artists, and local acts. The customers love hearing the variety! A few weeks ago, a local music reporter wrote a piece about our shop as the place that has the pulse of the local music scene and profiled Cory as the maestro. The kid was on top of the world and now I am convinced that he will be making espresso for the rest of his life.

Cory is also responsible for running our trademark daily contest. Every morning, either Cory or I will put a string of lyrics from a popular song on the message board by the entrance and invite customers to attempt to identify what song the lyrics are from. Some people get them immediately and others will come back at lunch to tell us that they got it. Obviously they could search the web for the song but that would kill the fun and there is no prize for knowing, other than pride. It's a silly little game, but it is one of those little things that make Beanfest a happy place to come to and leads people to us instead of our gloomy competitors.

Our goal with the lyrics is to make the clue familiar so that you will have some recognition, but not enough to make it obvious. We want people to feel like they could have identified the song when they didn't, and feel pretty smart when they are successful. I have watched customers come into the shop looking worn down and beaten, and leave smiling and self-contented simply because they solved the lyric riddle.

The game also demonstrates the nearly universal love of music. Music has always been in my life, although I lack any musical talent. My family is not musical, but I grew up on a steady diet of big band sounds that my mother would play as she worked around the house. I went through all the musical phases growing up and developed a love of all musical genres. I thought that my musical diversity was rare.

When we play our lyrics game, I find that I am not such a rarity and that almost all of our customers have a wide-ranging musical appreciation. We find twenty-year-olds who are die-hard Beatles fans, and fifty-year-olds who listen to Kanye West. It seems that while everyone may have a favourite type of music, most people will find something good in any type of music.

We also find that music has an unrivalled connection to memories. Like this past Friday, we had a tricky lyric posted: "Love can mend your life, but love can break your heart."

It is from a well-known song but the lyrics are clipped from the middle of the song, which makes them much harder to identify than if they were from the beginning of the song. The morning had passed by without a single customer identifying the lyrics, but at the beginning of the lunch rush, one of our semi regulars checked the board and yelled out the song's next line: "'I'll send an SOS to the world.' Those lyrics are from 'Message in a Bottle' by The Police," and he continued to tell no one in particular the story of him and two buddies going to see The Police on August 23rd—and he made a point of that—August 23, 1981, for the Police Picnic at the Grove in Oakville.

"I can't believe that it happened," he said. "It was one of the best days of my life. It was so long ago, but I remember everything. We were the first ones to arrive and got a place by the stage. We saw Oingo Boingo, Iggy Pop..." and he lists all these other bands, then says, "The Police were at their best! It was so raw, energetic, awesome."

Cory was amazed and said, "I can't believe that you remember the exact date dude."

"I can never forget it—God, what a day! Right before Sting and the boys took the stage I met this incredible woman at the concession stands. We danced to 'Message in a Bottle,' and last Tuesday, that girl and I celebrated our twenty-third wedding anniversary, so you can bet that I remember the concert date."

Not only did the Police Picnic guy leave feeling great, but everyone else in the shop got a lift just from sharing in his lyric-inspired memory. This kind of stuff never happens at Tim Hortons.

Grant

I would love a cappuccino this morning—please have no line up. Great—no one there—let's make this quick. This place is so weird and the staff must spike their own coffee with happy pills. What the hell can they be happy about? Getting up at five to come in and schlep coffee for minimum wage—some life!

"Good morning. Large, low-fat cappuccino right?" Big deal, you remember my order, sparky. That doesn't get you into Mensa. I just nod while checking my phone. "Would you like a blueberry muffin to go with your crackberry?"

Maybe it's the music that messes these people up—they're cranking out "No Woman No Cry" this morning—a little early for Marley and a reefer isn't it?

It's almost 7:30 and Caffrey will arrive in ten minutes, so I better move my ass. He still thinks that I am in the office before dawn, so it's key to look fully engaged by the time he walks by me. "Ev'rything's gonna be alright, Ev'rything's gonna be alright—shit, get Marley out of your head. That old bastard Caffrey should just retire and enjoy his money. I swear if he doesn't clear out of my way by Christmas, I am out of here. Remember that guy from the conference in Chicago said he would love to have you on his team. Chicago would be awesome.

Remember to return Dad's call from last night. He'll be fishing until noon, so call him at lunch. He watches the mutual funds in his RRSP like a day trader and his calls to me are almost always about his portfolio. When Lehman Brothers and the other big boys caused the market crisis in the fall of 2008, all investors lost a chunk of their assets but only I have a father who blames me for not seeing it coming and warning my dear old Dad. It's been almost a year since the crash and the markets have gained back almost as much as they lost, but Dad got spooked and so now he looks like a squirrel guarding his last nut. I keep telling him that while I may be a bank vice president, I am not an analyst or a trader. I have tried to explain that I am not a nickel-and-dime retail broker—I do deals. Well, not lately—but I am supposed to do deals.

Deals—let's go—we've got an offering memo drafting meeting this morning and the clients will be here soon. Time to find a dress for this pig. How are we going to spin this into the market? Argon Biotech—when these guys thought that they had cancer's silver bullet, they were so cocky that they wouldn't even consider doing a deal. Now they have one mixed-message clinical result and they want to cut and run. It is a very familiar story for these discovery companies—they have a smart hypothesis, which is supported in the lab, so they raise the money and take it into animal studies and eureka, they can help a cancerous mouse. The huge extrapolation error happens right here when they assume that if they can cure mice they can cure humans. Every group that I have ever met can cure cancer in mice, but can't add a single additional day of misery and suffering to a human cancer patient's life.

It doesn't really matter all that much to me because cancer will always sell. People are so afraid of it and have such an emotional connection to cancer that these deals always get picked up. When we sold Avimed to Bristol Myers, I ended the closing dinner party for the deal at the bar with the fat guy who led negotiations for Bristol. Over scotches and cigars, this guy was choking up as he told me that his momma died of lung cancer ten years ago and that he had to do this deal out of respect for her.

He said, "I think that we both know that I may have paid a premium for this deal, but I knew that it was a small price to

pay for a shot at curing this thing." Whatever it takes buddy—
I am just glad you did the deal, big boy. Now just finish that
cigar—out of respect for your momma's lung cancer.

"Mr. Woodyear—Argon is here."

. "I am on my way."

Well—not quite yet. I will let them settle in and let all of the
junior staff take their seats before I go in. The meeting starts
the second I walk in and if I go in early, it's too awkward. They
all have to recognize how busy I am and that I can't waste three
minutes talking about the weather and last night's game.

I check out the videos on TSN's website to kill a few minutes. All right—now it's time—let's go.

Grant

I have to say that I am still a little freaked out about a very close call that I had a few nights ago with a lawyer from the Apoptocom team.

We closed the Apoptocom deal a couple of weeks ago and so our grateful client hosted the closing dinner celebration for everyone who worked on the offering. These self-congratulatory events are part of the crap that I have to put up with as a player in this industry. Things started off pretty normally as I gave my patented bullshit speech about this being the most inspiring story and most dedicated and knowledgeable team that we have ever had the pleasure of serving. The truth is that Apoptocom is going to crash and burn within two years and no one on that team can see it coming.

Dr. Karl Kalinsky was a brilliant university researcher who made some important discoveries around programmed cell death that impressed some venture capital scouts attending the American Society of Clinical Oncology meeting that he presented at in Chicago in 2004. They quickly convinced him that he could build his discovery into a business, and with an initial investment of $2 million, Apoptocom was born and Kalinsky was the CEO leaving behind his university position.

Kalinsky may be a brilliant scientist, but it turns out that this guy has never been out of his lab and had rarely interacted with anyone other than his mice or lab techs. Four months into the CEO role and he was being asked to interact with bankers, lawyers, and various other navy suits. Most importantly, he

was charged with dealing with more potential investors to raise
Apoptocom's next round of money. Remember, biotechs never
earn money, they just spend it. Before they even scratched the
surface of the $2 million investment, Apoptocom had to turn
its attention to where the next round of money was coming
from. Kalinsky hated every moment out of his lab and it was
obvious to all of the potential investors who rejected him. He
was out of his depth in the boardroom.

The original VC decides that Kalinsky needs to focus on his
core strength (ya think?) and they move him into the ever so
prestigious title of Chief Scientific Officer. CSO is code for "put
out to pasture." That was when they brought in Philip Baron to
be the new CEO and here we are in 2009 with Philip as the shin-
ing star. Philip is referred to as a "professional CEO" because
he has done all of this many times before. It has always seemed
appropriate to me that prostitutes are also referred to as "professionals" for the same reason. Baron is a cartoon character—his
suit is perfect, his hair is perfect, his smile is a little too big, and
he speaks in that loud and rhythmic tone reserved for CEOs and
preachers. This is the fourth biotech that he has led and he was
considered a big catch for Apoptocom. Baron is well connected
with financiers and knows how to speak their language, so he
has had success raising funds.

He has also been viewed as a success in all three exits from
his previous gigs. In two, he managed to sell the small biotechs
to big pharma—he lost his job both times, but always with full
vesting of his stock options and a sizeable termination package. The third company raised a huge private round of financing and the new California investor group moved the company
and the CEO job to San Diego. Baron was again out of a job, but
again was left with vested options and a generous termination
package to ease his pain. He has made millions over these three
plays and no one seems to have noticed that not a single product has reached market from any of these entities and, in fact,
most of the science has long since died.

Baron's real skill is acting and he was at his best the other night,
starring in the role of gracious host and modest team leader.

"Tonight is a night for celebrating all that we have and will accomplish for the benefit of those battling cancer. I am honoured to play a small role in leading this team of scientific superstars to great things. I am further honoured to have had such a dynamic team of professionals leading us through this transaction. Lawyers, accountants and bankers rarely get credit, but in a few years, when Apoptocom is treating cancer patients, I hope that you will all remember your role in bringing benefit to those battling this horrendous disease."

If you didn't know his history, you could almost find him inspiring. I know that he'll be cashed out and gone by the time the rest of the world figures out that the only cancer that Apoptocom is going to cure is mouse cancer.

The night seemed like it was going to follow the same pattern as most of these events—excessive champagne reception, raucous meal peppered with a handful of puffed up speeches—but I picked up a weird vibe from the lead counsellor of the New York law firm that we worked with on the deal. My staff hated her and I had heard them talking about her as an ice beast after one of their technical document drafting sessions. I only saw her working twice when I was forced to join a couple of meetings to work out the "business points" of the deal that the lawyers had decided were not "legal points" and therefore required something more than their exclusively legal brains. Business points are usually common-sense decisions that are obvious to everyone, but the lawyers need to cover their own asses so they refuse to make such decisions.

During one meeting that was painfully too long, I remember letting my mind drift into the ice beast's underwear. A tiny swatch of a black lace bra was visible under the counsellor's perfectly professional and lawyerly two-piece suit. A lace bra showed more creativity than one would expect from the surface and I allowed my imagination to see the matching lace thong and some velvety smooth hips. "Quite provocative counsellor—what do you have in mind?" I felt my heart race as she leaned back and closed her eyes, her hand disappearing into those black lace panties.

I blinked out of my daydream and quickly scanned the table to see if anyone had noticed that my face had flushed.

Her name is Kate and she joined a group of us drinking champagne early in the reception and asked if she could have a private conversation with me later in the evening. It seemed like the kind of thing that a workaholic attorney would want to do during a night of fun so it was not a remarkable request to anyone else, but I sensed—or imagined—something unusual. She had a sparkle in her eye that I read as something more interesting than a legal question.

I spent all night at a table with my client's team and didn't talk to Kate the entire time. Things began to break up around eleven, and a group was forming to hit a jazz club a few blocks away. I declined that crowd and made gestures to head home, but my mind was on Kate. She caught my eye and motioned me to come over to her table, where she looked trapped in a conversation. As I approached, I heard her break off the conversation saying that she needs to bounce something off Woodyear before he bails out for the evening. She waved me to the bar and ordered two single malt scotches, which only heightened my interest.

Once she was certain that all of our colleagues had left, she laid it on the line in a way that I could never imagine having the courage to even consider.

"Grant—I just work. I have no friends, no romantic life and no sex. I don't want you to be my friend or start up a relationship with you, but I do want to have sex with you...tonight."

Guys in movies always know what to say and how to look cool at these times. I didn't say a word and I don't think that my bulging eyes and open mouth looked anywhere close to cool.

"I am attracted to power, Grant, and I do not want any strings attached. I have a husband and I know that you have a wife and so I know that after we go up to your office and do it on that black leather sofa, we will never discuss it again." I still said nothing—I was frozen.

A few seconds passed, maybe a minute, I'm not sure, but I know that I couldn't move or speak. Kate leaned in and whispered, "Get up and follow me to your office Grant—I'm about to fuck you."

We walked to the elevator and made-out like starving seventeen-year-olds for the twenty-two-floor ride. As the doors opened, Kate grabbed me by the belt and pulled me down the hall with purpose. The office lights were on, but it was too late for anyone to be there, so I actually relaxed a little and was focused on how expertly Kate was able to unbutton her blouse with one hand while loosening my belt with the other. That was the moment that a bucket of ice-cold water hit me right in the face.

One of the cleaners from the nighttime crew was emptying the garbage can from my office and stared right into my eyes with a judgment reserved for heinous sinners. She could see my loosened belt, Kate's unbuttoned blouse, and my red-faced guilt. I know that these women don't speak any English and would probably just vacuum around us if we were screwing in the hallway, but she freaked me out beyond belief.

I snapped out of the enchanted state that I had been in since the single malt at the bar and returned to the calm and cool banker. I stalled until the cleaner left the office and then I just explained to Kate that this was not going to happen and she needed to leave immediately. I guess I was fairly authoritative because Kate just turned and left without argument.

That was it—it was over before it really got started. I climbed in a cab and headed home, looking out the window wondering how the hell that almost happened. I could feel myself shaking in bed and I was just hoping that Ellen wouldn't be woken by my tremors. I barely slept all night and was out of the house before Ellen got up the next morning.

Some people just never do the math. Three of the floors that I clean are professional firms—lawyers, accountants and such—and you can tell how they operate by looking at who is working after seven o'clock. Almost every night, all of the corner offices are empty, most of the window offices are empty and the young prairie dogs in the cubicles are working like crazy. These firms are fueled by the sweat of the young who seem only too willing to let it happen. Good deal for the bosses who reap the benefits, but how do they get the young guys to push so hard?

I think that the answer is that no one ever really studies how to get rich and university profs can't tell you because they don't know. It still seems to me that these young guns should look at a little history and see if they are picking out appropriate role models. The guy—maybe it was a woman—who said that those who cannot learn from history are doomed to repeat it, could have been explaining the Groundhog Day experience of the average professional office. Every generation benefits from the sweat of the next because the new guys never notice that the path that they are stepping onto is a treadmill.

The law firm in this building is a great example because they are supposed to be the hottest firm on the street and every year the best new students wrestle for the entry-level jobs. The students are mesmerized by the allure of the firm and its three young hotshot senior partners. These guys wear $3,000 suits, drive sports cars, have trophy wives and live charmed lives. At least that is the façade that they work very hard to maintain. The true story is that one has just lost his wife, the other is in big financial trouble because his tax shelter deals were reassessed, and the third guy...actually I don't know anything about the third guy, but he seems like an asshole nonetheless.

There are some guys who know how to make money in those games by taking a cut of the deal or getting an equity stake in a client, but 99 percent of these guys just hump for their hourly fee and never realize any serious wealth. Most of them make more than enough money to be comfortable, however the other half of the equation is that they spend ridiculous amounts on things intended to demonstrate that they have the wealth that they only wish they had.

It is wonderful to make $500,000 a year, but people don't do the math. The government will take $210,000. Your semi-detached in the city will eat up $80,000 a year with the mortgage, taxes and maintenance. The hillside chalet takes another $40,000. The BMW will eat $40,000 a year. You get the idea. By the time this high roller is done, he will have maybe $50,000 to put away for retirement. The superstars in this world start making this money at forty, so realistically these guys are not able to retire until the time that most civil servants retire.

It all makes me want to scream at these young kids to get out now. For most of the kids it is already too late, as they are spending money on lattes and fancy martinis that they can't afford so that they can create the image of a successful young player. If you weren't fortunate enough to receive the lucky gene that entitles you to inherited wealth, then you should study how others in your situation have become wealthy because it isn't by working seventy hours a week for someone else.

Terry

One of our first customers every morning is an Asian woman who works nights cleaning the office towers. She is very pleasant but she always looks so worn out and tired, and she never says much. She is at the door by 6:00 a.m. and picks up a large cappuccino and a whole-grain bagel to go every time without fail. It actually bothers me to charge this woman $5.25 each day as I figure she works the last half hour of her shift just to pay for this small salvation. I try not to be judgmental about this as perhaps this is the one "luxury" she allows herself every day, but I can't help but think that she can't really afford it. If this woman just stayed on her feet long enough to make it home, she could make her own breakfast for pennies, but somehow our culture has adopted expensive coffee as a basic right.

Back in 1971 in Seattle's Pike Place Market, three friends had a fairly simple idea to open a store based on their shared love for coffee and tea. They were not hard-nosed business guys in navy suits—they were academics named Jerry, Zev and Gordon, and I suspect that they wore tweed jackets with elbow patches. When they opened Starbucks, it didn't even sell coffee by the cup. Instead, it sold fresh roasted coffee to take home alongside their exotic teas and quirky souvenirs. This business did not have a global domination agenda and although the friends opened a second store in 1972, there would be only four Starbucks stores a decade later and all were confined to the greater Seattle area.

The point was not to make profit but rather to make coffee. In a bit of Starbucks lore, there was a time when the partners were asked about maximizing profitability and Jerry replied, "We don't manage the business to maximize anything other than the quality of the coffee."

The boys learned how to do that very well during the seventies and worshipped at the altar of coffee legend Alfred Peet, who started his coffee house in Berkeley, California, a few years before our boys. They built a management philosophy based on the highest quality coffee and—probably because of their teaching backgrounds—educating customers about their products.

The history of Starbucks from this point on depends (as does most history) on the perspective of the teller. A young, bright executive named Howard Schultz convinced the partners to take him on as the leader of marketing and retail. The company would never be the same. Schultz is viewed as a corporate mastermind—a genuine hero—by many who see the value-creation that he led. Others view him as a villain who destroyed something good and pure, and replaced it with something deliberate and plastic.

He is the man responsible for introducing espresso bars to North America and in 1984, when Starbucks opened its sixth store, they began to sell coffee, espresso and the rest in single servings to customers. The corporate aspect gets complicated at this point as the original partners were all off in different directions and Schultz was moving at such a dizzying speed that the original three could not, or would not, keep pace. The long story made short is that Schultz ended up as the largest shareholder and the CEO of Starbucks by 1987 at the age of thirty-four. Schultz was responsible for the hyper growth mode that Starbucks thrived under, resulting in the almost 10,000 locations worldwide and an international brand that is almost as recognizable as the golden arches.

If I were pressed to cast a vote, I would say that I think that Schultz was a good guy with mostly good ideas. He held on to the guiding principles of the founders, devoted as he was to high-quality product and client education. He also under-stood that he had to treat his employees very well and he did many things to make Starbucks a good place to work, includ-ing a controversial decision to offer health benefits to part-time employees.

In the end however it was a business and not a coffee club. Schultz had a large number of investors on board who were demanding high growth and profits. In 1992, Starbucks became a publicly traded stock and the cry for high growth and profit only became louder. Ultimately this financial push is what sucked the charm and the pleasure out of the Starbucks experi-ence. It's no one's fault. The evolution had to occur and they did a great job to get it that far—it's just that I feel hollow when I go in there now, so I don't go anymore.

Schultz and Starbucks deserve credit for adding coffee shops to North American culture and for creating a very successful business. My gratitude to them is simply for convincing the planet that it is OK to pay $3.50 for a latte.

Terry

When we were beginning operations, we knew how to organize our mornings and what to sell, but we lacked a noon-hour plan. With thirty-four floors of captive hungry people above us, we knew that we could make money at lunch, but what was our identity? Then we got a gift from the gods. Three weeks before we opened, I was sitting on the sofa on a Thursday night laughing my head off at the Soup Nazi on an episode of Seinfeld. The Soup Nazi—what timing! We opened with six varieties of soup everyday served by our cook, Al, who was only too happy to yell at the occasional customer or staff member if it helped the image.

Prior to Seinfeld, soup was as cool as corduroy. The Soup Nazi made soup fun and edgy. The Soup Nazi made soup profitable. Big batches of soup cost pennies to make, can all be prepared in advance. And if you give them exotic names, you can sell them at premium prices. Sell pea soup and you may get $1.50 a bowl, but sell organic Quebec pea and curried ginger soup and that goes for $3.95. Take that with a bottle of water and we'll call it an even six bucks. Prefer chilled green tea? Make it seven bucks.

Watch how fast our line moves—ladle it in, move along. It's fast and frenzied and the customers think that we are doing them a big favour by moving so quickly. Look at those guys across the hall at Subway. Custom sandwiches made fresh for each customer. They're lucky if they serve one customer a minute. Eventually, people give up on their long line and decide to have some soup.

This afternoon, a young woman customer asked, "Can I have some crackers for the chowder?"

Al jumped into his role as outraged and tormented chef: "... and would you like some catsup for your filet mignon? Would you like a pen so you can touch up the Mona Lisa! No crackers! No crackers for chowder! No soup for one week for you." Al turned and stormed back to his pots as I passed her the crackers with a wink. She left beaming with a great story to tell everyone about being attacked by the Soup Nazi. She'll bring friends next time.

Al is tailor-made for this place. He is in is his early sixties and has a new lease on life. He took an early retirement from a career, behind a desk, with the RCMP over the last twenty years, after some accident took him out of the field early in his service. The five years before retiring were apparently pretty bad for Al, as he lost his wife (cancer, I think, although he has never said) and his only son moved his family to Los Angeles for some big career. Al stayed to himself and drew away from the world a little more each day over that period, and so when he retired, most people just thought that he would slowly rust and fade.

My sister-in-law's house backs onto his and she would talk with him while raking or barbecuing so she saw his societal withdrawal first hand. She was the one who suggested that I offer him a job when I was opening Beanfest. He had just retired and she was very worried that he would go from bad to worse and that his retirement would be miserable. It seemed like a bad idea at the time, as a gruff old man wasn't quite what I had in mind...until that Thursday night on the couch with Seinfeld.

I stopped by Al's place the night after Seinfeld and expected to meet an uncouth, unshaven, grumpy old man. Instead I arrived at a house brimming with energy and full of people. It turned out that old Al had spent exactly one day on the couch during retirement before setting his new life in motion. My unannounced arrival at Al's place was right in the middle of a script reading for a new play that Al was acting in with a local theatre group. He looked fit and energetic and his smile looked permanent. I described what I was doing and how I thought that he could fit into the new enterprise. His fellow actors jumped on the opportunity for him, describing the benefits of having a great character role on a daily show. It would refine his acting skills and his fellow actors convinced him that he absolutely must agree to do it.

Al asked me some questions about the café and his duties. He asked me about my life and my family. He asked me about other staff and I sensed that he wasn't evaluating the job, but instead was considering whether this would be an enjoyable daily social activity. He seemed to be looking to make friends in his retirement and I think that he and I instantly knew that we would become great friends.

I didn't get a grumpy old man to serve as my soup Nazi. I got a kind and wonderful man to play the role of a grumpy old man and that is much better. In the end he agreed to do it, but only if he could leave by 2:20 p.m. because he was also driving a school bus every day.

"It helps me to not miss my grandkids quite so much."

I love that guy.

Grant

The funny thing about the close call the other night is that I wasn't really all that fired up about sex with Kate. Maybe I am getting old, but I just didn't feel like I needed all the drama. If sex is put right in front of me I will take it, but I don't want to work for it. I don't want to woo anyone or concoct some romantic scenario to lead someone to bed—it's just too much work.

Sex with my wife is still good and I enjoy all three times a month, but I think that I could live without it. Weird. From ages fifteen to thirty, sex dominated my brain and now it occasionally creeps in between deal negotiation and hockey highlights.

I don't think that it is a problem with my marriage. My wife is okay. She couldn't get pregnant so we got a vacation home instead of kids and we maintain a pretty simple life. She has her life with her career, her friends, yoga class, book club, et cetera, and I play only a supporting role in her life. I may have been the leading man initially, but her world is really about her and there isn't room for two lead characters, so I am a movie extra. This would bother some guys, but I don't really care. I like that she never bothers me and doesn't need much from me.

This apathetic approach to sex and my marriage carries over into much of my life and actually may explain why I got mixed up with Kate the other night. I just go with the flow rather than resist anything—it was kind of like, well if you want to screw me then who am I to stop you? More passive than one would imagine for an extra-marital situation.

The other weird thing about that night is that it has never happened before and so technically I have never cheated on my wife. It is not that I am devoted to the sanctity of marriage; it is really just that no one ever offered before Kate.

Most people think that I have incredible vision and focus, and that such a one-track drive has propelled me to the exec ranks in a big investment bank. The idea of being on one track is the only accurate part about me. I got involved in investment banking because someone offered and I didn't have anything better to do at the time. When it was suggested that I move from the resource sector to biotechnology, I went with the flow. I have always put in long hours because that seemed like what you were supposed to do and now I guess I am pretty good at biotech deals, mainly because I have done so many. There was no great plan to get here—just some combination of apathy and the passing of time. Maybe having a one-track, focused perspective just means that you can't raise enough interest to switch onto another track.

I think that most people evolve into their life like I have. It seems exhausting to resist life's natural momentum and I think that those who do resist are most often viewed as a little crazy. There was a guy in my department for a few years who quit on short notice and opened up one of those fishing lodges that you have to fly into, far up in Northern Ontario. No one talks about that guy as having great vision and focus—they talk about him as the guy that flipped out for fish. If you think about the people that you know who have made radical changes in their lives, you view them as your radical friends, not your smart friends or your

successful friends. A radical friend is the guy that is fun to invite
to the picnic because he has great stories and everyone can feel
better about themselves because they are not as loony as him.

My path-of-least-resistance approach to my career is something that I have been aware of for some time, but it has been
my personal secret. The fact that I have been faithful to my
wife for the same sad reason is a secret that I had hidden from
myself. Weird.

Lee

My mother was already awake and making Jackson's school
lunch when I walked in this morning and, as usual, she smiled
like she hasn't seen me in months instead of hours. She has
lived with us since my father died when Jackson was only a
couple of months old. I can't imagine life without her and our
little trio makes for a great family.

I never married and can't tell you much about Jackson's father
because he was just a guy that I met in a half-marathon training
group and slept with half a dozen times. We had stopped seeing
each other before I even knew that I was pregnant and since I
had already decided that I didn't want him in my life, I didn't
see any point in bringing him into Jackson's life. Poor bastard
doesn't even know that he is a father.

Jackson is the most adorable ten-year-old on the planet. His
father was a very light-skinned Indian and Jackson inherited his
father's creamy pigmentation. His facial features are from my
gene pool and he is distinctly Chinese looking, despite being
taller than any of his classmates. He is a happy kid and he seems
to have his head on straight.

I do have a great man in my life, but we both have a good
thing going and neither of us want to mess that up so we stay
single and live apart. Gord sells corporate insurance for a big
broker but he is not a slimy sales guy. He is well dressed, well
spoken, and earns a solid income. Our schedules don't line up
all that well so we usually only see each other once or twice a
week and I will often spend Saturday night at his place. I am

not sure that there is a magic spark between us, but we do make each other happy and enjoy each other's company.

When I say "no spark," I mean that I am not convinced that he is my one true love. I do not mean that there is no sexual spark because there is plenty of that. To be perfectly honest, Gord has a unique strength in that he goes down on me better than any other man that I have been with. Way better. I was beginning to think that it was a lost art before I met Gord, but he has restored my faith in the arts. Too many men are in a hurry to get to the main event and go down like they are in the drive-through lane of a fast-food restaurant. They want to munch and move on as quickly as they can. Gord takes his time, but he can be aggressive when the time is right. He knows how to put it together—why aren't there courses that men can take to improve this vital skill?

Our relationship could go to another level someday and we have discussed the possibility of marriage, but there is no urgency. My mother gently needles me about getting married from time to time. I don't really think that she wants me to get married, but I think that she feels that she has to put forward such comments because it is some kind of Chinese maternal responsibility

My favourite thing about Gord is that he isn't always around. That is not to say that I don't enjoy his company, but simply that I adore my family trio. It would seem like an incredible intrusion to have an outsider join the family and change the rhythm. I have friends who have told me that Jackson needs a father figure in his life, but I am not convinced. If you are surrounded by people who love you, then gender doesn't matter.

Mom keeps herself busy with Jackson at night and housework in the morning. In the afternoon she alternates between yoga classes, some kind of sewing club, and an afternoon movie with two old friends. She has never pursued a replacement man for my father and she does not seem to have any interest in looking. I think that she has found a nice balance for her life and that she is happy.

I don't hide Gord or my relationship with him from Jackson, but I have not allowed a relationship to form between them.

I am dating Gord, but I am not auditioning him for the role of Jackson's father. I think that I need to be more committed before I ask Jackson to get involved. This position is annoying to Gord, as he would love to be Jackson's pal, but that is exactly what I am trying to avoid because in the unlikely event that Gord becomes stepfather, it will not be an easy transition to go from buddy to dad.

Gord has never married and when contemplating his future, he drifts between the desire to have a family and the conflicting desire to live a carefree, travel-filled life. I think that he romanticizes the notion of the single life, but would ultimately prefer a family. But he's hard to read and if I ask too many questions it sounds like I am trying to talk him into something—which I am not.

My mom yelled to Jackson that his bus was coming and he raced past me as he bolted for the door. Then he stopped, ran back and hugged me. He hugged me hard—so that I knew that he meant it.

"Love you, Mom."

I love you guys, too.

Track 4

Lee

I clean three floors every night with my cleaning partner Mrs. Chen, who is the person that all of the clients think that I am. Mrs. Chen speaks heavily accented English and although she is very smart and interesting, she is nervous around these big office guys. She structures her cleaning schedule to minimize contact with people and if she must interact, she bows apologetically and rushes away as quickly as possible.

She also works extremely hard, never misses a day's work, and has been with me for four years. She understands that I am the boss because the clients pay me and then I pay her, but she certainly doesn't understand that I own the business. If I really delved into it, I think that she probably believes that I am something of a working manager—a first among equals.

That image is something that I carefully craft by scrubbing my share of toilets and vacuuming offices for a few hours a night. The rest of the shift Mrs. Chen works alone because I need to manage my other staff at other locations.

The rest of my crew are almost all like Mrs. Chen and they all believe that Lee is their ever-so-friendly manager, rather than the proprietor. No one on my crew has English as a first language and most are terribly nervous introverts in the English-speaking world. They are very happy to have their jobs and they see me as their great protector against the clients, who occasionally complain, and the faceless people who own the company that they work for. I remind them that they should just keep things simple by showing up every day and working hard and that everything else will be fine. When I meet with anyone on my crew, they know that I recently had my hand in a toilet and thus my social status can't be much different than theirs and that leads to trust. Most of these ladies have experienced legitimate reasons to fear authority, so I try very hard not to seem authoritative. If they knew that I owned the business, I would not receive the strong work, dedication, and cooperation from any of them—not from a single one of my 126 employees.

Terry

On the evening of my forty-fifth birthday, Carol and I sat out on our back deck and enjoyed an Australian shiraz and some quiet conversation. It was a pleasant night, but was showing no signs of being a life-changing event until Carol asked a seemingly simple question:

"What are you going to do with the second half of your life?"

I explained to Carol that I was statistically not at the halfway point in my life and that the average remaining life for a forty-five-year-old male is only thirty-two years. In fact less than 10 percent of forty-five-year-old men will live to see their nineties. Her blank stare back at me told me that she was not impressed that I had gone technical on her. I moved away from my facts and figures, but reminded her that it was an occupational hazard for me.

I have always found that numbers come easily to me and the concepts around investing are intuitive. Add that background to the fact that I love to talk to people and that explains how I ended up as a personal financial planner. I worked for a company that sold insurance, mutual funds, GICs, et cetera, to the solidly middle class. I had been doing this for the fifteen years before my forty-fifth birthday and was reasonably successful. My boss left me alone because I always beat my performance goal. My customers were great and I had developed friendships with many of them over the years.

Overall I didn't hate my job—I probably even liked it, but while Carol sipped her wine and waited for my answer, I was struck by the thought that I didn't want to stay in the same job. Maybe I selected a career change because I was content with the other areas of my life. My wife was amazing, my son was great, and I had a great set of friends. I had never had any desire to rise to a higher calling in life, and although it did not seem very adventurous, I did not have an exciting list of exotic travel wishes.

When I blurted out, "I want to leave the company," Carol beamed with interest. "Are you finally going to start your own business?" Carol has always been my biggest fan and she has always thought that I am much smarter than I truly am. She had urged me to consider stepping out and running my own financial services business for years as she thought that I could do a better job than the guys at head office.

"I don't want to just leave the company, I want to leave the entire financial planning field."

Carol's excitement ebbed to curiosity.

"I don't have any idea what I want to do, but I do know that I don't want to do this for much longer." It felt so good to say that. A few minutes earlier I didn't even know that I felt that way about my career, and yet I was strangely liberated by announcing my desire to leave, as if it had been bottled up inside of me for years rather than minutes.

Throughout the evening we talked about a myriad of options, including switching roles within the same company, going back to school, and starting my own business. The only one that elevated my heart rate was the idea of starting my own business. The vantage point of financial planning gave me a great view of several entrepreneurial hits and misses and I felt that I had learned a great deal by watching others.

Our evening ended without conclusion, but that night established a point of no return the second I said that I wanted to move on.

In the end, I selected a coffee house when inspiration and opportunity arrived on the same day. While driving to meet a client downtown, I caught the tail end of a story on the radio about a Boston coffee shop owner who spoke so romantically about his shop and compared it to tavern owners of another era. "Except that the hours are better and you don't have to deal with drunks," he quipped. It did seem like a charmed existence and it was still in my head when I entered the lobby of a downtown office tower to meet with a customer.

I was waiting for the elevator when my client came up from behind me juggling a tray of Tim Hortons' coffees. "Hi Terry— my turn to make the coffee run for the office. Can you believe this frickin' building has thirty-four floors of offices and no coffee shop?"

For those who do not believe in fate, I present that moment in time as proof positive.

After my meeting, I went back down to the lobby and stared at the 2,000-square-foot vacant unit directly across from the Subway, the dry cleaner, and the convenience store. I vaguely remember that there had been a very greasy-looking cafeteria in that location for years, but I had never been brave enough to venture in and I guess that it finally just couldn't make a go of it. I took down the number of the agent on the "For Lease" sign and called later that day. The unit had been empty for a year and the price had been dropped twice since it went on the market.

I knew by the time that I arrived home that night that I had found what I wanted to do for the remaining 36.8 percent of my life.

Grant

I rarely leave the office at lunch but I make exceptions on a hot and sunny August day. It's not that I am craving the sunshine in the courtyard of the office tower, but the scenery is too good to ignore. Everywhere you look it is sundress, sundress, mini-skirt, mini-skirt—makes the summer heat worthwhile. I have a pretty quiet afternoon scheduled so I was able to take some time for sightseeing before heading down to the coffee shop for some take-out. I usually have my assistant order in a sandwich for me, but when I have time I prefer to go to the coffee shop— they have the greatest soup in the world. I don't know why they don't expand their lunch menu and make some fancy sandwiches and hot meals, but all they really carry is soup. Soup must be part of the official granola handbook that these laid-back coffee shop guys follow.

The people are so weird. The guy that serves the soup is the grumpiest man on the planet with absolutely no people skills.

He is amazing to watch because he has such a short fuse and he can yell at a staff member or a customer at any moment—it's hilarious, actually. It is like watching a car wreck; you just can't look away. Somehow the guy that runs this shop doesn't see what a whack job the soup guy is so he leaves him there day after day, scaring his customers. The owner actually looks like a guy who could work in our office if you bought him a nice suit. I wonder if he is one of those guys who flipped and left his real job to live out his bohemian dream of making coffee and soup?

The young woman ahead of me in the soup line was speaking with her husband on the phone—one of those sickly sweet new-lywed conversations. I hate those conversations at any time, but on a cellphone in the middle of the day it's just nauseating. It did remind me that I really want to talk with Ellen, but I am not one of those guys that calls his wife during the day. It would seem strange to her if I called, but I haven't spoken with her since all of that weirdness of the failed affair the other night. She was away for the weekend, so I haven't seen her and I need to know if I can talk to her and feel normal.

I briefly thought about telling her what happened, but I just can't see anything good coming from that and I don't feel any burning need to unload a burden. It isn't telling her about the encounter that would be hard—the hard part would be trying to explain why I went along for the ride, so to speak. Somehow I think that my explanation, that I really didn't see any reason to stop Kate, wouldn't be satisfactory.

I also don't want to tell her because I can predict her reac-tion. Initially she will fake an overly dramatic reaction, which will include some screaming, crying and long "how could you" speeches designed to make her feel bigger by making me feel small. After a week she will decide that we can save the mar-riage as long as we commit ourselves to strengthening our rela-tionship. That means we will be at a counsellor every Tuesday afternoon and we will take several weekend getaways to quaint bed and breakfasts so that we will have time to reconnect. We can rebuild our bond by antiquing.

I will just keep my mouth shut and pretend that it never hap-pened—and it didn't.

Grant

As the traffic crawls along at twenty kilometres per hour, I think back to the salesman explaining how this engine was inspired by the Formula One engine that the BMW team races. I remember that it redlines at 8250 rpm and has 500 horsepower, but this morning I am thinking that one horse would be faster. Certainly the subways, which are undoubtedly whizzing by underground, would be much faster but my reputation would never permit me to be seen on public transit. The M5 is the signature car for my job and all the young staffers in my office drool as they walk past it in the underground lot.

I am half listening to the classic rock station on the completely unnecessary fourteen-speaker system, when I am jolted by the line: "I know that the hypnotized never lie."

Wow—that was the line on the blackboard at the stupid coffee shop yesterday. I got another one—it's "Won't Get Fooled Again" by The Who. I always read those lyrics in the coffee shop and I am pretty good at getting them. I am still a rocker at heart, after all. I never tell the staff when I solve them, but my batting average is pretty good. I must be a bit of a nerd because identifying The Who song makes me happier than it should. One small thing that I love about the game is that the lyric board is part of an old CHEZ 106 poster and CHEZ was my favourite station when I was growing up back in Ottawa. I don't miss much about that one-horse town, but seeing the CHEZ sign always makes me happy.

Things went well at home yesterday and it seemed as normal as ever. My wife's younger sister is in town for a few days, so I stayed out of their way last night. They had already finished dinner and most of their first wine bottle when I got home, so I just made a plate for myself and ate in front of the hockey game.

I was in bed before eleven and had just flicked the lights off when Ellen came in and playfully whispered in my ear to see if I was awake. I gave a little laugh and that was enough for her to determine that I was up. With no subtlety at all she reached down and awoke my half-sleeping penis. I was game and we had a short but satisfying session. As soon as I was done, she rolled off me and was off to the washroom for her nightly rituals. I like that there wasn't a lot of frivolous romance and conversation— get on—get off—get off.

I guess that the wine and conversation with her sister was stimulating. Whatever the case, I didn't complain. This is the thing about my wife: she is okay—I am not all dreamy about her, but I don't mind her—especially in a mood like last night.

Some of these douche-bag executives like to be at work by 6:00 a.m. so my crews have to be finished by 5:30 a.m. It makes our cleaning window fairly small, because our clients also prefer that we don't start cleaning until their offices are virtually empty, presumably so that we do not do anything to remind their semi-slave labor force that it is getting late. Our earliest jobs begin at seven but most clients want us to begin after eight, so most of my staff work from 8:00 p.m. until 5:00 a.m.

All of our business is in the downtown core so I can drive to any customer in less than five minutes and, in most cases, I can walk from site to site. I drop by three or four sites between eight and nine in the evening just to touch base with the cleaners and see if they need anything. My visits are short and upbeat, and because I am always asking how they are and if they need anything, they don't realize that I am checking up on them.

I join Mrs. Chen cleaning our building around 9:30 p.m. and will clean until 2:00 a.m. Mrs. Chen starts at eight and will finish up after I leave so that we are both gone before five. Mrs. Chen works hard and can usually be finished by 4:30 a.m., and the fact that she is allowed to leave early while still getting paid makes her leave with a smile despite a full night of back-breaking work.

From two until six I will drop by at least another five buildings to make sure that the offices have been properly cleaned. I rotate the office locations from day to day so that the staff never know when I will drop into their building and therefore they do a good job every night. I occasionally have to deal with inferior cleaning, but these women take such pride in their work (and they really need the job) that they almost always do a great job.

By six, I am exhausted and need a little "me time" before I go home and help get Jackson up and ready for school, so I head to the coffee shop. There is a little place in the building where I park that makes the best cappuccino on the planet. I grab a bite and that cappuccino every morning and somehow it revives my strength until Jackson heads to school and I can finally fall into bed.

Most early morning places are dreary as people ease their way into the day, but this coffee shop seems to spring from bed with energy. I am always one of their first customers, so I usually hear the debate about what lyrics they will put on their black-board for this weird little tradition they have where clients try to guess the song that the displayed lyrics belong to. My brain isn't firing at full potential at that time, so I rarely get the song name right away but I usually let the lyrics roll around in my brain during the ride home and I would guess that I have about half of the puzzles solved before I hit my driveway. The next day the answer from the previous day is posted and I almost always know the song so I am convinced that if I played the game on a fresh brain I would guess almost every song. I never tell the staff that I can guess their songs because it seems like they put too much thought into it just to have their first customer pop their balloon. The staff seem to get a kick out of their own game and

I really enjoy the combination of friendly banter, roasting coffee smells and my piping hot cappuccino.

Terry

My mother asked if she could drive up for a visit and stay with us this weekend. I made up a lie on the spot and told her that we already had plans and that we would be out of town with friends. My mother is a wonderful woman who is intelligent, kind and pleasant to be around but I can't stand to be in the same room with her anymore. I like to think that I am a good father and husband but I know that I am no longer a good son.

This weekend is the second anniversary of my father's death and Mom doesn't want to face it without me, but I am too weak to offer any support. My feelings are selfish and irrational but they are not going to change any time soon I fear.

My father was also intelligent, kind and pleasant to be around. His career was successful and his life was happy and full. He retired on his sixty-fifth birthday and had enjoyed nine more years of a happy and healthy life with Mom before his death. What none of us knew was that over the last couple of years his little "senior moments" that we all excused were terribly worrisome to dad. His older brother had died ten years earlier of Alzheimer's disease and Dad had a front-row seat for the savage deterioration and cruel death that Uncle Richard experienced.

TV and the movies tend to depict only early stages of Alzheimer's because the final stage is just too hard to watch. In the last few months, Uncle Richard had not only lost all of his memory, but he had lost all of his verbal skills and only made a frustrated grunting sound. Physically, he was extremely limited—he couldn't walk or stand, and even sitting was a struggle, so he was generally confined to bed. He had no control of his bodily functions and didn't even notice when he had soiled or wet himself. Beyond all that, I think that the worst thing for all of us to see was the look in his eyes—he had a permanently panicked and frightened look on his face that was just heartbreaking. Most families stop visiting Alzheimer's patients at this stage because the patient presumably gets no benefit from the visit and the family members have their hearts broken on each trip. My dad, however, never wavered and sat with Uncle Richard every day and was holding his hand when he mercifully took his last breath. End stage Alzheimer's is as nasty as it gets.

Dad knew that his senior moments were a serious problem, but he kept it from all of us. In fact, the last time we were together, he was the life of the party. We had a Canada Day family picnic and all of his children and grandchildren were there. Dad manned the barbecue and made the grandkids line up and perform a song for him in order to earn each hot dog. The day was so much fun and I love the fact that all of his grandchildren have that day as the final memory of him.

A few days later, he surprised my mother with tickets to the opera at the National Arts Centre. He hated opera, but Mom loves it, so it was a grand gesture for him to take her. They had dinner, went to the opera and stayed at a hotel in the city. Mom says that it was a fantastic evening and that Dad showed no sign that anything was wrong.

The next evening, he drove to the hospital and parked next to the phone booth in the emergency room parking lot. He called 9-1-1 and simply said that they needed to send a police officer to the parking lot immediately as there had been an accident. He then went back to his car and shot himself in the head.

His suicide note said that he had been diagnosed with Alzheimer's two weeks earlier and he could tell that he was slipping fast, so he wanted to go before he became something that he didn't want to be.

Ignorant people say that suicide is a coward's way out, but I have come to think of my father's death as pure bravery. He chose the terms under which he would leave this earth. He decided to spare his loved ones from the burden of caring for an eroding mind and body. He chose to crystallize how he would be remembered.

Why should we be obligated to fight against an incurable disease? It is not brave; it's illogical. Make sure you say all that needs to be said, put your affairs in order and end it. That's brave and dignified.

I am not hurt by the suicide and I am not haunted by my father's death, which makes it hard to articulate why I can't reach out to my mother. The unwanted by-product of his death is that I find myself incapable of spending time with her. I have small panic attacks when I see her and I feel an overwhelming desire to flee. It is as if I want my memory of her to be locked at that point in time from which my final memory of Dad comes from. My sisters have told me that Mom feels crushed under the weight of my cold shoulder. I can't define the feeling, but it is strong and unbending even though I understand that I continue to hurt the feelings of a very kind woman.

Terry

A few days ago, I returned to the café after running some afternoon errands only to find that Cory was in a heated argument with two of our regular customers. My anxiety eased quickly once I realized that the argument was about the music game that we have been playing—find the top five musical remakes of all time. This debate over cover songs has been going on for a couple of days at the coffee shop and although I thought that it was a little nerdy, I realize that people are coming in and spending six bucks for a latte and muffin specifically so that they can weigh in with their opinion.

When I walked over, they were debating the rules of this recently made up game.

"Both the original recording and the remake had to be hits."

"And we have to know both versions."

"That's ridiculous because then you can't count "Cross-Roads" even though it is the greatest cover of all time."

"I know the Cream version, who did the cover?"

"That's the beauty, Cream was the cover and the original was Robert Johnson in 1936."

The place roars with laughter.

"In 1936? Are you kidding me? If the song was recorded before Terry was born, then it definitely doesn't count!" Cory has spotted me and works me into the conversation smoothly—mostly to be a nice guy, but also with the hope that I won't notice that the shop hadn't been cleaned after the lunch rush.

I decided to play along: "I think that it's hard to beat the Tesla remix of The Five Man Electrical Band's 'Signs.'" This sparked outrage, which is what I intended because I hate the Tesla version just like these guys do. "Well, Cory, what is the latest top five list?"

"Check out the blackboard Terry," Cory shouted and waved to the board by the front door.

5. "Knockin' on Heaven's Door"—Dylan/Guns N Roses
4. "Come Together"—Beatles/Aerosmith
3. "All Along the Watchtower"—Dylan/Hendrix
2. "Blinded by the Light"—Springsteen/Manfred Mann
1. "With a Little Help From my Friends"—Beatles/Joe Cocker

Actually, it was a pretty good list and for the next three days people were invited to come in and present a case to "Judge Cory" for not only why their song should be on the list, but for why one of the songs presently on the list should be removed. The arguments that were brought forward were fantastic.

One guy, who surprised us, is a fairly regular soup customer from one of the law firms in the office tower. He is always dressed very well and reminds me of an office guy from a different generation because he always wears a suit and tie—never a sports coat—and always looks pressed and shined. He is probably only forty, but he dresses like he is sixty. Well this guy came in and made a formal appeal to Cory: "I wish to take exception with song number two on your list."

Cory shouted over the crowd with perfect mock scorn, "This gentleman is going to skip the bottom rungs of the ladder and will attack our potential silver medalist!"

The crowd was interested and the man proceeded, "'Blinded by the Light' was indeed originally recorded by Bruce Springsteen on his *Greetings from Ashbury Park* album in 1973 and it was released as a single. However, like so many of Springsteen's early recordings, it was inexplicably ignored by the brainless buying public and it was never a hit. Not by anyone's definition, could a song that did not enter Billboard's top 100 list be considered a hit. I accept that Manfred Mann's version was indeed a better version than the original, but the rules are clearly

expressed and both versions must have been hits, so I respectfully request the removal of song number two."

Cory assumed a judicial formality and said, "Before I offer my
ruling, I wish to hear your suggestion for a replacement for the
top five."

Our new friend was ready: "I submit for the court's con-
sideration "Big Yellow Taxi," originally recorded by her royal
highness, Ms. Joni Mitchell and subsequently recorded by the
Counting Crows in 2002. Both versions were substantial hits
and satisfy your criteria." A small but enthusiastic round of
applause was offered to our customer's performance.

Judge Cory rubbed his chin in academic contemplation and
thanked the counsellor for his well-reasoned arguments and
announced that he was prepared to render his decision.

"I accept the reasoned arguments vis à vis Mr. Springsteen
and, by definition, will remove "Blinded by the Light" from our
top five. And I will temporarily move songs three to five up
one notch. As for your arguments with respect to "Big Yellow
Taxi," I must draw your attention to one fact that was overlooked by counsel. The Counting Crows version sucks! I love
the Crows, dude, but this tune is weak and Joni is a queen. The
cover version must be better than the original, which in this
case it clearly is not, and therefore I reject your nomination. We
will seek to fill the void fifth spot throughout the rest of the
week," concluded Judge Cory.

Over the next two days we heard passionate pleas for "Dancing
in the Street" (Martha & the Vandellas followed by Van Halen);
"Killing Me Softly" (Roberta Flack followed by the Fugees); and
"Land of Confusion" (Genesis followed by Disturbed).

Before long, we settled on "Loco Motion" with the original
by Little Eva and the cover by Grand Funk Railroad. This song
met all the criteria and everyone agreed that the Grand Funk
version was better. This song actually had the special distinction of being one of the very few songs by two different artists
ever to reach Billboard's number one spot. There are actually
eight other songs that share that accomplishment, and you can
look them up if you like or you can just trust me that the other
eight all suck.

I started smoking pot and hash in Grade 10 and I have always preferred smoking to drinking. Now that I am a bit older and can afford better quality wine, I enjoy the odd bottle, but I still prefer weed.

On the rare night when I have no plans and Mom and Jackson are gone to bed, I like to smoke a little weed and watch a funny movie. You need to be fully baked to fully enjoy the experience, so I always roll a fat one before I start.

I start by organizing my snacks—Orange Crush and Doritos. That combo has satisfied my stoned munchies cravings since the days before I learned how to roll my own joints. Then, I pop in a movie and spark up.

I remember a movie era of hilarious comedies with real people as the stars. When I was young we had Porky's, Ferris Bueller's Day Off and Monty Python flicks. Today, all of the funniest movies are animated and directed primarily for the children's market. When was the last time that you laughed out loud in the theatre? Shrek? Finding Nemo? Toy Story? All of the real laughs now come from Disney and Pixar.

Finding Nemo is probably my favorite and working on my Dory impression while high leads to uncontrollable giggling. "Just keep swimming, just keep swimming...what do we do? We just keep swimming...." Shrek is awesome and my ogre voice is pretty good. Last night I went old school with Aladdin and I almost peed myself during the genie scenes. Robin Williams was crazy good in that one.

I am a single mom running my own company. If I need a little joint to help me relax and enjoy an evening by myself, why should that bother anyone? I am not complaining—my life is awesome—but I do feel the weight of responsibility and occasionally it is nice to shed the load. My customers and employees count on me to run the company smoothly. Jackson and my mom are understandably dependent on me. It is all fine—I can take it—but it is a mentally exhausting to be everyone's rock.

For a few hours, I can get out from under all of that with some animation and a joint. When I wake up the next day, the power and stamina that I need to carry the load is restored to full power.

Grant

Caffrey was sick this morning and left at lunch so I had to cover for him on a handful of meetings and calls this afternoon, which was fine because I basically do his job anyway. The only interesting part of all of those calls and meetings stemmed from a call with two senior bankers out of San Francisco who called to engage our firm in the Canadian promotion of a new financing round that they will lead. The engagement is basic and the call was straightforward, but I was surprised by the opening banter of the two San Fran guys as we waited for the final participants to join the call. They have obviously known each other for years and spoke so openly about private matters that I felt like I was eavesdropping, even though they knew that I was on the call.

One of the guys was on his car phone heading up to Napa Valley for a two-night getaway. Buddy number two asks if he is meeting his wife or the skirt at the resort. Buddy one laughs and says that he is going specifically to get laid, so why the hell would he bring his wife. It turns out that the skirt is a regular companion of buddy number one and he pays for her Napa lifestyle in return for twice-monthly slam fests mixed with the valley's best pinot noir.

I can't believe that they spoke so openly in front of me, but truthfully I just can't believe that people actually do these things. It seems so risky, complicated, and frightening. This guy must tell so many lies. I can't believe that he never gets caught. Is he even afraid of getting caught? It doesn't seem like he is. Maybe his wife knows and accepts it. Maybe she has a lover on the side. I guess it is his casualness that has me confused. I always assumed that an affair would be a clandestine thing with whispering and secret messages, but this guy was talking about this rendezvous like he was discussing his weekend tee time.

Do guys like this really have that much of a sex drive? Is the sex so good that they would risk so much just for the gratification? It doesn't make sense—the risk/reward ratio is way off, but then I don't imagine that these guys are taking the time to fully compute the odds.

When I was eighteen, I dated Lisa Blair for a few weeks and we had a few great make-out sessions and a little touching, but it never went any further. Then one Sunday afternoon I was invited to a family picnic in her backyard and that changed things. The last place that I wanted to be on a hot summer day was in Lisa's backyard talking to her lame parents, but I put up with it and I could see that Lisa was really happy that I was making an effort and a good impression on her parents.

Lisa moved behind her parents' chairs and mouthed to me, "I'm horny," then asked her parents if we could watch TV in the basement since it was cool there.

I caught on fast and was excited by the opportunity for a little more touching, so I followed Lisa into the basement. When Lisa hit the bottom stair she smoothly unclipped her skirt and stepped out of it showing me her shockingly bare ass. My first thought was, "My god this is awesome." My second thought was, "Shit, her father is forty feet away!" Lisa quickly put a blanket down behind the couch so that we couldn't be seen from the stairs, which I guess was enough to level the risk/reward ratio for me and then we had thirty-five seconds of unprotected sex to the sounds of her little brother splashing in the pool. I was scared of getting caught, but not so scared that I would miss the opportunity so generously offered to me by the horny Lisa. That must be the way that the guy in San Fran feels about his affair. The difference is that he is fifty, not eighteen, and he is risking half of his assets and a great deal of his reputation. I was only risking a beating from Lisa's father.

With the events of the last week rolling around in my head, I can't help but wonder if I am the guy in the minority. How many guys would have turned Kate around just because some minimum-wage foreign cleaning lady saw him? Most guys would have found a way to close that deal, but I got scared. Actually, I don't know if it was fear—maybe I didn't want Kate in the same way that I wanted Lisa in her basement that afternoon. In either case, I feel like I am out of sync with other men my age and I can't seem to shake this feeling that I am missing out.

Grant

Ellen sent me an e-mail this afternoon to say that she is leaving the office to pack a suitcase as one of their regional offices out west is in a mess. She made the decision to just go out and fix it in person. She will be gone a few days, but it could stretch to a week. I don't really care, but I wonder if other spouses communicate this way. I am sure that most spouses would phone and at least discuss some plans, if not how much they will miss each other. My wife didn't even add any personal commentary in her e-mail—it reads like an e-mail to a distant colleague.

When she lands out west she will not call to tell me that she has safely arrived or what the weather is like out there. She will not connect with me at all while she is away unless she thinks to send me an e-mail announcing her return details, which again is nothing more than professional courtesy.

These are the kinds of things that I have never noticed before, but seem to be obsessing about now. I am now trying to measure my marriage against some objective standard with no idea what I would do with that measurement if it were available. I would never want some cute and cuddly marriage where the spouses wear matching sweaters and argue about who loves the other more. I have never been into public displays of affection, and I am not even concerned with how little time we spend together. I guess I have just noticed how businesslike we are with each other and wonder if that is abnormal.

We have been married for eighteen years, but really it has

been pretty much like this from the start, so it is not a case of a marriage running out of steam. I remember that Ellen and I made fun of other newlyweds while we were on our honeymoon because they would be all doe-eyed and sappy. That was just never our thing. The question is, what is our thing?

We do have a lot in common. We both are career-focused; we are both calm and logical. We have similar taste in food, wine, and movies, which are clear signs of compatibility. We have similar investment philosophies and never argue about money. We rarely argue about anything. We rarely laugh about anything, either.

The businesslike e-mail from her is a perfect metaphor for our relationship—we are solid colleagues or maybe even amicable business partners. I have nothing to compare this to, but I am beginning to feel that marriage should be more than this. There is nothing magical happening here and there are no violins playing, but what I don't know is, does anyone experience the magic and the violins or is my marriage the norm?

On Saturday night Gord and I went to a small dinner party hosted by Gord's best friend and his wife. I know Tony and Erica well, but had never met the other couple that made up our little party. We had a great meal, a little too much wine and some interesting conversations. The final subject of the night was my cleaning business and what I should do with it.

If I have any complaint about Gord, it is that he works a little too hard to explain to people that I own a cleaning business and that I am not a cleaner. I don't really see him as a status-conscious person and I am certainly no trophy girlfriend, but he is so quick to draw the owner/cleaner distinction for people that it makes me wonder just a little. At the dinner party, he spoke to the third couple at the table and went on at length about the size of the business that I had amassed. It could be taken as a compliment that Gord is proud of what I have built, but something needled me that it might be something closer to justification for why it is acceptable for me to periodically push a vacuum.

Well, it turns out that the third couple—Jennifer and Kevin, or maybe Keith or Kent—have considerable interest in my business and asked me a series of very insightful questions that suggest that they completely understand my position. Jennifer is a partner in a law firm that specializes in business law, including mergers and acquisitions. Her husband is a retail stockbroker and seems to understand a great deal about the value of my business. They bantered back and forth about my business worth, who I could sell it to and how long it would take to unload it.

The consensus around the table was that we are in a seller's market and that this is an excellent time for me to cash out. Gord was visibly excited by this conversation and insisted that I deserve a better life than working straight nights and cleaning. My default life plan was that I would sell the business in ten years or more and I have never given any thought to selling it now. I didn't share that thought with the dinner guests and instead chose to sip on a nice port and listen carefully as Jennifer outlined the process of "exiting."

She is familiar with a number of brokers or agents who would represent me and put together a "book," which would be used to drum up some interest in my business from a list of prospective buyers that my agent would identify. I would need to be involved in meetings to talk up the value of the business, but she made it sound like my role would be pretty small if I selected the right professionals. The whole process could take only a few months if a buyer emerges early, and I could be living the good life in no time, I was assured.

Gord talked about the merits of selling all the way home and up the stairs into the bedroom. I was only thinking that I don't want to waste my nice little buzz and was busy putting on every green light for Gord to get into the mood, but he drove through every signal. I got tired of waiting for him to stop talking and so I gave up on the sex and fell asleep while he rambled on. The sweetness of the port left me with a small hangover this morning so my thinking may not be crystal clear, but I can't stop thinking about the possibility of selling the business.

Terry

Ben was home from university for the weekend—well, sort of. I think he slept in his old room on Friday and Saturday nights, but Carol and I didn't really see him very much. He came rushing in at eight on Friday night and dropped a massive bag of laundry in the hallway, hugged his mom on the way to the kitchen where he grabbed a beer and then headed for his room and a shower.

I tried to stop him for a conversation as he bounded back down the stairs, but he was in a big rush: "Dad, the Arkells are on at ten at the Piccadilly. I'll catch you in the morning."

Well, I am one of the oldest fans (longest serving and by age) of the Arkells, but I couldn't help feeling like the father in that Harry Chapin song. The rest of the weekend was the same. Ben graced us with snippets of conversation as he ran from one thing to another. The boy is just too busy for his father. I have had a hard time adjusting to Ben growing up and Carol teases me because I tend to think of Ben as a shy, little, eleven-year-old boy rather than the young man that he is. When Ben was eleven, he needed me. We would talk for hours. Every night he sat on the edge of his bed and waited for me to come and say good night. Where is that kid?

On Sunday night I was telling Carol how annoyed I was about Ben, but she laughed it off and told me to remember what I was like at that age. I get it, and I get that in the two days he has back in town Ben would rather spend time with his old friends than his old parents, but it scares me. It scares me because I do remember what I was like at that age and that I was just like Ben. It scares me because it was at his age that I began to drift away from my parents—not in any deliberate or conscious manner— just that other things became more interesting than my parents.

When I became a young adult, I never found my parents that interesting and so I didn't seek out their company. I called on the appropriate occasions and would make semi-annual, brief visits, but all of those small gestures were done out of obligation, not out of desire. Then I married, had a kid and a job to worry about, so although my relationship with my parents improved as I matured, I never devoted much time to them. I have often wondered if they were disappointed that I drifted away from them.

Will Ben feel the same way about Carol and I? It breaks my heart to think that he will. He is one of my best friends and there are few people that I would rather spend time with. We share so many interests, memories, and philosophies that it seems that we should have a great adult relationship. Now that he is of age, we can sit and have a beer and watch Hockey Night in Canada and I can't think of a better thing to do...except, he didn't want to do that this Saturday, and he may never want to do that again.

I remember watching a nature show about the family structure of elephants. Throughout their childhood, male elephants stay within a herd of females that includes their mother, aunts, and sisters. The family unit is incredibly caring and protective. Everything that the young bull knows is in the context of that family unit and, even on film, you can sense that the young males are loved by and love their herd. This cocooned environment is abruptly shattered when the male reaches his age of sexual maturity. At that stage, the herd permanently banishes the bull from their group. The male is physically chased off with malice by the family that yesterday was perfectly loving. It is a shocking action that leaves the young bull completely dumbfounded. The male tries to return to the family and is violently rejected time after time. The male will usually trail the herd at some distance for a couple of weeks with the occasional attempt to be readmitted, but after repeated rejections he eventually drifts away and sets out on his own. It is cruel and sad. It must be the best thing for the survival of the species, but it is hard to watch as you can see the confusion and sadness in the eyes of this giant puppy. As a parent, you want to have a heart-to-heart talk, just man to pachyderm, to explain why this is best.

It may be natural for a child to drift away from his parents as he matures. School, work, a love life, a family, a mortgage, friends—where is the time to spend having a beer with your dad? It is natural and it may even be optimal for the species, but it is cruel and sad.

Lee

I became self-employed because I needed the money, not because I had a grand plan. I started cleaning homes on the day that I saw an ad in the local paper looking for a cleaner. The client wanted someone to clean her massive home two days per week. I called and told the woman that answered that I was a self-employed cleaner and would not work as an employee, but that my company would be happy to take on the assignment. I have no idea why or where I found the audacity to try that approach, but it worked and I secured an hourly rate that was 30 percent higher than the wage she intended to pay.

I did very good work and within two months I had been referred to other customers and had a full slate of houses that paid me well and helped me to establish a small but legitimate business. Over a three-year period, I added two staff members and many more houses and I was making a decent living. I didn't mind the work and truly enjoyed the sense of being my own boss.

The change from residential to commercial cleaning was simply a matter of good luck and good timing. Charlene Crystal had been a residential client for over a year, although I had only met her a few times as she had a busy career that I later learned was as the managing partner of a downtown law firm. I was just finishing the cleaning of her house one afternoon, when she came up the front steps screaming into her cell phone about a missing document. I overheard that the office cleaner had accidentally thrown out some papers that were on the floor of Charlene's office, and she was incensed. Apparently, there had been other issues with the cleaning company and she hit a breaking point.

I heard her shout, "Tell Bev that I want a new cleaning crew by next week." Charlene saw me out of the corner of her eye and more quietly spoke into the receiver, "Actually, just wait on that." She ended her call and then turned to me and said, "Lee, are you ready to clean commercially? I am a big fan of competent people who show pride in their work, so I don't care if you have never done this before, but I want you to take a contract to clean my firm's offices every night."

Charlene invited me to meet in her office the next afternoon, and when I arrived she introduced me to her office manager, Bev, who had clearly been given instructions to bend over backwards to make me succeed. Bev spent three hours with me that afternoon and gave me the best education one could ever ask for, and the kind of inside information that I was too naïve to appreciate the importance of at that moment. Among the information that Bev gave me were the confidential proposals that the top five cleaning companies in the city had submitted to her the previous year, when they were bidding for the work to clean Charlene's 35,000-square-foot office suite. These proposals not only taught me what my new competitors were charging, but also how they were marketing themselves. Over time, I would reread these proposals dozens of times and learn more about my competitors' operations, infrastructures and approaches. Those proposals were gold.

Some people would think that it was unethical of me to take those proposals. Those people are fucking idiotic and probably still poor.

Bev also gave me a contract with the same terms and rates that the soon-to-be-fired company had used. The only things that the contract didn't have were my signature and a company name. Bev sat with her pen ready and asked me for the company name, and although I had never considered a name before, I immediately said SunRay Cleaning for some profound but private reason. The following Monday night at 8:00 p.m., I was there with two assistants cleaning dutifully until midnight. For six months I cleaned houses during the day and the law firm at night. It was an exhausting time, but when I look back at that office job, I think about that time as the real start of my business and never think about the long hours.

Grant

If the reports of Caffrey's screw up are accurate, I may finally get his job. He was apparently on a call last night with one of our clients and the rest of the professionals who will work together to assemble the private equity offering that they are undertaking, when he stepped in deep shit. The client is now based in New York and Toronto but the business was formed in Montreal, and the founding scientists and the corporate accountants who were on this call last night are all in Montreal. The pre-call chatter among that group was in French, but when the call formally began, Caffrey just started speaking English.

One of the scientists interrupted and asked if everyone on the call was fluent in French and before anyone could respond Caffrey said, "This is a business call, so of course it is in English. French is the language of the farm and the factory and I don't see any fuckin' cows or machinery, so let's get on with it."

He's lost his mind and I literally can't stop laughing!

The client was actually so dumbfounded that they didn't reply and, after an awkward silence, the call proceeded in English without any mention of what was said. By the morning, however, the client had fired us. All of the lawyers and accountants on the call were buzzing about how Caffrey is a liability to the firm.

The coffee-room rumour mill says that the big boys are pulling together a meeting for this afternoon, which can't bode well for the old man. I haven't seen Caffrey this morning, and I wonder if he even knows that the shit has hit the fan. I could call him and give him a heads up—but I won't.

The old man should have left years ago. If he has passed up so many chances to leave voluntarily, maybe it takes an event like this for the firm to push him off of the ledge. Perhaps I should have a greater sense of loyalty, but Caffrey has never gone out of his way for me unless it was in his own best interest to do so. No one in this industry ever reaches out a hand to anyone until they have calculated whether or not it helps their own situation. Everything that happens is cutthroat, even if we all try our best to make it look friendly. The way that Caffrey treats me is the same way that I treat all those below me, so I don't resent him at all—I just don't feel any obligation to pull him out of a fire.

I have been a vice president in the firm for several years, but the only real power belongs to our three managing directors. Caffrey has been around the longest, but is probably the least influential of the three, although he does officially lead our health care practice. There are several VPs in this practice area, but I am by far the biggest producer and have the strongest reputation in the market. I don't have a flashy style, but I always hit my numbers and that is what these guys care about. I am certain that if Caffrey goes, I will get the call to take his place immediately.

I should be thrilled that I can finally have Caffrey's job, but I can't think of any reason to get excited. Caffrey's job has more prestige and money, but I wonder about the actual work. There will be more wining and dining, which I hate and I will be counted on to bring in new business, which I also hate. I will also have to manage more staff and take an interest in the macro-level performance of the firm rather than just the health care practice and I don't like that either. The worst part of my current job is that I have to endure a semi-monthly executive meeting and if I take Caffrey's job, I will undoubtedly be stuck in daily meetings like that one.

I am not sure the list of good things about the new job is very long, but I can't imagine how I would be able to turn the offer down. It would be viewed as crazy to build a career up for this crowning achievement and then decline the offer of the throne. There is just no way off of this career path and it will be easier to accept the promotion than make a career change. I am reminded of a Chinese idiom that says something like... the hardest part of riding a tiger isn't the ride—it is getting off without being eaten.

Terry

I overheard a conversation that a customer was having on her cell phone as she entered the shop this morning. It was obvious that she was talking with her elderly mother and was trying to end the conversation so that she could place her order. The mother must have been nattering on a bit because the lady could not get a word in to wrap up the call. The shop was otherwise empty so I didn't mind waiting, but the woman was terribly apologetic once she finally freed herself from the conversation. She explained that her mother no longer hears well and that she tends to repeat herself quite a bit, so phone calls are a challenge.

She asked if my parents were like that and I told her that my parents were dead. She mumbled the awkward words that one uses to reply to such stark news and quietly slipped out. I have never said that before and I don't know why I said it today, but it seemed like a perfectly natural thing to say.

Recently, during a late-night call with my sister, I was lectured about how my coolness to my mother was breaking Mom's heart and that I needed to snap out of it before Mom died and I would regret it forever. I caught myself thinking that I might feel relieved if Mom died, and maybe it was a hangover from that twisted thought that led me to tell the customer that my mother was dead today.

I never had a problem with my mother before Dad died. I was closer to my dad, but that just came from my family's tendency to line up activities along gender lines. Dad and I would fish or go to hockey games, while my mom would spend time with my sisters. In my weekly phone calls home in the years before Dad died, I would have my call with whichever parent happened to answer the call and I spoke as comfortably with Mom as I did with dad. I can't think of anything that she said or did to earn this irrational emotion that I am trapped with. She handled the death very well and everyone commented on how well she was holding up throughout the process. She even managed to find the strength to speak at the reception after the funeral about how proud she was of Dad to manage his disease on his terms and to shelter his family from a long, crumbling good-bye. Sure, she cried a bit, but not much, and we all followed her powerful example. But as I listened to her talk about what a great man she had married, I illogically felt anger not sadness. Now, whenever I hear or see her, that pot of rage begins to boil again although I don't know why.

One of my sisters will call again in a few weeks to encourage me to repair my relationship with Mom—I think that they take turns calling. It is a waste of time. Not every relationship in your life will work. My relationship with my mother is broken and I don't know how to fix it. More to the point, I don't want to spend the energy to fix it. I am prepared to accept one unhealthy relationship in my life and move on. My mother has two daughters and plenty of other friends and family, so she can learn to live without me in her life. She should move on as well.

Track 9

Terry

My father had a pet peeve related to how certain people would modify their behaviour towards others based on the social status of that other person. He called it the royalty factor. He never missed an opportunity to show his kids how someone would turn on the charm for their interactions with people of a higher social status. Then he would point out how that same person would treat the receptionist, the doorman or the waiter. He urged us to put some balance back into the world by not just treating all people equally, but by actually showing additional kindness to those who would generally be viewed as the lower rungs of the ladder.

I guess that the lesson stuck with me because I have a hard time with customers who are rude to "lowly" coffee shop clerks.

You need that background to understand the conversation that I got into with a customer today. The customer's name is Grant and he is a big time deal maker at an investment banking company. He is busy and distracted, and never really has time to stop and talk, but my sense is that he is an okay guy. My staff, however, refer to him as "FS" behind his back. FS standing for Fuck Stick. They see him as arrogant and rude, and they feel like he speaks down to them. Cory has been trying to convince Al to "go all soup Nazi on him," but Al says that it wouldn't be in the spirit of the role because he is never displaying any real hatred at the customers, but he would be if he were going off on FS.

When Grant came in this morning, he was talking on his cell phone and returned Cory's happy "good morning" with a severe look that said, "Can't you see that I am on a call?" Cory went to make Grant's customary cappuccino, grumbling to himself. He silently returned, set the coffee down, and had turned to the cash register when Grant snapped his fingers a couple of times and pointed to the muffins. Cory bit his tongue and retrieved the muffin, but I could see a red tinge forming around Cory's ears, so I slipped in at the cash and motioned to Cory that I would finish up with this customer.

Grant finished the call as I was making change from the fifty-dollar bill he flipped onto the counter. I politely said, "You seem like a good guy so I hope you don't mind me asking a favour. My staff find it degrading when you snap your fingers for your order, so would you mind just being a bit easier on them?"

As if not hearing my request he replied: "You own this place right? You can't make it big with one store, so you need to think about other locations and franchising. Christ, Starbucks is everywhere and they aren't much better than you. You need to expand your menu and define your identity, but there must be consultants who can help you with that stuff."

He gave me another two minutes of unsolicited, rapid-fire advice before I could finally get a word in. I feebly squeezed in, "Thanks for that...and about my staff?"

Grant turned and waved his hand as he walked away: "No problem, and your staff will be fine with the expansion." And he was gone.

Cory had a big smile on his face as I turned, open-mouthed, towards him. "He didn't hear a thing that I said."

Cory thanked me for trying to stick up for the staff and said, "There isn't much you can do for a guy like that. What do you call someone who is a really smart, successful guy but who is a moron outside of the office?"

"I think that you call him Fuck Stick."

Grant

I came back from a meeting and saw an e-mail from Ellen in my inbox. I felt embarrassed after I had just complained that she never contacts me during her business trips and here was an e-mail on her first day away. Well, it turns out that the e-mail was just to let me know that she forgot we had concert tickets for Thursday night, so I will need to find someone else to go with me. "Tickets are on the fridge—you will love Bublé!"

Are you fucking kidding me? Michael Bublé? I want to see Aerosmith or Rush, not some queer, pretty boy singing to girls that he probably secretly finds repulsive. How can we have been married for so long and she doesn't even know that I would hate Bublé—it's like she isn't even trying to understand me.

For a year in high school, I was the bass player in Fried Eggs, the hardest rocking band at Eastland High. The band was led by my best friend at the time, Alan Weir. Alan was a little cooler than me, but not much. He had long hair and played lead guitar, but he was the only child of very strict parents, so he also couldn't stay out on a school night. He won the math and science awards every year. We recruited a drummer that Alan had met at a summer math camp and a keyboard player through a flyer we posted on the school bulletin board. Our keyboardist, Sasha, was the only musician who gave us any credibility at school. Sasha was a grade ahead of us and had a reputation as a stoner, which made him seem pretty dangerous and cool to the kids in my grade. It was Sasha that came up with the name, Fried Eggs, because he thought it made us sound like bad-ass, drug-using rockers. Sasha never actually even smoked weed— the kid was clean—but his reputation was wonderfully dirty. The only thing that the Fried Eggs ever got into was Brador—a crappy-tasting beer that we drank as teenagers because the alcohol content was very high.

We used to practice every day after school at Alan's because his parents didn't get home from work until six. We put in the time to become a solid band—I'm not saying that we were world-class, but for high school kids we were damn good. We worked up an eight-song playlist including "Highway Star" by Deep Purple and our wicked version of Brownsville Station's "Smokin' in the Boys Room." Those were the two songs that we performed the day that we won second place in the school talent show. Truthfully we were robbed—there is no way that we should have lost to a jazz quartet, but when the entire quartet plays in the school band and one of the judges is the band instructor, what do you fuckin' expect? Still makes me mad.

The band split up because Sasha left for college that summer and Alan's parents freaked out when they heard some of our lyrics. I never really played again and I don't even own a guitar anymore, but I will never forget being in Fried Eggs. I still play a little air guitar in private and pretend that I am back on my high school auditorium stage. The thing is, I have told Ellen about the band many times. I was in a rock band. I rocked out. Michael Bublé doesn't rock out. How can she not see what a rocker I am?

"Smokin' in the Boys Room" starts with a hard-ass spoken part that I performed and still remember:

"How you doin' out there? Ya ever seem to have one of those days where it just seems like everybody's gettin' on your case, from your teacher all the way down to your best girlfriend? Well, ya know, I used to have 'em just about all the time. But I found a way to get out of 'em. Let me tell you about it!"

That was me in a pitch black auditorium under a single spotlight.

Fuck Bublé!

Fortunately for me I have to go to New York for the rest of the week, so I sent a note to Ellen telling her that I was giving the tickets to my secretary because, sadly, I will be out of town.

My business got to the next level when I decided to take the biggest risk of my life. After six months of cleaning the law office, I was awarded another contract by a close friend of Bev, the office manager in the law firm. There was no competitive bid process or anything—the contract was simply offered to me and I accepted it. I now had five employees commercially and the money looked good. The residential work was still good, but was physically wearing me down. I had to make a decision if I should try to expand into the commercial business or be happy with what I had at that point.

This is when the second piece of magical good luck/good timing occurred. I had seen Anne Tremblay many times without ever meeting her. We had similar running schedules and ran the same seven-kilometre route around the outer ring of my subdivision. One afternoon, she finished her run as I was stretching out after my run and she introduced herself. We had a nice talk and agreed to meet the next day to run together, and it turned out that we shared great conversations and the same running pace.

After a couple of weeks, we agreed to meet for lunch and that afternoon I learned about her professional life. She was in sales with a national office-equipment company and sold photocopiers, fax machines, et cetera, to the local business community. She liked her job and her customers, but was frustrated with her company.

She explained that the reason she was out running at three most afternoons was because she was finished work by mid-afternoon. Anne was paid on a commission basis and was an excellent salesperson so she made great money. In fact, four years ago her commissions pushed her earnings higher than the earnings of the regional vice president in charge of her office. Rather than thanking her for her effort, and for making them a lot of money, her company decided that it was offensive to have a sales person making more than a vice president so they introduced a cap on her income at a level just slightly below that of the vice president.

Anne tried repeatedly to explain why this was not in the best interest of the company, but apparently the bureaucracy was too thick to absorb the logic. She considered quitting, but she actually liked her job and her customers so instead she stayed and learned to play the game.

"I can work about five hours a day and earn enough commission to max out on the company pay grid. Beyond that, there is no incentive to sell more, so I don't. The company leaves all that sales volume on the table for their competitors to walk away with."

I couldn't believe that this level of stupidity existed in big companies and told Anne that I thought that stories of this kind of incompetence were left to the fictional moochers and looters in *Atlas Shrugged*.

She laughed and simply said, "Who is John Galt?" In that exchange, I learned that we shared a love for Ayn Rand's writing and that we shared a business philosophy that would allow us to form a partnership.

Before lunch was over, I knew that I could completely trust this woman and so I fully explained the decision point that my business had reached. She asked about my ability to quickly add staff to service contracts if the business was expanding, and I explained that my connection with the Asian community would provide a steady stream of competent and dedicated staff.

That Sunday afternoon, we developed a business plan that would see Anne become my one-person sales team. She would be paid a portion of all the contracts that we executed with no cap on her compensation. Why would I complain about paying her a dime if I picked up a quarter every time she found us more business?

Anne had long-established relationships—virtually friend-ships—with most of the office managers throughout the city. These managers were responsible for purchasing decisions not only including which photocopier to buy, but also which clean-ing company to hire. The managers trusted Anne and during her first week with me, she secured commitments to start three new office-cleaning contracts. We never looked back from that point and the business has grown steadily year after year. Anne makes more with me than she ever did with the office equip-ment company, and I couldn't be happier to pay her every dollar.

When people tell me how impressed they are with the busi-ness that I have built, I am always a little embarrassed because I think that a great deal of the success has simply been good luck. If I had not been cleaning Charlene Crystal's house on the day that she fired her office cleaner or if I hadn't run into Anne, I would have never have made it out of house cleaning.

Advice for becoming a business success? Have a good idea, work hard, and be very lucky.

Lee

I met with Jennifer—the business lawyer that I had met with Gord at a dinner party—to have a friendly discussion about options that I would have with my business. She had called me a few days after the party and asked me a couple of simple questions about the business before suggesting that we meet to discuss options that I may wish to consider.

Jennifer introduced me to two colleagues who were obviously more junior members of her team and we sat to talk about my business. I assumed that they would know little about my grimy world and so I started at a basic level. They began to interject with questions and it quickly became clear that they had keen insight on my business and industry. After twenty minutes, Jennifer suggested that they present a few ideas that they had been simply brainstorming to give me a sense of their thinking. The next forty-five minutes was a beautiful slide presentation that began with the delivery of bouquets of verbal flowers that saluted the strong growth and profitability of SunRay Cleaning. I admit that I was drawn in and appreciated the recognition.

The presentation discussed types of transactions that could be of interest, including mergers, equity financing, and various forms of sale transactions. I was about to interrupt to say that I was not interested in selling, when they launched into a summary of comparable transactions that had been executed in the cleaning sector. They had the buyer names, the seller names and, most importantly, the price of seemingly dozens of transactions. Jennifer had saved this as a hot button to push to get my interest, and it worked. I think that I maintained a look of professional indifference but internally? Fuck me, my mind was blown.

Jennifer spoke slowly and calmly, and with just a hint of a smile said, "Lee, it is enough money to never have to work again. You can keep going and build the value higher, but once you are past $10 million the next million will not change your lifestyle. Having money is about having time—time to do the things you want and time to spend with your son while he is still young."

She was completely right. It was enough money and I would love the free time.

Enough money.

I am not a lavish person, so if I had millions I would buy a nicer car and take more expensive vacations, but I can't think of anything else that I would spend it on. So if the business is already worth more than I need, why would I keep growing it and risk fucking something up?

Enough time.

My schedule is odd but it works. I see Jackson for breakfast and I am home when he returns from school and well into the evening when I leave for work around eight. Despite working nights I probably spend more time with my son than a parent who works nine to five. My weekends are free, so I see him then and squeeze in a bit of a social life for myself as well.

However, not being home at night takes a strange toll on me. A few weeks ago, I came home from work expecting to see my mother and Jackson starting their day, but the house was completely quiet. I went through the quiet kitchen and up to the bedrooms but both Mom and Jackson's rooms were empty. My heart raced. I came down to the living room and, to my relief, I saw both of them curled up together sound asleep on the couch. I touched my mother's arm to wake her and she smiled up at me like a sleepy angel.

I asked, "Is everything okay?"

She whispered, "Jackson had a high fever and a bad night—he couldn't sleep and he was overtired and frustrated. I just laid him down here with me and we both fell asleep. His fever has dropped a lot."

She is so loving and caring and perfect. And at that moment, I was overcome with anger towards her. I had to fight back this emotion, which I knew was completely irrational. At that moment I was jealous of her bond with Jackson and overcome with guilt for not being there for him. More time sounds good.

I agreed to meet with Jennifer and her team the following week to discuss what steps, if any, that I wished to take. Jennifer's professional courtesy and tact are impeccable, so there was no hint of pressure in her suggestion to meet again and yet when I agreed to meet, I had the very real sense that I had set something unstoppable in motion.

Grant

When I was in school I was a bit of a late bloomer. My parents never really pushed me to achieve anything better than the Bs and Cs that I was picking up without any effort, and it never occurred to me that you can't get into the best universities with those marks. When it came time to apply, my high school guidance counsellor suggested a short list of schools and programs that might accept me, and that is how I ended up in an unrenowned commerce program.

School began to make sense for me the moment I stepped onto campus and I just couldn't get enough of it. There was a sense of maturity about university that was so appealing in contrast to my high school days. The professors were so sophisticated and the courses seemed so relevant to the real working world that I would soon face that I was finally turned on to education. There was a clear rhythm to each day at university and I always knew where to be and what to do. I went from the classroom to the library, to the cafeteria to the classroom to the library, and it all felt right.

I ended my first year with an 88 percent average and pushed that to 90 in year two. My parents were delighted and perhaps shocked to see my success and quickly suggested law school as the next academic stage. I saw no reason to object and when I was accepted into the across-town law program at the University of

Ottawa, I simply changed my bus route and found a new library and cafeteria but basically maintained my pleasing routine.

While my classmates fell for the intrigue of criminal law or the heady issues of constitutional law, I felt the real-world pull of business law and learned to love a well-drafted agreement. Even though I have lawyers who do the leg work of agreement preparation for my deals now, I still love the sense of order and logic found in a well-constructed document.

When I think about my university days, I remember them as extremely happy times although I can't remember doing many things that would objectively be considered fun. I never really partied at university and although I did occasionally socialize with classmates, I never really had many friends. I remember that I was happy about knowing what to do and where to be all of the time. I remember enjoying that your performances were scored by a numbering system and that I could determine if I was doing better than the next guy by comparing grades. You never receive such ordinal rankings in any other part of your life and that makes it harder to determine if you are winning.

When I listen to other people talk about their university days, they tell stories about frat parties, football games or sexual discovery. They never discuss key moments of learning or specific exams or essays that they succeeded on, but those are exactly the moments that make me smile when I think back on those wonderful years.

Terry

Everything is bothering me today. The smell of foaming milk is nauseating to me for the first time in my life. The weather is beautiful and everyone is happy and that is really pissing me off. What the hell is this music?

"Cory, this music is terrible. Find something else."

"I'll change it, but you need a doctor because this is amazing stuff. This is The Drive By Truckers, my friend, and 'Carl Perkins Cadillac' is one of the best songs you will hear all week."

I need a doctor? You don't know the half of it. I have an appointment next week to perform a test that I think I will fail. Damn, I can barely breathe. If a doctor who thinks that you have cancer tells you to come back in a few days for testing, you are a dead man walking. I'm going to hyperventilate. If I could talk to someone about this maybe it would be better, but I don't want to freak anyone out so I haven't said a word. I guess I will need to tell everyone after the appointment. I can't imagine what I will say—I guess it depends if they give me weeks or months to live. Oh my God, I'll be dead in a year for sure.

I guess that I should sell the shop. It seems silly to spend your final days working so that you can save for retirement. I could travel and maybe hike Kilimanjaro like I've always said that I would. I can't do that—I'll be sick. Chemo kicks the crap out of you. Maybe I shouldn't go through all of that—no one ever gets cured, they all just lose their hair and puke a lot. Why should I even try to fight it? I could just make the most of whatever time I have and die with all of my hair.

Listen to me—I sound like some kind of tree-hugging homeopath. I believe in doctors, I believe in our health care system, I am getting way ahead of myself.

Last week, my GP sent me for a follow up on some bump on my shoulder and it leads to this mania. My family doctor is hard to stir up, as she believes in letting the body heal itself. She tends to let things run their course, never overprescribes, and has never referred me to a specialist. My blood pressure climbed a bit when she told me that she wanted me to see a dermatologist and have the thing on my shoulder checked out, but I really wasn't worried.

Her receptionist would make the appointment with the dermatologist and the receptionist would call to give me the details. That night, there was a slightly apologetic message on my answering machine from the receptionist telling me that all of the dermatologists are very busy and that my appointment was in five months on such and such a date. I was actually relieved to hear that, as I figured that anything serious would not be cued up with the acne kids for five months, which is exactly why I almost fainted when the next day the receptionist called to say that my GP was not happy with the dermatology booking and so the doctor made a call on my behalf and now my appointment had been magically moved to next Monday morning—wasn't I lucky? Holy shit!

The dermatologist is Zsa Zsa Gabor or some close relative of Zsa Zsa. In an accent that is half thick Hungarian and half Hollywood, she asks me to "Please take your shirt ovv, darlink." Her version of comforting small talk was to describe to me how the city now has half as many dermatologists as they use to and now they must rush through every patient. She removed a pair of diamond-studded glasses from her silvery hair and moved in to take a look at this thing on my shoulder, which now occupies my every waking moment and thus feels like it weighs eight pounds.

She feels obligated to put me through mini med school as she assesses the mole. She explains that one evaluates such things by following an A-B-C-D-E checklist. A is for asymmetry—one would like to see a nice symmetric mole rather than this oddly shaped one that I have. B is for borders—a nice, regular border would be preferable and while my border is somewhat irregular she says that it is not too concerning. C is for colour: "see how you have a range of colours in your growth…that concerns me, for most regular moles are a consistent colour." D is for diameter—the boulder on my shoulder measures five millimetres, which coincidently is the break point between worry and don't worry.

By the time she is set to explain E, I have already jumped ahead to F which I am certain stands for fucked. E is for evolutionary change and when I explain that the growth was something that I only noticed a few months ago and that it seems to have grown a lot since then, she lets out a resigned and exaggerated puff and pursed her lips as if she is thinking about how to explain this to me. She actually didn't say anything for five seconds, which must be her Hollywood half working up the drama.

As she put the glasses back up in her hair, she explained that she would like to take a biopsy because she is concerned that this is not a conventional mole, but instead may be melanoma. For five more minutes she talked and handed me pamphlets, but I really never heard a word. I felt blood draining from my body and I was close to vomiting or fainting or both. The dermatologist can do the biopsy herself but not today because the city has half as many dermatologists as we used to and her schedule is so tight...

I will have to come back next week—her receptionist will call with the date and time. I got out of there as fast as I could and raced back to my car where I sat shaking for ten minutes before I could start it.

Since then, I have been a wreck and my nerves are on a thin edge. Cory has changed the music from the Drive By Truckers to Lauryn Hill who is one of my favourites, but I can't stand her voice right now. I went over and turned the music off and returned to preparing for the lunch rush.

Grant

I am beginning to be haunted by the woman that I never had. Last night, I had a dream that Kate was lying in my bed at home in near ecstasy touching herself as her hips pushed up into the air. In her ice queen voice she ordered, "Finish me off—get down on me now," as she rolled onto her back. The dream blurred into a whirling haze, but I could feel Kate's wet heat as she frantically drove herself into my chin. I could feel the smooth, firm, hard peach halves of her ass in each of my hands and I could feel my pulse racing. I remember that I was excited by the passion, but I was frightened that Kate's moans would draw Ellen's attention. I moved faster to work Kate to climax and I could feel her body tighten and freeze in that split section before she released into a fitful orgasm. Her voice rose and she moaned loudly, and her call was shockingly echoed with another loud moan from a different voice. I kept my head down but heard this moaning call and answer several times before I lifted my eyes to see Ellen's rocking ass as she sat perched on Kate's face above me.

I awoke panting and with a rock-hard dick in my Manhattan hotel room. I got up and splashed some water on my face, and as my breathing and erection subsided, I returned to bed. I have no idea what meaning that I should take from my dream, but it left me with a guilty anxiety that I don't deserve.

If this were the first time that I dreamed about Kate I would blame it on the drinking last night, but I have had a series of dreams about Kate and I can't explain why because I don't feel any particular desire for her and my only daytime thoughts about her relate to questioning my own sanity for letting things get as far as they did.

If alcohol was the trigger for my dream, then last night was a great set up. I had way too much to drink. I am in New York to help my client, Aziq Therapeutics, negotiate a license extension with their Japanese partner. Aziq has little experience working with the Japanese and they need my guidance. The challenge that the Aziq team has is that they cannot adjust to the pace of negotiations with their Japanese counterparts. I continue to counsel the Aziq team to slow down and allow the Japanese team to work through the agreement in their own style, but Aziq is a fast moving and direct company and that sometimes leads to impatience.

There are no quick agreements with Japanese companies. The Japanese simply do not like to have open disagreements in their negotiation, so while you are at the table with them they seem to agree to everything. The next morning, a memo arrives saying that they do not support deal points numbers one, three, six and nine, and that we need to have more discussion. Things would be so much easier if we could openly disagree, but you have to accept the business culture if you wish to complete a deal and not become completely frustrated. Unfortunately, less experienced groups like Aziq don't appreciate this subtlety, so each time a meeting concludes the Aziq team walks away thinking that they have a final deal.

We finished the negotiations with the Japanese by about 7:00 p.m., but the Japanese team declined the dinner invitation saying that they needed to meet internally to discuss how to present the solution back to the Tokyo office. That probably means that the deal that we reached will not be the final solution, but my client thinks that they have a final deal and I really didn't feel like getting in the way of their celebration.

The Aziq team is led by a senior VP named Jerry Quinn, who is originally from Boston. And although I am certain that he has never been to Ireland, he insisted that we honour his heritage at his favourite New York City Irish pub.

As we arrived, our Bostonian host insisted on taking care of the drink order so the rest of us filed into a booth while he headed to the bar. A few minutes later our host returned with the bartender in tow. The bartender carried a tray of Guinness and some dark liquid in shot glasses.

"Have you ever had an Irish Car Bomb, boys?" asked the bartender with a smile that suggested that it was a dare.

As I was about to learn, an Irish Car Bomb is a fast way to get drunk. You fill a shot glass to about two-thirds full with Baileys Irish Cream and then top it off with Irish whiskey. Then you shout "Bombs away!" as you drop the shot glass into a pint of Guinness and drink it fast before the cream begins to curdle.

As I was downing my third car bomb of the evening, the thought struck me that the drink probably will curdle in my stomach whether I drink it fast or slow but I didn't want to break protocol, so down it went. I don't know the history of that drink, but it can't be politically correct to make Irish Car Bombs, but no one in that pub seemed to care.

Before the fourth round arrived, I excused myself and went to the bar for water. Jerry dropped a hand on my shoulder a few minutes later and suggested that we dump the corporate crew and have some real fun. I told him that I wasn't feeling up to it and that I was heading back for a good night's sleep because I was expecting that the Japanese would be keeping me busy the next day. Jerry waved off my concern and told me that instead of a good night's sleep I just needed to get laid and that he was the man to see that this would happen.

Jerry told me about a couple of "cougar bars" in the neighbourhood where the women are not looking to get into a long romance or anything complicated. These women just want to meet a decent guy with a strong libido who can meet their needs and allow them to be home at a decent hour so that they can get up and go to work tomorrow. I played it cool and told Jerry that I know exactly the kind of place that he was talking about, but that I would have to take a rain cheque because I just wasn't up for it tonight.

Truthfully, I have no idea if it is as easy as Jerry says, but my guess is that there is a little Irish exaggeration in his story. The idea of women showing up at a bar ready to go home with the first guy who has no visible signs of excreting wounds seems farfetched. The other problem is that I am quite obviously married—if my personality doesn't give it away than the distinct ring finger tan line would be a clincher. If such women exist, they are certainly not looking for a married man and I think that Jerry overlooked that point.

I escaped back to my hotel without a trip to the cougar bar and only one more Irish Car Bomb, but Jerry said that he had a concrete plan for cashing in the rain cheque that I used to get back to the hotel early. So this morning I have a hangover, a sense of worry about Jerry's plans and a request to meet the Japanese negotiating team at 11:00 a.m. for a discussion to clarify some deal points—it's going to be a long day.

Terry

I psyched myself out on this one. I was back at the dermatologist's this morning for a punch biopsy of my mole. The receptionist told me to allocate an hour for the appointment: "Although," she added cheerfully, "it doesn't usually take that long."

I steeled myself for an hour of agony as I confronted the physical torture of the biopsy and the mental anguish of getting closer to the inevitable diagnosis. Doctor Zsa Zsa didn't provide any mini-med-school lecture today and initially didn't really say much at all. She came in and quickly swabbed alcohol on my shoulder, then injected the area around the mole with an anesthetic and said that she would return in a few minutes. When she returned, she obviously saw some stress on my face and I think that made her slow down and talk me though the procedure as some odd way of providing comfort to me.

As she worked, she explained the she was just stretching the skin, twirling her device into the mole a couple of times, giving it a little clip, setting the sample in a test tube and putting a Steri-Strip over the mole. It took less than a minute; there was no pain, no stitches.

Zsa Zsa explained that not only did the city not have enough dermatologists, but we lacked pathologists as well. "You should be able to get this result in a day or two ,but we will be lucky to have it in a week. Let's book you in for two weeks today to review the results because we will have the report back by then for sure."

I left feeling a little silly about the anxiety I had for this appointment. I shouldn't have worried about this appointment—I should have saved that worry for the next appointment. With an appointment only a couple of weeks away, I have to decide if I will tell Carol what is happening. I want to protect her from the stress, but she will probably take greater offence to being kept in the dark—a lose-lose situation.

Lee

I was the only customer in the coffee shop this morning, so as I waited for my coffee and bagel I was able to listen clearly to a beautiful version of "Over the Rainbow" that was playing in the quiet shop. I closed my eyes for a few seconds to let the music wash over me and maybe because I was so tired I was nearly overcome with emotion. Not sadness or happiness or any easily defined emotion. It was as if I were struck by the sheer beauty of what I was hearing. It pulled on my heart and I felt tears well up behind my eyes.

The young guy who works there—Cory, I think—says, "That's not Judy Garland, you know. It's a woman named Eva Cassidy. When you have more time, come back and ask me to tell you about her."

I thanked him and left, but I couldn't get the song or the singer's name out of my head.

When Jackson left for school, I found the song on iTunes and downloaded it and began to search for the story that the coffee shop guy was prepared to tell me.

Eva Cassidy was born near Washington, D.C., and was singing by her teens. Her voice is special—it is smooth and soulful and beautiful. She performed in different groups and on various projects within the D.C. area and was well respected locally. Her style of music is traditional with a jazz feel and her song preference favours old classics like "Somewhere Over the Rainbow" and "Danny Boy." This was not the kind of thing that was going to make her a pop star or sell millions of albums, so she enjoyed only limited and exclusively local success.

She recorded a duet album in 1992 and in 1996 she recorded her own album called Live at Blues Alley, but it was not a commercial success. Shortly after the album release, Eva died of melanoma. She was thirty-three years old.

If that were the end of the story, it would be sad but not remarkable—there are many talented singers who never achieve success despite their obvious talents. But Eva Cassidy would find success—many years after her death. Almost four years after her death, a U.K. radio host stumbled across an obscure recording and played Eva's version of "Somewhere Over the Rainbow" and the audience clambered to discover this fresh voice. Apparently the radio host had no idea who she was or that she was deceased. When he researched her on behalf of his listeners and reported back that she had died at thirty-three a few years earlier, his listeners became even more interested. Over the months and years that followed, her career caught fire and her songs began to sell throughout the world. Other recordings have been assembled posthumously from her unreleased studio sessions and they have also sold millions.

How strange and how sad that she never found her audience when she was alive. I listened to the song one more time and didn't try to fight the emotion as I let the tears roll down my cheeks. Eva's story was sad but my tears were not sorrow. They were just the cleansing tears that wash away fatigue and stress when you listen to certain music at a certain moment.

Lee

I met Jennifer's team for the second time this afternoon and we got into the specifics, including what their firm would do for me, who else would be involved, how they all get paid, et cetera. There was undoubtedly some momentum created in the meeting and if I allow it to carry on, I will probably face a life-changing transaction in no time.

The team is excellent. They are competent and well prepared. They gave me the sense that they have done this type of thing dozens of times (which they have) and I took great comfort in that experience. We reviewed the types of transactions that were possible and quickly struck down alternatives. I do not want to consider buying other companies to start my own conglomerate. I do not want to sell equity in SunRay because that will essentially establish an ownership partnership and I don't want to share decision-making. Plus that situation will mean that I get some money for the shares I sell but it won't give me any more time as my job will require at least as much time as before. If I am going to do anything with the company I have to get money and time.

As we systematically ticked off the alternative strategies, it was clear to all of us that the only scenario of any interest was an outright sale. Everything else that we discussed sounded like it would complicate my life. Selling is clean. Cash out and leave.

The meeting ended with an agreement to meet again next week after I have some time to digest the discussion and the team has time to prepare a timeline of the intended process. It was a great meeting but, as I pulled away from the parking lot, I could feel my pulse racing as the implications of a sale swept over me.

As if reading my mind from sixteen stories above, Jennifer called my cell phone at that moment. She told me that she didn't want to get into the personal aspect of this transaction in front of her staff, but that she suggested that I not focus on the transaction details for now and that I instead spend my energies in thinking about the personal issues over the next few days. It was the kind of call that a friend makes and one that I didn't expect from my lawyer. She ended the call by assuring me that she would support my decision not to sell if I opt for the status quo, and that no one but me could decide if this was the right time to sell.

I certainly have plenty to think about. It is interesting how the value of the business just gradually ticked up over time without my noticing—I had my head down for so long that I didn't look up to see what had been amassed.

Selling my business wasn't even on my radar a few weeks ago and now it seems that I am one decision away from making it happen. I didn't know that such a big change was possible, but now the opportunity to change is staring straight at me.

Grant

It is so embarrassing when lies are told and everyone knows that it is a lie and the liar knows that everyone knows but goes ahead with the lie nonetheless. The firm announced that effectively immediately, "Caffrey would be stepping down for personal health reasons. On behalf of the partners and all staff, we would like to thank him for his tremendous contributions," blah blah blah. I guess that they are trying to protect his reputation, but his reputation is shot, so why not just say that he was fired for doing something stupid? He isn't going to care—no one will ever see him again because he will be living on some beautiful island counting his money within a week. I hope that there are no francophones on his island.

So Caffrey's gone and the managing partners have asked to meet with me at the end of the day. I guess that I better decide if I will take this job that I don't really want. I have tried to develop a refusal speech, but no matter how I phrase it I just sound like a coward. Everyone will see a refusal as me shrinking back from an opportunity because of a fear of failure. People will wonder why I want to stay in my cocoon when I am being offered so much more. People will question my commitment, my drive and my manhood.

Two of my junior VPs stopped by my office early this morning and they were bubbling with enthusiasm because the grapevine had told them that I was getting the big job. I wish that I were as excited for me as they are. I know that they are not really excited for me. They are excited because if I move up then the potential for them to move up is created.

Everyone will be shocked if I say no, but that is what I want to do. I need the words to reject the offer. I could try honesty and just tell them that I prefer my current job to this one. As sad as it sounds, there is no respect for honesty in this business. The senior partners will look through what I want and will focus on what I should want and see the incongruity as a character flaw. I could lie, but all of the potential lies don't seem like things that I could sustain over time—if I say that I have health issues or that I am going through marital problems to avoid the new job, will I have to die or divorce to maintain my story?

I am trapped and I know it. For all of my brave thoughts of taking a stand and rejecting the promotion, I know that I will take the job. It is the path of least resistance and that is apparently what I am all about. My life has some problems. I don't love my job and my marriage isn't magical, but nothing is perfect so I will accept this promotion and accept that nothing in my life has to change.

I called and left a message for Ellen to suggest that we go out for dinner tonight because I have news to share with her. I made reservations at our favourite restaurant and asked for champagne to be ready for our arrival. If I am going to pretend that I want this job, I may as well pretend to celebrate it.

Terry

I have spent the last two nights on the Internet learning so much about melanoma that I think I should be close to earning a degree. Doctors must hate the Internet. They probably pine for the good old days when patients didn't know anything and never asked any questions. Now every guy with a computer arrives at the doctor's office with a list of questions, challenging every statement that the doctor makes.

I started with the website from the Canadian Cancer Society. They had an incredibly cruel teaser link on the home page under the title Statistics. Who can get past that first page? It's really all I want to know—what are my odds? I downloaded the statistics PDF file and found 116 pages of charts and graphs that convert life and death into bar graphs and pie charts. I scrolled through, looking for melanoma and found lots of facts, but not much meaning. In 2007, they estimate that there will be 4,600 new diagnoses of melanoma and 900 deaths in Canada.

Another graph stated that I have a 1.3 percent chance of getting melanoma but only a 0.3 percent chance of dying from melanoma. Did that mean that about one in four who get it will die? That's harsh. A survival chart on another page said that melanoma patients have an 89 percent survival rate. Both charts couldn't be right. Which way is it? The chart listed cancer by type and at the bottom of the survival chart was pancreatic cancer, which has only a 6 percent survival rate. I seem to remember that point from Carol's uncle's death when many people were saying that he had the worst kind and that no one survives pancreatic cancer. Now I know that 6 percent have a shot.

I read about diagnoses from a few sites and they were consistent in the message that everything begins with a biopsy. I can imagine my sample sitting unattended in a dingy basement pathology lab. I have read all about biopsy analysis and how to "characterize" melanoma, so I am now anxiously waiting for my Clark and Breslow scores. Clark will tell me the level of skin penetration for the growth from level one to level five. Three or higher is bad and I feel like I am at the casino craps table cheering for level one—come on snake eye. Breslow is a measurement of tumor thickness and obviously thick is bad. So I will ask about Clark Breslow and will be listening for low numbers on both.

I spied on a couple of melanoma patient chatrooms last night to see if I could learn something of what to expect from my upcoming appointment. It is clear that I need more focus than I had with my initial appointment with the dermatologist, or else I will miss all of the important information after the initial diagnosis. I need to stay focused and get my treatment going immediately. I need to make decisions and that means I need to understand the facts, the unknowns and the odds. Most of the chatroom people said that you should take a loved one with you to the appointment just for that reason. That seems like good advice, but I don't have a loved one who knows about this appointment.

I managed to hide the little wound from the biopsy from Carol by sleeping with a t-shirt on for the last few nights. I want to tell her and I have rehearsed my speech a few times, but I can't get it right. I really don't want to scare her. At the same time, I don't want her to think that I am not taking this seriously, which will be her first instinct. I need a balanced message that says, "I am concerned and proactive, but not really worried as it is unlikely to be cancerous." If I could say something like that without bursting into tears, it might be convincing.

I can't shake the sense that my life is about to change. Maybe I am wrong and all my worry is for nothing, but I really feel that the next part of my story will not allow me to enjoy my status quo. I wasn't looking for a change at all, but life throws curve balls.

Part Two

"No Games Today"

Terry

I am down to a week before the results appointment and I am a bit of a wreck. I didn't sleep all night and was out of bed half an hour earlier than usual. In my frazzled state I struggled with my morning rituals so despite the early wakening, I got to the shop a little later than usual. The staff had everything under control and Cory was writing the day's lyrics on the board as I arrived. That normal daily activity that is such a hallmark of our shop was completely intolerable for me today. It all just seemed so insignificant and routine. People need to wake up and stop drifting—people need to make the most of their opportunities.

I asked Cory to step aside and I wiped away what he had written on the board. I replaced the lyrics with the following written scream: "No Games Today! If there are things in your life that you don't like, fix them today!"

Cory stepped back and asked if everything was okay. I said, "Yeah, everything is okay, but just watch how many people come in here today that are unhappy and accept their unhappiness. What are they waiting for? They need to fix their life before it is too late."

The next person that came into the shop was the Asian cleaning lady. She read the sign and then waited for her order. When her bagel was ready, she reread the sign and then casually looked at me, smiled and said that she thought that was good advice and then turned and walked out. I never noticed before, but she actually doesn't have any accent at all—that's strange.

But why doesn't she get it? I wrote that message on the board for her—and others like her. I can tell that her life is miserable and that she is in a hopeless rut, but what I can't understand is why she doesn't change it? Why doesn't she at least try to change it? If she were facing death, she would regret that she led an unhappy life working nights to put food on the table and would curse herself for accepting that fate.

I spent a couple of nights thinking about what I should do if I am given bad news. It wasn't that hard to come up with the list of things to do if the news is bad because that will mean that my time will be short. The shorter my time, the shorter my list. I will spend time making sure that my family is looked after financially and that I spend as much time with them as I can and that I say everything that I wish to say. Interestingly, when faced with death I have no physical desires—no wish to run a marathon or climb a mountain. I have always said that I want to climb Kilimanjaro, but it doesn't seem important now. Instead, everything is related to my heart and mind—I want to be sure that I squeeze out all of my parental advice to Ben and that I leave no feeling unexpressed to Carol.

Most people are not as fortunate and their lives are difficult and unhappy. If they were facing the urgency of cancer, I am certain that they would want to fix their problems, so I am simply lending them my urgency and imploring them to make the changes. I want people to stop accepting their unhappiness— stop choosing the same shitty status quo. These people have big problems, but they are not even trying to fix them. That is why I wrote a note that screams at them to change. That is why I put the message on the board. I hope the cleaning lady gets it—I hope that someone gets it.

Last night was a truly enjoyable night at work. All of the jobs seemed to go smoothly and my own cleaning time sailed by quickly. I get a sense of accomplishment from a night like that, which makes me a little happier. It is the same sense that I get from checking off another day on my training schedule when I run. I am not going to win any races and no one but me would know if I skipped a day, but I still feel a small happy pride when I finish each training session.

I had that happy step in my stride as I went into Beanfest on my way home, but the Beanfest vibe was off this morning. There was no music playing and the lyric board didn't have any lyrics on it, but instead had a message reading: "No Games Today! If there are things in your life that you don't like, fix them today!"

What a terrible thing for them to put on their sign. People come here for respite and refuge from their problems. They want the pleasure of a coffee and maybe a biscotti. They want to share a smile and pleasant snippets of conversation with the familiar staff. They should not be reminded of their problems, their disappointments and their pain. It is arrogant and preachy to put such a message in front of paying customers.

I was actually so annoyed by the sign that I was going to say something to the staff, but as I met the eye of the guy who owns the place, I saw that there was something deeper in the message and I immediately knew that it wasn't written from arrogance. It was written from pain. The owner stared at me as if imploring me to read the sign. I glanced once again at the sign and then looked back to the owner and said in the most casual and calm voice that I could muster, "Thanks, that's good advice." I left quickly, but I have been thinking of that sign all day.

I spent the first half hour wondering what was wrong with the place or the guy who wrote the message. Is the store in financial trouble? Is the owner having a mid-life crisis? He must have something in his life that needs changing or he wouldn't be instructing others to do so. I found myself worrying about this relative stranger.

My worry turned to introspection and I began to think of what I would fix in my life if I could wave a wand. I had been feeling good about my situation lately as the job was good, the company was in good shape and my home life was great. I was fairly close to deciding that I would not pursue the business sale with Jennifer and her team because my instinct was it wasn't yet my time to sell.

But "if there are things in your life that you don't like." There is really only one thing that I don't like and that is that I don't have enough time to do all the things that I wish I could, specifically being home with Jackson throughout the night. If that is my problem, I could "fix it today" by following Jennifer's suggestion to sell SunRay. Benjamin Franklin probably reversed the order when he said that time is money, because as I contemplate selling my business, I really see that money is time—luxurious time.

That coffee shop sign was probably intended for people with unhappy lives who are stuck in bad jobs and have terrible family lives. I have a great thing going on all fronts and I am not calling out for change. But the sign didn't say: "If your life is a mess then fix it." It just said, "If there are things that you don't like, fix them."

The last part of the message is what is most striking for me—the part that said "fix them today." There is urgency in that statement. The author must be watching hourglass sand. It is compelling logic to immediately modify an unsatisfactory state rather than passively accept dissatisfaction. The reality is that no one ever takes such action urgently. Think about the people you know who accept their bad situation because of some terribly lame excuse: I think that he will change; I'll go back to school once I save enough money, maybe after the kids move out. What are we waiting for? What am I waiting for?

I recently read Suzy Welch's book 10-10-10. It is the current flavour of the month in a never-ending series of self-help books. I can't help it, but I buy them all. Welch's book is typical of most in this genre—it contains a handful of thoughtful ideas that would make a very compelling seven-page essay. There is no commercial market for seven-page essays, so instead it is stretched ad nauseam into a 240-page book.

The book focuses on why we make certain decisions and provides guidance on making important decisions. The premise is that when faced with an important decision, one should ask herself three questions: What are the consequences of my decision in ten minutes; ten months; ten years? I like the idea behind the book and today it seems to connect to the urgency within the coffee shop message. People could make decisions today that will obviously improve their life in ten years and maybe even ten months, but they don't take that decision because it will make their life worse ten minutes from now. The reality is that, when most people are faced with short-term pain for long-term gain, they do nothing because they do not want the short-term pain.

Many people hang on longer than they should in dead relationships simply because they don't want to experience the drama of the break up. It sounds ridiculous, but virtually everyone will make a bad long-term decision or at least defer a good long-term decision just because they don't want to face the implications of the first ten minutes of that decision.

What if I were to use the 10-10-10 method on selling my business? Would I be better off in ten years? Seems obvious that I would. In ten months? Maybe I would struggle with the adjustment, but I think that it would be net positive after ten months. Ten minutes? My heartbeat quickens when I think about the near term. I would have to make a big jump and I feel paralyzed on the edge of that cliff. I think about the conversations that I would need to have with my office staff, my cleaning crew, my customers, my family and it all seems stressful. It is all just short-term pain but isn't it logical that the pain that you fear the most is the one that you will face next?

When I went to bed this morning, I was mentally preparing the pro-con list on selling SunRay and fell asleep without resolution. I can't say that I woke up with a decision, but I can say that the first thought that I had when I woke was "Fix them today." It's crazy that a random message on a coffee shop blackboard has me reevaluating my life plan.

Grant

Jack Cash is joining the firm.

When I walked in to meet with the two remaining managing directors last night ,they were smiling like little kids bursting with a happy secret. I actually felt a rush of emotion as it seemed obvious that these guys were very happy about asking me to replace Caffrey.

They wasted no time and said, "Grant we have unbelievable news—Jack Cash has decided to join us and take Caffrey's old job. He will breathe new life into the group and we will be number one in the field in months. You are going to be busier than ever with huge new deals. We had been talking to Jack for months, but had a hard time fitting him in with Caffrey here. So you see, Caffrey leaving is actually great news for us and for you."

As they went on to tell me how exciting this was, my mind was focused on not showing the pain from this insult.

Jack Cash is the rock star of our industry—the name helps, and he is most often referred to as Jumpin' Jack Cash. He is a Canadian who has been running Merrill's New York life-science practice for a decade and is always the man to beat when competing for clients. His personality is huge and he backs it up with excellent work. He is smooth, articulate, confident and yet humble and likeable. He has a loyal customer following and it truly is a great catch for this firm.

And it still feels like I was kicked in the stomach.

"Grant, we want you to work directly with Jack for the first few weeks to get him up to speed with our shop. You will be his right-hand man anyway, so it makes sense that you are his chaperone for a while, right?"

I think that I conducted myself well in the meeting and that I said all the right things and smiled and laughed at the right times—it is good to have that autopilot setting available for moments like that—but really, the meeting was a twenty-minute blur.

I called Ellen and told her that something came up and that I had to cancel dinner and that I would be home late. I left the office and drove for an hour in no particular direction, trying to vent the anger that I had from the news of Jumpin' Jack Cash. I understand that Jack is a better candidate than I am. He is a better deal man than I am and, more importantly, he is the rain-maker that I will never become and don't really want to become. I think that what has me pissed off is that the managing directors never even saw me as a candidate.

I pulled into a sports bar for dinner and stayed for the night because I didn't want to go home and really had nowhere else to go. The only game on was Tampa at the Blue Jays and, despite it only being late August, neither had a shot at the playoffs. It didn't matter to me and I focused on the game like it was the seventh game of the World Series. I drank too many beers and drove home well over the limit, but steered the car safely into the laneway and ended my night falling asleep on the couch with one more beer and Sports Centre.

And this morning, I was supposed to walk into the office and share in the excitement that Jack Cash is coming. I delayed the inevitable by stopping for a cappuccino. And this is where things got weird. The sign for the music game in the coffee shop didn't have any lyrics.

Instead there was a message on the board that read: "No Games Today! If there are things in your life that you don't like, fix them today!"

Why would they post that on this day of all days? I wonder if this sign was just for me, like the voice in Field of Dreams that says, "If you build it, they will come" and only one guy can hear the voice.

Fix them today. I can't fix them today. My problems are complicated and need to be carefully analyzed. I need to work out a new long-term plan and think through all of my options. It is just like those bohemians in the coffee shop to think that you can fix problems instantly but they are right about the need to fix them.

I took my cappuccino into my office and closed the door. For the next two hours I sat with only a yellow legal pad in front of me and wrote out two columns: 1) Problem; 2) Solution. Problem: Job is boring. Solution: New job. Problem: Don't love wife. Solution: New wife. Problem: No friends. Solution: Get friends. Problem: Leafs suck. Solution: Cheer for someone else.

If the coffee shop had its wish for me, I would have a big day ahead of me. By day's end I would be unemployed and divorced, looking for friends in the chatroom of fans of the Chicago Blackhawks.

Grant

The buzz around the Jumpin' Jack Cash news is still going strong and probably will get even louder when he arrives next week. Not one person has given any thought to the possibility that I may be disappointed that I was not offered the job. It now seems as if I was the only one who saw me as the rightful heir.

When I told Ellen that Cash was getting Caffrey's job even she was excited, as she had heard me speak about him on many occasions. She said that Cash will put some energy into the tired old office and she is right on that point. I never explained to her that I was a little hurt by the hire, but she certainly never sensed anything was wrong with me, either. I guess that she is not all that tuned in to my feelings these days.

Ever since I wrote out that problem/solution page, I feel like my chest is tighter and that it is harder to get a deep breath. I fully realize that I am not in a happy place. I don't want to be dramatic because I know that I am not in a terrible place either—I may be at mid-life but there is no crisis. It's just that I think that I should have more in my life than what I've got.

What I don't understand is how I let this happen and why did it take me so long to recognize it. I can't follow the coffee shop instruction and fix them today, but I have decided that I will fix them. I don't know what I will change or when I will make the changes, but I have recognized the problems and that is a big step toward the solutions.

I have a trip to Miami at the end of the week and I am think-ing about taking the weekend by myself on the beach to clear my head and think about the solutions to these complicated questions. I have already committed to staying Friday night to be entertained by Jerry Quinn of Irish-Car-Bomb fame. Jerry and I are meeting with a company that Aziq is looking to license a product from in Miami and he has already warned me that he and I are hitting the town on Friday night. I think that I will just pretend to have fun with my client on Friday, so that I can be on my own for the weekend and relax. It's crazy that when I thought that I was getting the promotion, I was willing to accept all the negatives in my life, but my vision is finally clear and I am determined to fix my problems.

Terry

I didn't cry. Carol didn't cry. We were having tea after dinner and although I had resolved not to tell her until after the biopsy results, it suddenly felt like I needed to share this with her.

I said, "Hun, I have a little medical thing that I have been dealing with for a few weeks that I want to tell you about. I had a mole on my shoulder that our doc didn't like, so she sent me to a dermatologist who removed a piece last week so that she could assess it. The results are back in a couple of days and I have an appointment to hear the assessment." God, it felt good to say it and to stop deceiving.

Carol asked for details and listened carefully. She knew that I must have been doing research on my own and asked me to explain what I had learned. We talked at length about the possible outcomes from the biopsy and the corresponding paths that would follow each possible diagnosis.

We just talked. We never cried or yelled or argued. We just talked like teammates who were now united against a common foe.

Carol did not criticize me for not telling her earlier—she never mentioned it, although I am sure that she was privately upset about it. Her focus was on the immediate future and determining how to beat the foe and so it seemed that anything before this point was irrelevant.

When confronted with stressful situations some people will drink, some will smoke, some will become frantic. Carol makes lists. Her solution always begins with a list of action items and copious note taking. She made a list of questions to ask the dermatologist, a list of things to look up on the Internet, a list of personal questions that we would have to evaluate, including do we say anything to Ben? It is obviously a coping mechanism for her, but it felt good for me to have a partner to develop strategy with and I knew that getting organized was going to be beneficial.

Our night was not full of emotion and drama. We didn't profess our undying love or cry like we were in some Hollywood chick flick. We drank tea and made a list, which was exactly what I needed. I got into bed and I could hear Carol starting to brush her teeth in the next room. She stopped, spit and came into the bedroom.

She looked me straight in the eye and said, "We are going to be fine," then she turned and went back to finish brushing her teeth. She was probably trying to convince herself, but I took great comfort from her assurance. I rolled over and had the first good night of sleep that I have had in a week.

You have probably met people who fear spontaneity the way that Gord does. Gord is not controlling per se, it is just that he can't stand to see things out of control—things don't have to go his way, but he needs them to go in a predictable way. So Gord plans and schedules and rehearses every aspect of his life. I wish that he would—no, could—loosen up a bit, but it is more likely that he will continue to micro-manage all aspects of his life.

Gord hosted a small dinner party last night and rather than allowing a conversation to naturally develop among the eight around the table, he put out place cards to drive and direct our conversation. It actually went well and was fun but it wasn't necessary—we would have had fun without Gord's structure.

Anyway, let me tell you about the conversation place cards. Gord stole an idea from the Bravo TV show Inside the Actors

Studio. On the show, the host interviews famous actors and has a relaxed conversation about their background and chronologically reviews their career—it's actually a pretty good show, even though the host is an uppity dick. At the end of the show, the host always asks the same ten questions that come from some famous French guy that are supposed to illustrate the responder's true character. So Gord has these ten questions printed out and we went around the table so that we could each reply. I am not sure that anyone's true character was revealed, as most of the time the answers were just kind of funny or silly to entertain each other.

A couple of times things did get deep, like when Gord's neighbour answered the question, "What is your least favourite word?" with the word "malignant." His wife was not at the dinner, as she was ailing next door from a recent chemo treatment, so things got quiet and heavy for a moment after he gave that answer. Most of the time it was just fun and I especially liked the responses to: "What is your favourite curse word?"

"Shitballs, pantalones, fucknuts, jerkwad…"

This morning, the place card was on the kitchen counter so I thought that I would try all ten questions over coffee—it might actually reveal a bit of character.

What is your favourite word? Warmth. Heat can be positive or negative and so can coolness or cold, but everything about warmth is good.

What is your least favourite word? Pus. Most people can't hear that word without feeling a little repulsed.

What turns you on creatively, spiritually or emotionally? Debate—not Fox News debate, but intelligent and respectful arguing.

What turns you off? Ideology.

What is your favourite curse word? There are so many good ones. I'll go with fuck because of its general utility.

What sound or noise do you love? Music. Any music

What sound or noise do you hate? Closing doors or gates. Jail cell bars slamming is the absolute worst. I toured Alcatraz once and the tour includes an audio tour that has the sound of inmates and cells slamming closed and it absolutely freaked me out.

What profession other than your own would you like to attempt? I would like to run a government. But I don't want to have to get elected or re-elected or worry about popularity, so I guess that I want to be a dictator.

What profession would you not like to do? Teach. It's really just babysitting.

If Heaven exists, what would you like to hear God say when you arrive at the Pearly Gates? "If you thought that Earth was great wait until you try this!"

Track 15

Lee

I was vacuuming in something of a trance last night, preoccupied by the question of selling the business and, specifically, who I could talk with to help me make this big decision. My daydream was broken by a roar in the vacuum that told me that I had pulled in something that was blocking my suction. I stopped the engine and pulled out a neon-green bracelet.

Here I was at a time of need, asking for a source of guidance and what do I pull from my vacuum? A "What Would Jesus Do" bracelet. Was it a message? Should I seek guidance in the church? Had I found the answer?

Of course not, it was just a shitty piece of molded plastic with the ridiculous WWJD stencil meant to remind someone that in a time of trouble they should ask what an uneducated carpenter from 2,000 years ago would do. Who are these mindless sheep that need shit like that?

I was raised without religion. That is not to say that I was raised to be an atheist as my parents never tried to convince me that there wasn't a god. It is just they also never told me that there was a god. It would seem bizarre to most people, but the whole question just didn't come up. I remember asking why my friends went to church and we didn't and being satisfied with the answer that we were Chinese and didn't share the beliefs of the Canadians. In matters of language, food, dress, and so many other things we were different so it was no big deal to be different about church.

Both my parents were raised without a major world religion. My father's family were longstanding members of the

Communist Party so by definition there could be no god. My mother's family had something of a folk religion that sounds like it was a mix of Taoism and Buddhism but was mainly just local morals and customs. Mom says that there was never any godlike figure, no heaven or hell, and certainly no prayers. She describes it as an understanding that life would be enriched if you were kind and considerate. She taught those ideas to my brothers and I but not in any way that I would associate with religion.

As a parent, I have told Jackson that people here and around the world have a wide range of beliefs and that when he is older he will be able to study the beliefs for himself and decide if any or none feel right for him. He has some concern about honouring his Chinese heritage so he asked what most Chinese Canadians do for religion and he seemed relieved when I told him that the majority never go to any church or temple.

So if there is no guidance to be gained from a plastic bracelet or a statue of a fat-bellied man, where do I turn for insight? My family is out—I can't really talk about money with my mom because she just wouldn't understand, and I can't talk with my brothers because I don't want them to know how much money I have.

My brothers and I have a friendly relationship as long as we keep our distance. They live in the US and we only see each other a couple of times a year, which keeps us from arguing. I know that they do not understand the size and scope of SunRay, and they both think that I am just getting by month to month. I don't need to impress them, so I let them keep that belief.

Anne has been the one person that I can have heart-to-heart business discussions with, but she is an employee and her life will be affected if I sell. I can't expect her to advise me.

None of my friends are business people. I tried talking to Gord, but he has already made up his mind and is convinced that I must sell. When I tried to explain my reservations to him, I could tell that he faked his expression of understanding before returning to saying, "Yeah, but you will have all that money and no more working nights."

He might be right, but he is not the unbiased listener that I was hoping for.

So maybe I need to face this decision on my own. I have written stacks of pro and con lists but I don't think that you can make a life decision based on which column is longer. My hang-up is that the status quo is pretty good. I can sell and that might change my life from good to great, but what if I sell and that changes my life from good to shitty. What if I find that I spend all my newfound time drinking vodka from the bottle and playing online poker?

The coffee shop guys who wrote that stupid sign probably intended it for people with totally fucked-up lives. It was meant for stupid people who accept their shitty circumstances without realizing how easy it would be to change things. I agree that those people should "fix them today." Fat people should stop eating and start exercising—drop the excuses and get started today because it is an obvious problem and an obvious solution. Women in abusive relationships should leave today—there are social service agencies that will get you through the mess, so just walk out. It's obvious. It's interesting that the bigger your problem is the easier the solution is. If you are in a bad marriage, divorce. If you hate your job, get a new one.

If you are in a good position, it is harder to consider a big change. Life would be so much easier if you believed that in times of trouble you could simply stop thinking and just let Jesus take the wheel.

Terry

As we sat in the dermatologist's lobby, I teased Carol that she had brought enough notepaper to complete a thesis. She reached for a Sports Illustrated and handed it to me in a manner that suggested this was not a good day for me to play class clown.

We were ushered past the treatment rooms and into Zsa Zsa's personal office. The precipice from the tile and cold steel of the patient areas to the posh and elegant personal office was a strange crossing. The first step onto the thickly padded carpet made me feel like I was leaving a medical facility and entering a high-priced lawyer's office. High-back leather chairs and a massive mahogany desk seemed wrong in a place in which one usually sat on a table lined with butcher paper.

Zsa Zsa rose from her desk and warmly greeted Carol, who I introduced.

When she returned behind her desk, I knew that we would be forced to watch a little overacting before we learned the results, but I had neglected to explain this to Carol who was becoming impatient. Zsa Zsa explained the procedure in which the biopsy was taken and the nature of the tests that were run by the pathologists in painful detail—all irrelevant, but seemingly part of her performance.

When she finally opened the results folder I struggled to control my breathing and felt Carol squeeze my hand a little too hard to be considered comforting.

"The results are mixed. As I suspected, the biopsy supports the diagnosis of melanoma."

I felt my stomach contract.

"The key measurements are called Clarke Breslow scores and you are about a two out of five on each of those, which is fairly good. You are listed as stage one melanoma, although you are almost at stage two, so we are going to move quickly."

I reached for a tissue because my nose was bleeding. I heard something about mitotic rate, lymphocytes, growth phases but nothing was registering. Carol was writing as fast as she could, but I could see a tear rolling down her cheek. Ten minutes went by in an incomprehensible flash and I found myself rising because Carol and the doctor were rising. Carol was given an appointment card for an oncologist appointment and we were ushered out with some recycled positive words from Zsa Zsa.

This was one of the most important scenes in my life and I virtually missed it. Shouldn't it have taken longer? Shouldn't there have been a soundtrack of crescendoing violins? It was over in minutes and I missed most of the dialogue in my shocked state.

We stood in the hallway outside her office and held each other for a minute. Carol pulled back and looked me in the eyes and said, "We are going to be fine."

This time I didn't take any comfort from it and I could tell that she didn't believe it either.

Grant

I flew into Miami on Friday morning and met up with Jerry from Aziq at the airport. We shared a taxi directly to the scheduled meeting with a young biotech company that Aziq is considering licensing some technology from. I had reviewed the material during the flight and failed to see any complexity that required my presence. My feelings were confirmed during the meeting.

The respective teams had previously agreed to the major deal points and this meeting seemed to be a goodwill trip on Jerry's behalf to demonstrate that Aziq saw this partnership as important, and to stroke the management team of the young biotech. We covered some details on what the remaining elements of the due diligence process would be and what legal steps would be required to complete the transaction, but it was obvious to all that Jerry and I were both too senior to be involved in this level of detail and that the remaining work would be completed by junior staffers. Jerry must have sensed that I was thinking that this meeting was a waste of time because he looked over at one point and gave me a mischievous smile that suggested that he had another reason for me to be in Miami.

We had checked into our hotel in South Beach by five o'clock and were back in a cab ten minutes later.

"Here is the plan Grant—some eye candy and a good meal to get you primed. Then we are going to let you loose on the wild women of the beach." That was the only itinerary that I got from Jerry before we entered another world.

Our first stop was a beachside bar called Nikki Beach. Nikki is the answer to the question: Where do all the wealthy supermodels hang out? The bar was packed with all of the beautiful young things retreating from a day on the beach, and the handsome business crowd heading for after-work drinks. Like a movie scene, the terrace was furnished with beautiful oversized chairs, sofas and beds (really!) that guests lounge in to sip their champagne. White is the key colour here and everything from the umbrellas, to the staff wardrobe and the linens on the beds (really!) is eye-popping white. Two-thirds of the bar is actually on the beach and even the sand seems shiny white. All that white provides the perfect contrast to the stunning tan bodies that are on display in some of the smallest bikinis ever made. At one point I forced myself to close my mouth and narrow my eyes so that my shock wasn't obvious.

Jerry waved me over to the bar and ordered a couple of Heinekens.

"Grant, this place is better than Viagra. Look at those two." Jerry pointed out two gorgeous and slightly tipsy blondes who were having the most arousing play pillow fight on their bar bed. I had to acknowledge the accuracy of the Viagra comment, as I shifted on my bar stool to make room for my erection.

Within an hour, the bar was packed with not only beautiful women, but also beautiful men. It was as if a high-pitched whistle that only the most stunning people could hear had beckoned them all. I was happy to sip Heinekens and watch, but I said to Jerry that I felt a little out of place with all of the beautiful people and asked why the ordinary-looking people don't come to this place. Jerry explained his theory that any woman who is less than a nine out of ten will stay away for fear of the contrast to a roomful of tens. As for feeling out of place, Jerry told me not to worry because this first stop is just for our eyes.

We walked a few blocks to grab dinner at South Beach institution Joe's Stone Crab. Joe's has been serving stone crab since 1913 and it is a classic. One of those places that you sense has never changed and never will.

Joe's doesn't take reservations and the bar and lobby were packed when we arrived. I said to Jerry that I was starved and didn't want to wait if it would be long for the table. Jerry agreed and tried to block for me as we knifed our way through the crowd to the hostess counter. I reached the counter first, but instead of the beautiful young hostess that I had expected, I met a six-foot-five black man in his later years who had the personality and authority of a circus ringmaster. I sheepishly asked how long the wait was and was just being told to grab a drink at the bar because the wait was about ninety minutes when Jerry caught up to me.

Jerry confidently shook hands with our host and handed him a couple of bills and said, "I am sorry I couldn't hear how long the wait would be?"

Our host smiled and waved to a young woman who seated us immediately.

I didn't know how to react because I had never paid someone off to get my way. I felt like I was cheating and must have been a little red-faced as I took my seat across from Jerry.

"You Canadians really are too fucking polite. If you are going to get things done you need to know how the world works."

I learned that for the seemingly small sum of twenty dollars, Jerry had saved us a ninety-minute wait. It was another small eye-opener that I received last night, but it would soon seem insignificant to the rest of the education that I was about to receive.

Grant

After our crab dinner, we stopped in for scotches at the side bar in the Versace Mansion. I had some vague sense of Versace as a fashion line, but I didn't know much about it and truly didn't even know that it was named after a real person. Jerry found my ignorance humorous and waved over a staff member who kindly explained the history of the man and the building that we were in. I learned that Versace was a flamingly gay Italian who made a ton of money in the fashion industry, as well as in perfumes and other queer things. He was a jetsetter who partied all the time and was friends with Madonna, Elton John and Princess Diana. In the nineties, he was on Ocean Drive in South Beach and saw this classic Spanish-looking building that was being run as a small hotel or apartment and he decided to buy it for his own residence. That was a pretty flashy play to make your home right in the middle of the Miami Beach strip. He redecorated the place in a decadent way and lived and partied there for years.

It wasn't a very interesting story until the staffer told me about how Versace was gunned down on the steps of his mansion one morning in 1997. Jerry and the staffer insisted that I must remember that—it was front-page news for days. I assured them that I had never heard of it and Jerry apologized that his friend was Canadian and apparently lived in a fucking igloo.

Now Versace's former mansion operates as a small hotel with a restaurant and bar. It has also become one of the great Miami photo ops, as tourists line up to take their picture on the steps where the guy was shot. Pretty twisted, actually.

While I was being told the story, I could see that Jerry was watching a group of older women by the fountain one level below the glass terrace that we were on. I hope you are getting the picture that this was a really gay guy's house because it had fountains and flowers and art everywhere. Anyway, Jerry asks me to grab another round of drinks and meet him by the fountain.

Before I tell you what happened at the fountain, I have to tell you about the bartender. This girl had the biggest tits that I had ever seen. Not big tits like fat girls have. She was thin. It was just that her tits were massive and really round—like she had a couple of dodge balls in her t-shirt.

I was obviously staring and so she pointedly asked, "Is everything okay?"

"Yep. Two single malts on the rocks."

She poured the drinks and then, just to show you that stereotypes are sometimes deserved, she used a calculator to determine that two drinks at $20 each would be $40 dollars. I saw the worry come over her face when I handed her a hundred-dollar bill and she knew that she had more math to do. I decided to help and told her that I just wanted fifty back.

She handed me back the change and said, "It's not cool to stare at my chest like that."

I just took my change and walked away, but give me a break. Her boobs were like some kind of neon-lit, mystical orbs that were mesmerizing—of course they are meant to be stared at!

When I found Jerry, he was engaged with two women who were actually around our age. They were attractive and they were dressed in bright sundresses with high heels and high hair. Both were thin but shapely and they had bright eyes that suggested that this was a big night out. I had a fleeting thought that they looked like they were going to some event like an informal wedding or mature student prom.

"There he is. Thanks for the drink. Grant, this is Erica." It wasn't a random selection that led Jerry to introduce me to Erica first, as he had clearly staked claim to Lynn. Erica shook my hand and put her left hand on my shoulder in a way that suggested I was being measured for size. Jerry used the story of my Versace naiveté as a way to get the girls laughing and we talked and laughed for another ten minutes before Jerry asked if the girls were going to be out clubbing tonight or if they were looking to get off the bar strip for a small party.

The ladies made eye contact with each other and some telepathic message was quickly exchanged before Lynn said that they were going to hit another spot, but that they would look for us at The Clevelander later. Erica leaned in and hugged me as they got up to leave and, as she did, she pushed her pelvis firmly into mine. Shivers rushed down my spine as she turned and left hand in hand with Lynn.

"We're in the game now Grant." Jerry decoded the conversation for me because there was clearly a lot that I didn't understand. The ladies had just set us up as their default men for the night. Their plan was to hit another club to see if they could upgrade from Jerry and me and meet some guys who were younger and/or better looking, but if they don't find such an upgrade, they will go to The Clevelander and hook up with us.

They didn't reject Jerry's invitation to leave the strip (decode: have sex), but instead said that they would meet us later (decode: unless something better comes along).

We went to the Rose Bar at the Delano Hotel next because Jerry said that we needed to fish for our own upgrades. The Rose Bar is an older bar that looks like Bogart or Sinatra should be hanging out at it. We took a small standing table near the bar and I asked Jerry to slow things down for me and educate me with what was happening. I should say first that I had had at least five or six drinks up to that point so my decision-making faculties may not have been at peak performance. I wasn't thinking about what I would do, but I was very curious about the scene that I was in. Jerry gave me a full explanation of his cougar bar story that he had started to tell me back in New York. As he explained it, I still could not accept that there were women who were out for the night with the sole purpose of getting laid.

Jerry encouraged me to look around the room and I confess that it was packed with a strong Friday-night crowd of mostly thirty-five to fifty-year-olds and more women than men. The women were generally attractive, but not perfect like the hard-body super models from early in the night. These women had some miles on their odometer but they were still in good shape. Some had a few extra pounds, one had an obvious Botox mishap, and several were prominently displaying some expensive plastic surgery, but they were all dressed well, all had plenty of makeup, and all smelled great.

"Stay away from big groups Grant—cougars don't travel in packs. Those girls are just out with friends and will end up drinking themselves silly and dancing together, but none of them want to give their girlfriends the gossipy ammunition from seeing them leave the bar with a guy tonight. Be careful with women who are here on their own—they could be freaky. Pairs are great—two women can share their plan for the evening and they won't be judgmental if one scores and the other doesn't." It all made so much sense.

"Jerry, you seem to be a happily married guy, so why do you know all of this?"

"I am happily married because I know all of this. I think that because I can have anonymous sex a few times a month, it keeps me from taking a mistress or resenting my wife's limited sexual imagination."

"A few times a month? Holy shit!"

I was telling Jerry that this was a lot of fun, but that I wouldn't actually go through with anything when two beautiful women arrived with four glasses of tequila.

"Welcome to South Beach, tourists," was the greeting of the first woman. She was wearing tight jeans with sequins and a low-cut yellow shirt that said Victory on it. Her friend was in a business suit with her hair pulled back tight with small black glasses. But she didn't look like an office geek; she was hot. The conversation was almost too fast for me to participate in.

"We aren't tourists. We live around the corner," shot back Jerry.

"Right here on 12th Street?"

"For sure."

"This is 17th Street, tourist. Where are you from?"

"I am a priest from Rome and my friend here is the drummer in Springsteen's band."

"Nice to meet you. I'm Betty and this is Veronica. We are high school students over at Riverdale High."

"We are hoping to meet some local girls who know how to have fun."

"Tough luck, boys. We are the two last virgins in all of South Beach."

We shot back the tequila and crowded around our little table. The girl in the suit was Stephanie and the jeans belonged to Melanie. Because Mel, as she called herself, had started the verbal jousting with Jerry, they matched up and Stephanie sidled up to me. It seemed like the girls were old friends, but we learned that they had only met a year ago when they connected in the lobby of the divorce attorney that they shared. Both ladies had dumped their cheating, pieces of shit husbands and were happy to spend their divorce settlements together—on tequila, it seemed.

Within ten minutes of meeting them, they were sharing details of their lives that most people would never share with anyone. I learned that the first thing that Mel did after her divorce was get a tattoo and a Brazilian wax. Her husband hated tattoos and didn't want her to trim. So in acts that signified the end of the relationship, she got a tattoo of a dove on her hip and a clean shave because "the carpet didn't match the drapes anymore, anyway."

Stephanie shared that she hadn't had any sex in the last two years of her marriage and only when she divorced did she remember how much she missed sex and how good she was at it.

We switched from tequila to wine, and as we neared the bottom of the bottle my pulse quickened, as I could see that I was getting closer to having to make a big decision because we seemed like winning choices as far as Stephanie and Mel were considered. I was enjoying the racy discussion even if I added little to it and I confess that I was beginning to fantasize about Stephanie completing every man's librarian fantasy—you know, the one where the uptight woman with her hair tied back suddenly tosses off her glasses, shakes her hair out and rips her blouse open.

Jerry was a maestro in this setting and he had played everything perfectly as far as I was concerned, and it seemed that Mel was drooling at the prospect of taking Jerry home. That is why it was like a slap back to sobriety when Jerry announced that we had to leave for an hour because we promised colleagues that we would meet for a drink. If they would wait for us we would be back and we would show them the time of their lives.

Mel tried to ensure Jerry's return by getting her tongue half way down Jerry's throat. I avoided any of that with Stephanie by turning my head as I leaned in for a departing hug. As Stephanie hugged me she pulled me forward with a hand on my waist and pushed her pelvis firmly into mine. Two pelvic pushes already and the night was young.

In the cab, Jerry apologized and said that he just wasn't into Mel and that all he could think about was that he would prefer to fuck Lynn instead, so we were heading off to The Clevelander. It seemed like an abundance of fucking options for a married man, but I was just rolling with things by this time.

The Clevelander is a hotel on the South Beach strip with a large outdoor bar on the ground floor and a late-night club upstairs in the hotel. When we arrived, things were still rocking at the outdoor bar. There was a live band and the dance floor was jammed with people dancing to the hip-hop crap that the band was playing. The patio is massive and has three or four different bar areas throughout. We squeezed into two spots at the main bar and Jerry ordered two mojitos. I had no idea what a mojito was, but I drank it anyway. The crowd was a mix of tourists and locals, and the age range was massive—from early twenties to mid-fifties. It was almost 1:00 a.m. and it seemed like everyone in the place was hammered.

We stayed for another half hour, but when the band finished for the night it seemed like the party was heading inside as the crowd began to thin. There was no sign of Lynn or Erica despite their promise from the Versace Mansion that they would meet us here. The remaining crowd was mostly couples lingering over a final drink and a few large groups that seemed like tourists. Jerry had concluded that there were no "targets" here and that we should hustle back to The Rose Room.

Just as we were about to step into a cab, Lynn put her hand on Jerry's shoulder and calmly said, "I think that you would prefer to go home with me rather than him."

Jerry looked over to me and I was able to read the situation quickly, which was impressive given that I hadn't been this drunk since university. Erica wasn't coming and he wanted to go with Lynn. I gave Jerry a knowing nod and shut the cab door behind me and watched out the rear window as Jerry and Lynn entered the next cab. I told my cab driver to take me to the Rose Room because I was still following the plan that Jerry had set out for me. As we neared the Rose Room, I realized that I didn't have the guts to go back in there alone, and so I told the cab driver that I had changed my mind and that I wanted to go back to my hotel.

I was exhausted—not because it was late or because I was drunk—but because I had just explored a brave new world. I somehow navigated the hotel lobby and made it back to my room where I fell asleep with the lights, television, my clothes and my shoes all on.

I will admit that my opinion is in the minority on this issue, but I really can't stand The Beatles. I know that they are iconic and had a tremendous influence on music and stuff, but I really just don't like their songs. I mean, I like some of their songs well enough, but I think that they benefit tremendously from the halo effect. They had some great songs, which created an audio halo for them that everybody still hears in all of the other ordinary songs.

Gord has every song ever recorded by The Beatles on his iPod and it is the only music that he ever plays. I can't stand being in his car simply because I know that I have a choice of listening to shitty Beatles tunes or getting into an argument about it. Gord is like most Beatles fans in that he can't accept that differing musical tastes exist and that I do not have a taste for The Beatles. He insists that I have an illness that must be cured and so he continues to dose me with "Sergeant Pepper."

I can break this down for you. Listen to the early Beatles.

Listen to "Love Me Do" or "Please Please Me." These nursery rhyme lyrics are made worse by the simple beat, bad harmonica and slightly off-key harmonies. The best thing that you can say about these songs is that they are wonderfully short. I was too young to witness Beatlemania, so all Beatles songs have always essentially been oldies to me, but when you focus on the early Beatles—the oldest of the oldies—they are just not very good. If they were recorded by other old acts like Herman's Hermit or Gerry and the Pacemakers, no one except old people would listen to them today.

The middle Beatles? A little better than the early years, but this is also when they recorded "Yellow Submarine." Have you listened to that? Barney the Dinosaur would reject that song for his show because it is too immature for his audience. Once as I was complaining about "Yellow Submarine," Gord flipped to the next song to make a point that The Beatles were trying to show their diversity with songs like "Yellow Submarine" and the song that he was then playing "Tomorrow Never Knows." I didn't know this last one, but it sounded like a song from a Bollywood film score. I am happy to concede that it was musically innovative and that this period was a demonstration of The Beatles' diversity, but I am really just conceding that they had a wide repertoire of shitty songs.

The last couple of Beatle years are actually tolerable for the most part, although there is some shit mixed in here, too. Don't believe me? Go listen to "Octopus's Garden" then come back and apologize to me. My point to Gord is that the few good songs are what make people revere everything that they have done. But Gord is relentless and he defends The Beatles like a Jehovah's Witness on a recruiting drive.

My iPod has every musical genre on it and I certainly love listening to the oldies, but most of my music is from the current century. The old tunes that I grew up with are still favourites, but I love that music evolves and that I can find new music that I enjoy. I find music initially because it is great to run to new songs and then I fall for the songs while I am out on the trails and end up listening to them at home and in the car. I like a lot of hip-hop stuff like Kayne, Akon, Wyclef, Rihanna... I also like some of the upbeat Latin stuff that is great to run or dance to. It is fun to find new music and I love searching for new artists.

I played dirty the other day by playing some recent downloads while I was driving with Gord in my passenger seat. I knew that he wasn't enjoying the music but he didn't say anything until I played a Wu-Tang Clan song called "The Heart Gently Weeps," which rips off "While My Guitar Gently Weeps" in a way that I knew would piss Gord off. I thought that he was going to have a stroke at my act of sacrilege, but I loved every minute of it.

Terry

If you have to have cancer, melanoma isn't a bad choice. I am reminded that the odds of dying from melanoma are still low even if you are bordering on stage two. After the hysteria of hearing the C word, I am trying to get my head back in the game. This is a serious disease and the potential for things to go bad exists, but it is also most likely something that will be beaten. I will have to go through a lot of treatment and may feel pretty crappy for a while, but I am most likely going to live. Most likely. I am going to work and stay busy and see what happens when I meet with the oncologist. No one but Carol will know for now and that should keep things simple.

I actually managed to find a decent mood and headed into Beanfest, but found that the shop was somber. The staff seemed quiet and looked at me curiously. David Gray was playing over the sound system and although I love his stuff, it isn't exactly high energy. I went over to the music system and dialed in "Rubberband Man" from The Spinners—one of the happiest songs I know.

Cory sidled up to me and said, "Dude, you don't have to fake being in a good mood. We all know. It's okay to be sad."

"You all know what?" I said bravely, hoping that they knew nothing.

"We know that Carol left you. We have been trying to figure out why you have been so weird lately—you know with the grumpiness, the music, and the freaky sign the other day.

We started piecing it together yesterday afternoon—no one has seen Carol in here in weeks and you guys are empty nesters, so the odds were good that you guys would split."

I laughed so hard that I was almost crying and that got Cory and the others laughing. I finally composed myself and said, "Listen, everybody. First of all, you are all a bunch of idiots; second, I love each one of you idiots; and, finally, my wife and I are still together and very much in love with no risk of break up. If I have been acting weird lately, I apologize but there is nothing wrong except maybe some middle-age mood swings. I will try to control them." To my great relief, everyone took me at my word that there was nothing wrong.

We had all just got back to work when I noticed the lyrics that Cory had put on the board before I came in: "When you're weary, feeling small, when tears are in your eyes, I will dry them all. I'm on your side when times get rough and friends just can't be found..."

"Bridge Over Troubled Water" by Simon and Garfunkel. I swear that I have never mentioned that song to anyone in the shop nor have I ever played it while I have been there. I think that I would be embarrassed if everyone were to know that it is my favourite song of all time. When I saw the opening lyrics on the board, I was stunned. The staff was trying to send me a message that they were there for me and that I could count on them through my upcoming challenge. They were wrong on the nature of my challenge and hopefully now had the impression that there was no problem at all, but I was touched that they had reached out. I was shocked that they had reached out through the uncanny selection of such personally significant lyrics.

"Hey Cory—those lyrics are too long—you are giving them half the song—and it's a cheese-ball song anyway."

"You're the Grande Fromage, so I thought that you would like it, but feel free to change them."

So I went to the board and wrote, "What would you do if I sang out of tune"—the opening lyric from "With a Little Help from My Friends."

Terry

People commonly complain about the lack of speed in the Canadian health care system, but I don't think that the criticism is valid for cancer. Two weeks after meeting with my dermatologist, I had an appointment at the cancer centre. Among the various centre staff members, I met two that I could tell will become key people in my life. They identified themselves as my treatment team. Dr. Isabelle Ryder and Carmen Begin are my physician and coordinator and I instantly liked them. They were friendly, but not fake cheerful. They know that their patients are scared and that being too upbeat would be off-putting so, instead, they are nice but with a no bullshit sensibility.

Dr. Ryder started by telling me that she had worked with my dermatologist many times and that she is an excellent physician who diagnosed my melanoma expertly. She patiently explained to me that melanoma was treatable and not terribly disturbing, but what we need to worry about is the cancer spreading. If the cancer is localized, they can just cut it out and keep a good eye on me to make sure that it doesn't come back. If the cancer spreads to other places—from my online research I recognized the word "metastasize"—then we have a more complicated scenario.

She went on to describe the ways in which they could assess the possibility of spread, including various tests and scans, but she indicated that her preference for me was to have a minor surgical procedure called a Sentinel Lymph Node Biopsy. This procedure involved removing a few of my lymph nodes closest to the melanoma site so that they could definitively tell if the cancer had spread to my nodes.

Carol was ready for this and flipped through her papers until she found a list with a heading "SLNB Questions." She asked about the nature and the number of nodes that would be removed, any side effects that could arise from the staining dye, and so many other things that I felt like I was watching a conversation between respected colleagues rather than my doctor and my wife. Dr. Ryder answered every question patiently and respectfully and I could tell that she was impressed by Carol. After a few minutes, the two of them agreed that I should have the procedure as soon as possible—no one sought my opinion.

We spoke a little longer about possible outcomes and courses of action post-biopsy and then Carmen escorted us back to a scheduling area where we booked my surgery for a week and a half later. We received an information package explaining the surgery and more information on melanoma treatment. We received instructions on when and where we should report for the procedure and were given a list of websites, e-mail addresses and phone numbers that we could contact if we had questions. It is a very organized place and I realized that they treat so many cancer patients that they have developed a set of highly evolved standard operating procedures to guide them. In some places that could seem like a cold way to treat such a frightening problem, but the cancer centre staff emitted warmth, not cold. Everyone that I encountered was kind and patient and I appreciated it. There is something to be said for the professionalism that experience brings.

Grant

I slept until eleven on Saturday, which was fine because I was staying until Sunday with nothing booked for Saturday. I checked my cellphone for messages and there was only one— Jerry had left me a message at 8:00 a.m. from a taxi on his way to the airport. He spent the night with Lynn and had only slept for two hours, but his wife had plans for him that afternoon so he couldn't miss his flight no matter how tired he was. He said that he couldn't wait to hear how I did with the Rose Room girls and he hoped that I talked them into a threesome.

I walked back down the strip and had the all-day breakfast at The News Café—another renowned South Beach establishment that deserves its fame. As I flipped through the morning paper and drank my coffee, I looked back on the events of last night like it was some kind of crazy dream. The pounding in my head assured me that it was not a dream.

It is crazy to think that with no effort and no strings attached, Jerry met and had sex with a very attractive woman. I met two attractive women who were seemingly prepared to have sex with me. Granted, one of them bailed because she probably found a slightly better catch, but I was in the running. The question that confronts me now is what would I have done if Jerry hadn't left and I was directly offered sex? One day ago I would have said that the idea of me having a one-night stand was impossible, but today I cannot convincingly say that I would have stopped the path to infidelity that I was on last night.

I didn't do anything wrong—a couple of pelvis-linked hugs do not register—but I might have. I still could. It seems that these women are out there every night if you know where to look. I could leave my wife and play the field and have some success. I could meet a nice woman and start a new relationship. Or, I could just meet women and have regular, casual sex. Actually, I don't even have to leave my wife—I could just be like Jerry and stay married but step out a few times a month for fun. I swear that I didn't know that any of these options existed.

It seems that you can teach an old dog a new trick. I showed a shocking amount of self-restraint today and it worked to my advantage. What I did was not remarkable for most people, but a bit out of character for me.

From the time that I was in high school hanging out with my pseudo counter-culture crowd, I have always fought authority

and raged against the man—even if I wasn't clear who the man
was. I had a badass poster in my bedroom that read, "Speak
Truth to Power" and I viewed that adage as my rallying cry. The
worst thing that a parent, a teacher or a boss could say to me
was "Do it because I told you so." I rebelled against anyone who
outranked me unless they could out-reason me. It was my job
to speak truth to those who lacked logic but possessed power.
It was my job to educate the powerful and I fully expected that
I could rehabilitate them with a few edgy sentences of truth.

The problem is that people in power often get intellectually
lazy. If you have the power to make me do what you want, why
would you invest the time to reason with me? Obviously I am
not cut out for a military career, but this chain-of-command
thinking is not confined to the army. I have rebelled against all
kinds of powerful people. I wish that it was always a noble act,
but most of the time I lacked valid reasons to oppose the man
and mostly I was a rebel because it seemed pretty cool. It wasn't
a universally good idea.

I have had problems with teachers, cops, security guards and,
notably, border agents. When I was in my twenties, I went on
a cheap, all-inclusive trip to some Cuban fleabag resort with a
couple of girlfriends. I was determined to take full advantage of
my time in the sun, so I left home in sandals, shorts and a short
t-shirt—I looked out of place in a Canadian airport, but I didn't
care. When I went through security, I beeped and a slimy little
security fuck told me that he needed to wand me.

He gave me a gap-toothed smile and said this isn't going to
take long because "you don't have many places available to hide
anything."

It was a stupid but harmless comment, but I didn't like it
so I spoke truth to power and told him that he could stick his
wand up his ass. I had four officers with me within the minute
and I was escorted to a small office that was locked from the
outside and in which I sat alone until shortly after my flight
had departed. I joined my friends in Cuba a day later having
missed my flight and only narrowly missed joining the banned
flier list. Others would have learned their lesson that day, but

I have three similar stories—remarkably similar stories—that I will spare you from.

Today, I was flying back from a two-day service sector conference in Calgary and encountered Mr. Nerdy McNerdnuts manning the security scanner at the airport. In my typical style, I was a little late and scrambling to make my flight, so I absent-mindedly walked through the metal detector with my belt on and it set the alarm off. Nerdy points me back to the entry side where I take off my belt and go through again. I beep again and realize that I have bracelets on. Nerdy approaches quickly and asks if I can speak English—I resist a tirade about cowboy-hat-wearing, pickup-truck-driving, redneck Albertans and simply bite my lip and say, "Yes, sorry about the metal."

McNerdnuts—who is all of twenty-five years old—feels the need to lecture me. "It's called a metal detector and the way it works is that if you have metal on you, it will detect it. Do you understand this?" Speak truth to power! Speak truth to power. Speak truth to power?

I wanted to get home to see Jackson, so I smiled and went through the detector for the third time without incident.

It has taken me a long time to learn to pick my battles carefully. I hope that I can teach Jackson how to find that balance at a younger age than I did, but this is a delicate balance that can be elusive. It would be easy to live a quiet life simply deferring to power whenever you encounter it, but there are definitely situations in which you have to step up against power. Those times should be few and they should be in support of a worthy cause—not because you think that it is cool to be rebellious.

It turns out that my stick-it-to-the-man saying of "Speak truth to power" didn't arise from any radical group, anyway. It wasn't some mildly violent hippies, as I had always assumed. It comes from some Quaker group that adopted the slogan decades ago as the tagline for their anti-violence ideas—so lame.

Lee

One thing that I like about Jennifer's team is that they are not hesitant to openly discuss money. In our last discussion, we focused on the value of my business and what I could expect to net from its sale. The range is huge, as it totally depends on how many potential buyers emerge and who they are, but the range that they have given me is $12–$20 million.

So, let's be conservative and call it $12 million. Change that—call it $12 fuckin' million! That is like winning the lottery—three times. It is enough money that I would never have to work again and I could live an attractive life. Strangely, I am not worried about what to do with all of that money. I am pretty certain that I wouldn't do much with it. I don't have a wish list of expensive purchases and I don't want a rich and famous lifestyle. I once spent $600 on a purse and the guilt made me nauseous every time I picked it up. I would have to learn how to invest it and manage the money, but I am confident that I can do that so it isn't a question of what to do with the money.

It is a question of what to do with the time. If I sell, I will have enough money for life and I erase the one thing in my life that I don't like, which is working at night. But what will I do after I sell? I know that this is a nice problem to have, but I am worried. Jackson is in school all day and most adults are occupied during the day so what will I do from nine to five? Hang out with my mom? I love her, but no thanks.

I would love to travel and leave for months at a time to hike the Silk Road or safari in Africa, but Jackson will be in school for another ten years so that is not an option. There would be enough money to send Jackson off to private school while I travel or even enough to bring him and a tutor with me, but neither of those options reflect our real pedigree.

I could go back to school and maybe finish university. I am not sure what that would prove—isn't making a bunch of money proof enough that I deserve a lousy B. Comm? I could go back to university to study something new. But while I think that I may enjoy the odd course here and there, I can't imagine that I would feel sufficiently devoted to undertake a full degree. Not to mention, I think that I would feel weird hanging out in the cafeteria with a bunch of twenty-year-olds.

I have about five year's of reading on my wish list, but wouldn't it be some kind of sin to spend my day curled up on the couch in my pyjamas with a good book? I don't really want a life of leisure—I'm not cut out for the spas and frou-frou luncheons.

I know that most people would be laughing at me fretting over this problem. I get how fortunate this position is and I am not unhappy about it. I am just saying that it is not such an obvious decision. Intellectually, it doesn't make sense to keep working when I could sell and have enough money for life. In my gut, however, I am worried about what I will do and who I will become if I am no longer at least partially defined by my job and my company.

Terry

The surgery was indeed "minor" after all. The explanation seemed complicated. "The surgeon will inject a radioactive substance and some blue dye near your tumour, then we will put you out under a general anesthetic. The surgeon will use a scanner to find the sentinel lymph nodes and then she will make a small incision and remove the nodes."

The experience was simple. I arrived at the hospital and was put in a bed in a big open area, then they gave me a pill that made me sleepy, Carol kissed me and I was wheeled down a long hallway. Dr. Ryder said good morning and I was given an injection, then Dr. Ryder said good night as a mask was placed over my head. I woke up a few hours later and, after a couple of staff members checked me out, Carol took me home. I have had more complicated dental appointments.

They told me that I should expect the incision area to be quite painful, but I don't feel any pain, which is probably partially from the painkillers and partially because it is too soon to feel anything around the incision. Incision is a big word for something that is covered by a single Band-Aid. I feel a bit ridiculous lying at home in bed and taking painkillers for the "boo boo" on my shoulder.

I have been dozing in and out all day. I can't focus on reading, so I have been watching TV and trying not to think about the slab of stuff they cut from me. It will be a week before we get the results, so I keep flicking through the channels. I stumbled onto the Seinfeld rerun of the Soup Nazi episode that was responsible for Beanfest's lunch menu. I felt a twinge of guilt for lying to my staff that I was taking a few days off to visit out-of-town family, but I really didn't want them to worry. If the results of the biopsy are good, I will have nothing to tell them, and if the results are bad I can cross that bridge at that time.

The spacey feeling induced by painkillers led me to call my mother this afternoon. I think that it is instinctive to call your mom when you are feeling bad or sick. She was surprised and happy that I was calling, but as soon as I heard her voice I no longer wanted to talk to her. I struggled through a few minutes of light banter about what my nieces and nephews were up to and steered clear of any deeper subjects. I got off the call without harm but certainly didn't get the comfort that I was aimlessly hoping for.

I imagined the conversation that I would have had if my dad had answered the call. I would have told him about the cancer and my worry. He would have been calming, strong and reassuring—you could never rattle my father. I closed my eyes and as I drifted into sleep I clearly heard my dead father tell me, "You're going to be fine, son."

Grant

Do you want to know how good Jack Cash is? He called my assistant the day before he started and asked if he could meet with me before the day started, so she set up a 7:30 a.m. breakfast meeting for Jack and me. Jack and I have known each other for years as we have attended the same conferences, battled with each other for business and even shared a couple of engagements. We have always been polite and professional with each other and, if we weren't competitors, we would probably be friends. Now that we are on the same team, Jack greeted me just like that old friend that I could have been.

Jack spent an appropriate amount of time on small talk—how is your family, did you travel this summer, have you had a lot of business travel—and then got down to the reason that he wanted to meet with me.

"Grant, I was very surprised to get this offer when the firm already had you in place. You are a force in this sector and could handle my new job in your sleep. I don't know what the senior partners told you about why they didn't give you the job, but I think that we can agree that whatever explanation they gave you was bullshit. The truth is, they knew that I was determined to get back to Canada and they knew that if they didn't get me on their team, I would set up shop across the street and slug it out with them. That was too risky for them so I think that they figured, if you can't beat him, have him join you."

In general, Jack speaks in a manner that is relaxed and enthusiastic at the same time. He looks you straight in the eye, but not in a manner that makes you self-conscious or uncomfortable. Even his style of dress has that perfect balance of formality and friendliness. He wears a clearly expensive navy suit with a beautiful purple dress shirt but no tie—the clothes say, "I am so competent and successful that I can afford to be relaxed."

"I don't want this role if you are going to feel any resentment toward me. I only want it if you and I can form a tandem that will dominate this sector."

I assured Jack that there is no resentment and that I am excited to work together. I let him know that if the senior partners had brought in anyone but him that I would have been offended and walked.

For the next half hour, we sketched out a plan of what Jack needs to do over the next thirty days to get up to speed with our operation and current engagements. I know that he will power through that daunting thirty-day workload in fifteen days because the subject of our second half-hour breakfast discussion is what Jack is excited about. We spent the time talking about prospective clients, potential deal lists that Jack was tracking and a marketing plan of how to position the firm. I learned more in thirty minutes with Jack than I learned in all my time with Caffrey.

I also found myself turned on to the work for the first time in years and the ideas that I was coming up with were good. It was a true brainstorm by two senior colleagues and it was fantastic. When we stepped off the elevator laughing together, I could sense that the whole department was looking at us and were inspired by their new leadership team.

After an hour alone in my office, I realized how good Jack Cash is. He seduced me. I should be bitter and resentful towards him, but he had me energized and supportive after spending less than an hour together. I really like Jack, but I can't be talked into staying with this company. I need more in my life and simply changing bosses from Caffrey to Cash isn't a big enough change. I will work with Jack while I figure out how to make these big changes in my life, but if these guys think that they can play me, they have another thing coming.

Lee

I know that the cleaning industry is not sexy and that no one grows up dreaming of becoming a cleaning lady, but don't be so quick to dismiss my industry. The dot-com companies and high-tech companies get all of the press, but few of them have the stability that the cleaning industry has experienced. No one thinks about such businesses and therefore the norm is to assume that it is an inconsequential industry, when the truth is that the commercial cleaning industry produces annual revenues of well over $100 billion.

It is also an industry that lacks a dominate player, as no single company has more than a 6 percent market share, which makes it a little easier for companies like SunRay to carve out their spot in the market. I have been tracking the industry news and trends via the web since I took on my first commercial assignment, so I can keep an eye on potential competitors.

I have definitely learned from these industry associations and have incorporated many bright ideas into my business. Some of the information on contractual terms, financing, et cetera, has been great, but much of the basic business management for the industry is, in my humble opinion, misguided. I have to believe that a lot of these bad ideas come from old white men who own big cleaning companies. If these fat bastards did an honest cleaning shift like I do, they would see things differently.

The industry accepts two things as fundamental truths, which I fully reject—that employees within the industry are transient and that customer turnover is high.

Regarding employees, the industry trade talk assumes that because cleaning jobs are relatively low paying, all employees are just doing this until a better job comes along. The conventional approach is to make the job robotic so that you can just plug a new employee into the spot when the old employee quits. Hire efficiently and always have your next employee identified because someone on your staff is about to quit. Various sources quote different statistics, but I am safe to say that the expected turnover rate for employees is 35-55 percent per year. That means that you have to replace about half of your staff every year.

That's fuckin' crazy.

At SunRay, we have never experienced double-digit staff turnover. We don't pay much more than anyone else does, but we are very selective about who we hire. We screen out those employees who we sense are just taking the job as a temporary thing and those who we do not feel can work our strange hours into their life. Our "night shift" business is not easy to manage for many, so if we sense from an interview that the candidate does not have a long-term plan to manage her family life while on the night shift, then she won't get the job. We also clearly have the Asian connection as a unique strength. It just works—these women work hard, are happy to have the job, and are introverted in English and therefore not likely to look for another job.

Similarly, the industry assumes that customer turnover will be high and I routinely read about companies congratulating themselves for getting their customer turnover rate below 30 percent. It is assumed that customers will experience some level of bad service during the year and, as a result, many will switch cleaning companies. I know that bad service will happen sometimes, but to accept it as an expected norm is ridiculous. Furthermore, to accept that the service is so bad that a customer will fire you is incredible—my customers don't want to give office cleaning a second thought, so for them to notice it is bad and to be so annoyed that they have to spend time to hire a new company is wild. If more than 30 percent of my customers dropped me every year, I would lose my shit.

The two issues are linked very closely for me. I treat my employees well and they know how to do their job well so the number of service issues that we experience is incredibly low.

Sometimes I wonder if I could have had success in a different industry. Maybe I needed this combination of a low-tech service in an unrecognized industry to permit me to get started. I don't have a MBA—I don't even have a B. Comm.—so the complicated industries might have been too much for me, but when I see the errors that the big companies in this industry make, I feel that I might be okay in any industry.

Grant

Ellen's eyes are uneven—her left eye is clearly higher than her right eye. I have never noticed before, but it is obvious and it looks weird. It's really disturbing and it is putting me off.

She also has no body left. I remember when she had shape, but now all of that exercise has made her a fit and toned person with no shape. She has no ass, no tits, no waist, and even her legs are kind of like bird legs. She has the body of a ten-year-old.

I don't think that she tries to look good any more. She probably thinks that she is off of the market and that her husband will love her no matter what she looks like, so why waste time with make-up or fashion. The women in Miami were working hard to impress. Okay, they were working too hard to impress. I am not suggesting that Ellen needs fake boobs or Botox, but it wouldn't kill her to wear a push up bra or some heels occasionally.

I didn't do anything in Miami, but it is Ellen's fucking fault that I even looked. She is not competing anymore because she doesn't think that there is any game being played, and I am beginning to think that there is always a game being played. She doesn't have to compete with the mid-twenties starlets that are way out of my league, but she should at least be able to compete against the cougar crowd that was there for the taking. She could be better than any of the women in that class, but you can't win if you don't even know the game is on.

The young guys at one of the bars in Miami were bad mouthing the cougar women for pulling out every desperate stop to snag a younger man for a one-night stand. What is there to criticize? They know what they want and they are putting out an effort to get it. You can't turn a man on by putting on a ragged terry-cloth robe and watching Survivor while you drink your tea. Especially if your eyes aren't even level!

She could probably make similar comments about me and my lack of effort, but it is obviously not the same. Men don't try to look any certain way to impress women—we are who we are and women respect the honesty in that view. That is why men are allowed to age without resistance, why grey hair is distinguished. I am not a looker and I have never been known for my fashion sense, so I am certain that Ellen is still attracted to whatever it is that attracted her in the first place. She, on the other hand, has changed.

Terry

Waiting for medical results must make everyone philosophical. I can't watch a TV commercial these days without pondering some deeper meaning. Certainly I have been thinking about death, or more specifically what happens when you die. I have been thinking about God, which shouldn't be a surprise, but it is a surprise for me because I never really give religion any time. When I say that I have been thinking about God, I don't mean that I have conveniently found faith now that my days may be numbered. I mean that I am thinking about whether there is a god, an afterlife, a soul, anything other than a box and dirt.

I certainly do not feel any need to repent or start praying to some omnipotent being. If there is a god, he would understand me and accept me for the generally well-intentioned but practically flawed person that I am. The fact that I skipped the last 2,500 Sunday meetings will not count against me. If anything, I would expect my god to congratulate me for not wasting time sitting in a stuffy church singing stupid platitudes to a being who clearly doesn't seek my idolization. My god would be pleased that I spent my time more productively reading the Sunday paper or taking my dog (and dog spelt backwards...) for a long run in the park.

My focus in this contemplation of God's existence is rooted in the selfish yet scientifically inquisitive thought: What happens to me next?

The most logical answer is that nothing happens. Our whole being is dependent on a beating heart and when that stops, presumably all aspects of who we are come to a non-pulsing end. No bright light, no Pearly Gates, no grandma waiting with cookies. It certainly defies the mathematical odds to think that all living things or—if you think that we deserve a higher status—that all humans will progress to an afterlife.

Yet that answer is just too cold and final for my ego to accept. Surely I am so special that I must continue in some capacity. Could there be an infinite warehouse capable of storing mankind's history one-by-one on glorious end? This would be some kind of miracle and that is the source of my quasi-spiritual journey.

I went through my bookshelves last night to see if I had any sources of enlightenment there because it just seems like too important a question to trust to Google. The books that I found included *The God of Small Things*, a highly overrated, depressing half a book that I couldn't finish; *The DaVinci Code*, a guilty pleasure because I am supposed to be above pop books but I don't remember finding big answers in that book or in Tom Hanks' movie, either; and *God Emperor of Dune* (book four). When I was in university, I smoked a little weed and read all of Dune one semester. I hope Ben does the same thing. *The Satanic Verses*— wow, that was a great book. I didn't experience a spiritual awakening, but I remember reading until 4:00 a.m. to finish it.

I ultimately decided that the best thing on my bookshelf was a fifteen-year-old Glenlivet. I am not supposed to drink while on these meds, but I promised myself that I would not operate any heavy machinery as I poured myself a double, neat. I flipped through some very dusty pages of the Bible, but decided that the Bible belongs to believers and makes a pretty poor recruiting pamphlet for Team God.

It occurred to me that I was looking for some relief in either religion or whiskey and I was reminded of the Marx quote about religion being the opiate for the masses. I went to my computer to find the quote on Wikipedia and in part it reads:

"Religion is the sigh of the oppressed creature, the heart of a heartless world, and the soul of soulless conditions. It is the opium of the people. The abolition of religion as the illusory happiness of the people is the demand for their real happiness. To call on them to give up their illusions about their condition is to call on them to give up a condition that requires illusions. The criticism of religion is, therefore, in embryo, the criticism of that vale of tears of which religion is the halo."

Even as a translated quote it reads poetically, but Marx has a position to defend in this debate so he can hardly be viewed as independent or in any way close to confirming an absolute truth.

I need proof if I am going to invest in religion, and proof is illusive. I don't want a mathematical measure or a set of probabilities either. That is why the concept of Pascal's wager has never convinced me in the same manner that it has been adopted by some agnostics as an ultimate bet hedger. As described to me many years ago at the grad school pub by a philosophy major, Blaise Pascal was a seventeenth-century philosopher who reasoned that the repercussions from believing in God's existence and being wrong are very small, whereas the repercussions from not believing in God's existence and being wrong are monumental, therefore the safe bet is to believe in God. If I believe in God and I am right, then I will be rewarded with an eternal heaven. If I don't believe in God and I am wrong, I may be sentenced to a perpetual hell. And if there is no god, then whether I believe or not will have no consequence. The smart money therefore believes in God.

There is perversion on multiple levels. The first level was the most practical, as the philosophy major was gorgeous and I recall the stress of trying to focus on this deep discussion rather than the more primitive impulses that tried to interrupt my thoughts. The second level of perversion is the cosmic coin tossing around such an enormous question. And finally, the assumption that people can will themselves into believing or not believing based on the prevailing odds is ridiculous.

I think that I am either going to have to feel it or not feel it and no amount of willing religion into my life will matter. Neither side of this debate has proof. I wish that either side could recruit me to their team because I would be less frightened of either answer than I am of the unknown.

I do know that if I were told that my death was scheduled for tomorrow, I would not run to organized religion. I am certain that if God exists, every organized religion that I am aware of has fundamentally misunderstood him or her. Think of the kind of people who are devoted followers of an organized religion and you may understand my reluctance to enrol. The first group of followers includes the naïve lambs that Marx felt required religion's opium. These people generally lack the will or ability for critical thinking and instead prefer to be given an instruction manual on how to live a good life, so they can blindly follow without taxing their brain with the cumbersome and massive questions that those outside their faith have the burden of evaluating.

The second type of devoted follower is what I refer to as a religious traditionalist. Their belief is not deeply rooted in serious contemplation of their god, but is based on a family tradition that obligates them to include certain religious rites and rituals in their life. Most people follow the religion that they were born into because it is expected of them by their family, and because they have never challenged the tenets of their religion nor compared it to the other offerings on the religious menu. Touch football games, grandma's recipes, and campfire sing-a-longs are wonderful family traditions, but I just can't group the selection of a set of religious beliefs on the same list.

My least favourite group is the people that I call the equalizers. This group holds tightly to the concept that their shortcomings will be forgiven if they simply hold tight to a belief in a supreme being. All is forgiven if I attend service regularly and contribute significantly to the offering plate. The hypocrisy of this group who commit to a puritanical lifestyle at each service, but complete an under-the-table deal that afternoon or commit adultery that night are the hardest to stomach. If there is a god, he will punish this group twice—once for their sins and a second time for the mockery of belief.

The opposing team does not look attractive to me either. The atheists that I have encountered justify the stereotype of a beret-wearing pseudo-intellectual who is too cynical and jaded to entertain the possibility of a higher being. I have rarely found reasoned arguments against God stemming from this group and have never been motivated to commit to their team. Being cynical and sarcastic is easy and it is intellectually and emotionally lazy. The negative and pessimistic aura of these people is enough to turn me away from them, but I guess that my real opposition to them stems from my hope that they are wrong.

I am not prepared to fake a belief to fulfill Pascal's wager, but I hope that there is a god. If this is the end of my time on earth, the possibility of a full stop in a cold dark place is an overwhelming fear. I don't believe in a god, but I hope for a god.

Track 26

Lee

All of our cleaners are taught to stop cleaning and get out of the building if they feel unsafe for any reason. They are told to err on the side of caution and if we learn subsequently that they overreacted to a situation there will never be any reprisal. It can get pretty creepy in an empty office building in the wee hours of morning, so they need to know that if they are freaked out, they can run.

We have had some legitimately dangerous situations, so this is not some hypothetical policy. We had a cleaner walk in on a break-in. We once had a situation in which one cleaner physically threatened her co-worker. We have even had someone attempt to molest a cleaner. In every instance the potential victim escaped unharmed because they just got the hell out of the building.

A few weeks ago we had to reassign Mrs. Wei to another location because she ran out of her office building on four consecutive nights. Michael Jackson died earlier this year and, according to Mrs. Wei, he can now be seen moonwalking across the kitchen floor of Price Waterhouse Coopers. She seems fine in her new location and to the apparent disappointment of her replacement at PWC, the Prince of Pop hasn't been seen again.

Part of the safety instruction to get out of the building is to call the police if they feel that it is a police matter and to text the message 9-1-1 to me whether they call the cops or not. Just after eleven last night, I got a 9-1-1 text from Bao, who is one of my longest-serving employees. Bao is a sweetheart and has never caused me a moment of worry and had certainly never rang my 9-1-1 alarm before.

I immediately called her, but could barely hear her as the wind rushed into her cell phone. I could tell that she was frantic and crying, but I was only catching every fourth word that she was sobbing to me. I instinctively began to walk out of my building and head toward the next block where Bao and her partner Han were, but my walk changed to a run when I caught the word "gun" in the garbled call.

It took me less than three minutes to sprint around the block, but somehow two cruisers were there before me. A female officer had her arm around Bao's shoulder and was encouraging her to catch her breath and slow down. Han seemed confused and was trying to get the story from Bao just as the officers and I were. It took several minutes for poor Bao to let us know that she heard a gunshot from the corner office of the floor she was cleaning. She was collecting garbage from the cubicles just thirty feet from that corner office when she heard the loud bang and she immediately ran for the exit. On the way out, Bao pulled Han onto the elevator with her, and here they were in the cool night air in the outer entrance of the building just minutes later.

Three officers rushed to the bank of elevators with their pistols drawn and waited to see if anyone would emerge from the elevator or the staircase. The other officer made radio calls and, within what I guess was fifteen minutes although it felt like two minutes, a tactical squad was racing into the building.

By now there was a small group outside the building as paramedics and more officers had arrived. As the wind whipped our faces, we waited for the sounds of a shootout, but it was eerily quiet. Five minutes went by. Ten minutes went by. Finally, we heard the radio of the officer we were with crackle and an "all clear" message was given together with instructions for the paramedics. There was no murderer on the loose—there was just a victim of suicide.

Neither Bao nor Han knew anything about the man in the corner office. Bao apparently had seen him a couple of times, but had never spoken with him and in fact she didn't even know that he was in the office that night. Both cleaners were understandably rattled and we will give them some time off and then reassign them to a new building.

I am a little rattled, too. While the police were active, I was only thinking of murder. Suicide never entered my thoughts. It was a little bit of a letdown to go from a shootout scenario to a solo sad shooter, which I know is crass but it was my honest initial reaction. Now I am able to process this more intellectually than emotionally and I am left wondering why this happened.

How do things ever get so bad that there is no better answer than to shoot yourself? I have always thought that suicide seemed valid when it was to end the excruciating pain of one who is terribly ill, but that has been my only allowance for an act that I have viewed as cowardly. As far as I know, the guy from last night wasn't terminally ill, so what made him pull the trigger?

It's not appropriate for me to start asking personal questions, so if I can't invade the privacy of our shooter, I could at least learn about suicide in general. I found the website of a non-profit organization, suicide.org. What I learned is that there is a very legitimate reason why I cannot imagine being suicidal and that is because I do not have any mental illness. It seems that over 90 percent of suicides are committed by people with a mental illness. Of that 90 percent, the largest sub-category is people with untreated depression. As I read on, the judgments that I had formed about the shooter begin to melt. It was unlikely that he was weak or selfish. It was unlikely that he was taking a coward's path away from his problems. It is instead extremely likely that he had an illness that I do not fully understand but can appreciate is real.

Last night's events will stay with me for a long time. The pure sadness of it all will not be easily shaken off. Being in a big empty office in the middle of the night can play tricks on your brain at the best of times. I hope that Bao and Han will not be permanently freaked out by this and will be able to get back to work soon. I will be back at work tonight and will put on a brave face, but I can assure you that I will be fully freaked out.

Grant

While I am trying to decide what to do about my career and marriage, I have decided to take on the two easier items on my fix-it list: I have no friends and the Leafs suck.

Technically, the Leafs have won a Stanley Cup in my lifetime, but I was too young to remember it. My earliest memories are of my father drinking beer on the couch and laughing at Harold Ballard sitting in his bunker in Maple Leaf Gardens. Before The Senators arrived in Ottawa, Dad cheered for the Bruins and they pounded the Leafs fairly steadily during my early hockey-watching days. I think that I began to cheer for the Leafs because it gave me a way to oppose my father without any penalty. We could tease each other about our teams and it felt oddly empowering to be allowed to disagree with my father about a subject as important as hockey.

It has been a challenge to be a loyal Leafs fan because they have offered so little reward to their fans over the years. Most nights I turn off the television in frustration, and Ellen has asked me dozens of times why I continue to watch if I don't get any enjoyment out of it. It is hard to explain my loyalty, but I think that a fan devoted to any team would struggle to explain the bond that you have with your team. And like a true Leafs fan, I think that the team will be great next year so I can't change now.

So if I can't change my allegiance to the Leafs, I will have to work on finding some friends. How does a forty-nine-year-old man do that? First, one has to consider the very real possibility that you could be accused of being gay when you try to make friends with another guy. Any man-on-man advance is analyzed through a gay filter. Every time a guy asks another guy if he wants to go for a coffee, a beer or to catch a ball game, the second guy is trying to see if there is a gay code embedded in the request. This means that, generally, a man cannot directly ask out another man in the same way that a woman can call another woman to go for lunch or shopping just for fun.

If you can't be direct about inviting men to become friends, then you have to find subtle ways to let friendships emerge. When I see men who have lots of friends, I notice that the friendships have just developed from situations that they shared. Guys meet each other at work, they play on the same sports team or they have kids in the same gymnastics club.

I don't want to be friends with any of the guys at work because I prefer to keep my work life and private life separate. I don't play any team sports nor do I have kids, so that kills a couple of places to meet men. See what I mean? "Places to meet men." How faggy does that sound?

I knew that I was never going to get to solve the difficult items on my list if I couldn't take any action on the Leafs or friends issues, so I took one action. A couple of weeks ago we were at a dinner party with some of Ellen's friends and one of the other husbands was telling me about how much he was enjoying a new running group that he had joined. So this morning, I called the guy up and asked him about the group and if there was room for one more. He was really enthusiastic and happy that I called and now I am going to go for my first group run with Chad (gay sounding name) and the rest of the running group this Sunday morning. It's a first step, but I will be careful to see if Chad wears tights or runs like a homo before I take it too far.

Terry

I am keeping myself fully immersed at work as much to keep from thinking about the looming diagnosis. We have had a very focused music week at the shop, as we have been playing exclusively Canadian artists. There was an era not so long ago when it would have been tough to string together enough Canadian artists to fill a day, let alone a week. Not anymore—the volume of fantastic Canadian music is incredible.

When I was in my musical youth, we had a handful of good Canadian bands and a lot of mediocre bands that we listened to because our local radio stations had to play Canadian content.

We had the Guess Who and they deserve our admiration (as do
the post-Guess-Who careers of Mr. Cummings and Mr. Bach-
man). We had legendary musicians like Ms. Mitchell, Mr. Light-
foot and Mr. Young, but none of them oozed cool when I was
twenty. We slugged through bands like Lover Boy, Chilliwack,
Glass Tiger, Trooper, and Triumph. You may have some fond
memory associated with one of those bands or one of their
songs, but with the benefit of hindsight none of them were very
good. Things got better with Rush, Our Lady Peace and Blue
Rodeo, but today we may be in the midst of the greatest era ever
for Canadian music.

We played all of those older bands this week, but we also
played some fantastic bands from a more modern era. I had a
sixty-year-old man ask me about the Sam Roberts song that we
were playing and when I explained that Sam was a great straight
up rocker from Montreal, the customer wrote down the details
and went out to buy his music. If you are feeling a little out of
touch with Canada's brightest and best, get started with this
list: Arcade Fire, Hey Rosetta, Kathleen Edwards, Arkells.

There is one band, however, that stands above them all and
Cory and I took the very bold position at the beginning of the
week in crowning them as the greatest band in Canadian music
history. We were met with outrage from many customers who
insisted that no one could top the Guess Who, or Rush or, for
one very delusional customer, the Barenaked Ladies.

So we spent the week defending the greatest Canadian band
of all time: The Tragically Hip. The Hip have energy and grit.
They are musically complicated and as talented as any band I
have ever heard. Best of all—they are wonderfully Canadian.
Any band that can sing about Bobcaygeon, the Millhaven prison
and Bill Barilko wins the award on patriotism alone.

Musical taste is unique, so games like "who is best" are really
just for fun, but the takeaway is that the depth of our musical
talent is now another source of Canadian pride.

Grant

After months of taking on any assignment that would pay the bills, we are finally working on the kind of deals that we should have been doing all along. I know that Jack is responsible for bringing the business into the firm, but I am the one leading the engagements. He can have the glory as long as I get the fun of assembling the deals.

We are leading a cross-border Initial Public Offering (IPO) of an emerging biotech company named Brighter Day Pharma that has a new technology platform to attack central nervous system diseases such as Alzheimer's and Parkinson's diseases. More specifically, their products focus on treating symptoms of the diseases and their lead product targets depression for Alzheimer's patients.

The original investors and the current management team are going to get rich off this IPO and our firm is also going to do extremely well. There isn't much to criticize with this opportunity as the clinical data seems sound, the management team is good and the drug will sell like hotcakes. Brighter Day will be a Wall Street darling in just a few weeks and they will have me to thank for it.

I have had a big hand in developing the strategy for how we will position the IPO and the investor presentations, but I can't take too much credit. The real credit goes to the wizards behind the curtains in big pharma companies that keep identifying new diseases that society didn't know that we had. Brighter Day is pushing a drug to combat depression for newly diagnosed

Alzheimer's patients, as if depression was some virus attacking the body. I am not a doctor, but doesn't it seem natural to be sad about a death-sentence diagnosis? Why is anyone trying to prevent depression when it seems like the most human reaction possible? Why must one intervene and stop people from feeling what they should naturally feel?

Apparently, suicide rates are very high with Alzheimer's patients and one of the Brighter Day guys was telling me that at least 10 percent of Alzheimer's patients will attempt suicide and that their new drug will help to reduce attempted suicide rates. I wonder if chemical interference is the right answer for these people. Anyone who would contemplate suicide is troubled and anyone who would prefer suicide to a dignified fight against Alzheimer's is, by definition, weak.

If I were diagnosed with Alzheimer's, I would be sad—or "depressed" if you want a medical definition—but I would get over it on my own and then buckle down and battle. I may be a bad Catholic, but I still remember that suicide is a mortal sin. You can commit all of the murder you want, but if you can receive last rites on your deathbed, you still have a shot with St. Peter. If, however, your final act on earth is the sin of self-murder, then there will be no opportunity for last rites and you will burn for all eternity. So suicide is something that I would never consider, no matter how sad my diagnosis makes me. I guess that a drug that reduces suicide is good, but it annoys me that we have to try to intervene medically on behalf of those who are so fundamentally weak that they can't get over their depression on their own.

All of these thoughts I keep safely packed inside my head while I publicly sing the praises of the new wonder drug and how grateful we all are for the opportunity to help needy patients. The pitch to investors is a straightforward financial message. We are going to fulfill a medical need for a rapidly growing patient group with a disease that has no cure on the horizon. Our drug is very safe, with minimal side effects, so essentially every Alzheimer's patient can be thrown on our anti-depressant immediately after diagnosis and stay on the drug until the final stage of the disease.

The slightly twisted part of this success story is that because there is nothing coming that looks like a cure or treatment for the underlying Alzheimer's disease, this drug will sell for years and years. A bit perverse to list the hopelessness of Alzheimer's as a financial windfall for the drug, but that is the truth.

It's part of the game and no one is a bigger fan of the game than Jack, who stopped in to tell me that he just got off of the phone with the Brighter Day CEO who couldn't have been happier with the spin that I had put on his investor presentation. It is a good spin and I am good at this job. I wonder how good I could be if I worked on a product that I actually believed in.

I took another big step toward selling SunRay today when I signed an engagement letter with Ironside Capital Partners, which will now represent me in the sale of the business. Jennifer's team at the law firm helped me to find Ironside as an appropriate niche investment-banking group that would serve as my promoter and agent in the search for a buyer. Ironside is based in Manhattan and they have significant experience and connections within the cleaning industry.

When Jennifer's team gave me the shortlist of agents to consider, they were surprised that I eliminated the only local firm without even meeting them. I offered a fairly convincing lie that I thought that it was best to have a U.S. rep given that we already know the Canadian players. I think that Jennifer's guys bought into that logic. The truth is that I personally clean the office of the firm that they suggested—it's the one that includes my asshole past classmate from ECON 101—so I just thought that it would be too weird to work with them during the day and then scrub their toilet at night.

I have managed to avoid seeing that old classmate since the night when I interrupted one of his flings in his office. I am a little grossed out when I clean his office, now that I know that he brings women back for late-night flings. I haven't witnessed any of these rendezvous lately, so maybe he now does the decent thing and springs for hotel rooms for his mistresses. Douche-bag. I feel sorry for his wife because she probably has no idea that she is married to a pig. This guy isn't great looking, but he has a big job with fancy suits and probably drives a flashy car, and so he is able to prey on naïve women. I guess that power is attractive to some women, but the fact that this guy gets away with sleeping around so freely is frustrating to me. Prick.

Before I selected the guys at Ironside, they had hinted that they may be aware of certain companies in the industry that would be interested in adding a Canadian company to their organization, and that Ironside had a direct line into those potential suitors. I discounted this as part of the sales pitch, but Jennifer, who has infinitely more experience than I in such matters, smelled something different.

She counselled, "Lee, I think that Ironside has already identified a buyer and that they will connect you to them as soon as you sign the agreement. With all respect, this is a small deal for Ironside, so they wouldn't take it unless they thought that they could make their percentage on the sale quickly and easily." That was enough for me to sign with Ironside and now I guess we will find out if they have a buyer standing off stage.

They are certainly not wasting any time in getting things moving. We had a three-hour meeting today to put together "our book" which is a thirty-page summation of the company and everything that a prospective buyer would want to know. We protected some confidential information such as the names of my customers, but at some point I will have to reveal everything if a buyer shows that they are serious.

The book contains all of our factual details, including financial statements, tax information, et cetera. But it also tells a story. Ironside identified the characteristics of SunRay that they think will be most attractive to buyers and they wrote the story around three key points: The above average profit margin—we run a lean ship and avoid a lot of expenses associated with hiring and training new staff since our staff rarely leave; our customers are very loyal as evidenced by our high customer retention rate; and our staffing model is viewed as a unique asset and one that can be mined for further expansion.

The slightly disturbing thing about the book is that I am barely mentioned. The fact that I started the company and have led it thus far is in there, but Ironside deliberately played me down. They explained that if it sounded like SunRay was successful exclusively because of me and the buyer knew that I was leaving upon sale, then the price would drop because a key factor to the company's historical success was not going to stick around. Instead the "small but knowledgeable management team" was emphasized. The book included the slightly offensive line, "Despite being the sole shareholder, Lee prefers to leave macro business issues to her team, while personally focusing on certain administrative tasks, as well as spending over 50 percent of her time in her original role as an office cleaner." I understand the rationale of getting a higher price by diminishing my personal profile, but it stings a bit. Okay, it stings a lot.

Ironside explained what I should expect over the coming weeks. They will get things kicked off by passing word around to their contacts within the cleaning industry and their investment colleagues that SunRay is in play. That will generate a number of calls to Ironside. Most of these calls are "tire kickers." Some tire kickers are trying to see if there is a huge bargain to be had and will not be interested in paying the appropriate price. Ironside told me that most tire kickers are actually not buyers at all, but instead are other business owners who are thinking about selling their business and want to see what the going prices are like. Dave Watts, the senior man on the Ironside team, explained that it is just like residential real estate—three quarters of the people who show up at an open house are not interested in buying your house, they are interested in selling their own house and want to see how your house measures up for the listed price. Ironside will filter out all of the tire kickers so that I don't have to deal with any of them—sounds like they are earning their fee already. When serious buyers are identified, Ironside will engage them in discussion, review the book with them and answer as many questions as they can without involving me. They will also have a preliminary discussion about price to ensure that the buyer will make a respectable offer should an offer be made.

The next stage involves me and is part of a "due diligence" process. The buyer(s) will want to speak with me and ultimately visit me and check out the business firsthand. All of that seems normal so I was feeling relaxed about the process until Dave said, "...and then the buyer will want to meet with your key employees."

Oh shit! It makes sense that a buyer will want to do that, but I had overlooked this point and naively thought that I could shield the sale from my staff until a deal was done. I now realized that I will have to share my plan with Anne and a couple of other key staff and I felt a panic sweeping over me.

I tried to push back: "Dave, I don't want them talking to staff. Nobody should know until the deal is done."

Dave didn't budge: "Lee, no one will buy this business without talking to staff. You said you want to sell the company and this is how it is done. Delaying the inevitable will not make this go away because your staff will find out at some point."

I know that he is right, but delaying the inevitable sounds fine to me for now. I can at least delay until a prospective buyer emerges—maybe no one will be interested.

I have always expected that the big changes in my life would be connected to a birth, a death, a marriage. I never expected that something as simple as signing a contract would be the big pivot, but this Ironside deal feels like I am about to start a new chapter in life.

Terry

My cancer coordinator, Carmen, gave away nothing as we walked with her from the lobby to Dr. Ryder's office. She was cheerful, but not too cheerful, and she was serious, but not too serious. A good poker player.

Dr. Ryder greeted us at the door and, thankfully, skipped the small talk. In her no-bullshit manner she said, "As you know, we removed three lymph nodes and while two of them were clean, the cancer has spread to one of the nodes. This is not what we were hoping for and this makes matters considerably more serious."

Maybe it was my right brain kicking in, but for some stupid reason I loudly blurted out, "What is my score? What stage is this now?"

Dr. Ryder calmly replied, "Everyone's cancer is unique and those scores are just for statistical purposes, but if it matters to you, you have been upgraded from a stage one to a stage three."

Upgraded? How the hell can this be an upgrade? Do I get more legroom or free drinks? And what happened to stage two? We just blew right past that!

Dr. Ryder continued, "Although the cancer has spread, we are still hopeful that the spread is quite limited. The fact that you and your dermatologist found this so early may be our biggest advantage. My recommendation is that we assess further spread so that we can treat quickly and aggressively if needed."

I was irrationally angry. I didn't want to moan or cry, I wanted to punch someone. I knew that Carmen, Carol, and the doctor were on my side so there was no one to fight, but I felt my fists form and my nerves twitch like I was preparing for an alley scrap.

Carol stoically asked a string of great questions and dutifully noted the answers. She reviewed all of what was said for me at the kitchen table hours later because she knew that I wasn't capable of following the conversation at the time. I sat through the brief meeting with my hands balled into fists and my eyes set on the floor as if I were trying to burn a hole into it. I felt like I was going to explode.

It wasn't until we got back to the car that I was able to speak without fear of shouting or hitting. The first thing that I said as I handed the keys to Carol was that she should drive because I was too rattled. She took the keys and as she started the ignition the world crashed upon both us. We sat and cried uncontrollably for several minutes as the bright, cheerful sunlight of a perfect, late summer day poured in through the windshield. Carol was the first to find composure, and she finally put the car in drive and said that we had to get home to start developing a plan to beat this thing.

Her list-making, survival instinct was kicking in and, as I didn't have my own instinct, I was happy to do whatever she wished.

Across the kitchen table that afternoon, I learned what it meant to be upgraded to stage three. When the step before dead is stage four, it isn't great to be at stage three. Stage three is further broken into three—A through C, with C being the worst. I have stage 3A, which means that the spread or metastasis is a micro one. I guess that means that even though it spread, the new cancer is very small. Carol explained that I am actually very close to the line between micro metastasis and macro metastasis and therefore I am almost at stage 3B. Furthermore, there is no cancer left in the original tumour—they cleaned all that out when they removed the mole. I also learned that the cancer has not spread to any other organ. They apparently tested or scanned for that, although truthfully I don't remember them doing that.

I did hear Dr. Ryder say that she was recommending another surgery, but now Carol was giving me the details that I missed. The suggestion is to have a therapeutic lymph node dissection, which will remove all of the lymph nodes that are close to the original tumor and close to the cancerous node that they just removed. Carol explained that Dr. Ryder said that this isn't usually done until stage three-B or three-C, but she was suggesting that we go after this aggressively now with the hope of preventing further spread later.

I countered with what I thought was a pretty logical argument, "They just took some of my lymph nodes, so I am not sure it is a great idea to allow them to take more."

Carol nodded at my reasonable question but then a small smile came across her face, which eventually grew into laughter. I didn't know what she was laughing about, but found myself laughing along with her. It felt good to laugh.

As Carol controlled her laughing, she said, "We barely know what a lymph node does, we don't know if you have a dozen or a million. We don't know if anything bad happens if you remove them, yet we are ready to debate this whole thing with our oncologist. We are ridiculous."

We recognized that despite all of our research to date, we were still fairly unprepared and that we needed to do more reading. We trust our team at the cancer centre, but blindly following their advice is not our style and we need to understand all of the pros and cons of their recommendation as well as available alternatives. We made a list (of course) of the things that we needed to understand and questions that we wanted to answer. Then we set the list aside for the night as we were both too emotionally drained to start the research. We ordered pizza and watched mindless television before going to bed. Strangely, I slept like a baby, but I woke this morning with the thought that this shit is about to get real. My cancer status upgrade takes cancer from a concern to the thing that will dominate the next part of my life.

Part Three

Sittin' in the mornin' sun,
I'll be sittin' when the evenin' comes.

Terry

I woke early this morning, but with the upgraded cancer status in my head I couldn't bring myself to go to work. I called Cory with a lie about a head cold and he assured me that he had everything under control. I asked what lyrics he had selected and he said that he was just about to write them on the board. We have a printout from the internet of hundreds of great lyrics that we can use on a day like this when nothing significant comes to either of us. Cory randomly selected and wrote out "Sittin' in the mornin' sun, I'll be sittin' when the evenin' comes." Nice little throwaway lyrics from a nothing song by Otis Redding.

Carol and I each brought our laptops to the kitchen table, poured morning coffee and started to surf the web for melanoma information. Carol began working systematically through the list that we developed last night. As usual, I couldn't get past the statistics. I learned that if my SNBL had come back clean, my survival rate would have been over 95 percent. Now, the survival rates were much lower, but each website offered different rates. Some say as low as 40 percent and some as high as 80 percent. One site had a macabre tool called a prognostic calculator, which promised to reveal your specific expected survival rate if you entered a few data points regarding your own cancer. I couldn't resist. I entered my stage, my tumour thickness, age, sex and a few other things before hitting "submit" and received the instant reply that my expected survival rate was 75.13 percent. The precision of the two decimal point prediction offered, without any examination from medical personnel, kind of made me chuckle and head off toward more reliable sources.

The most comprehensive stats package was on the American Cancer Society website, which listed the survival rate of a stage 3A melanoma patient as 78 percent, so maybe the crazy prognostic calculator isn't so crazy. If I were to slip to phase 3B, my survival rate would drop to 68 percent, and if I slide all the way to stage four, I would be down to 18 percent.

I stopped myself from dwelling on what all these stats meant and decided I better get down to work if I didn't want to piss off Carol.

One article I read about my upcoming procedure talked about one risk that is present in tumours originating, like mine, on the trunk of the body. Apparently, the way that a cancer spreads could vary, depending on the lymphatic draining patterns, which are not as predictable when the tumour is trunk based. That means that a tumour could spread down a different lymph path than the one that we are focused on. I explained what I had just read to Carol.

"Finally, you are getting serious and doing some real research. That is a good question, but you can move on because this isn't a concern for you."

I was a bit indignant that my finding was being pushed off the table, so I challenged Carol's basis for dismissing me.

"You have already had a lymphoscintigraphy performed, so we know where the tumour could potentially spread to. Remember when they gave you that injection and then used the fancy camera to see where the radio-labeled colloid traveled? That procedure tells us where a tumour would travel to if it was going to spread and they learned that your case is pretty simple as the path is only to the closest nodes."

My open-mouthed, wide-eyed look was enough to convey to Carol that I was stunned by her medical rant.

Carol blushed a little and simply said, "I am a good listener" with a coy little smile.

We read site after site as the morning progressed. We read about the risk of lymphedema as a side effect of the procedure and the risks generally associated with surgery, but by noon we shared a sense that nothing was as risky as not knowing if the cancer was spreading. The best information that we found was in the materials provided by our cancer team. Their documents were complete and very direct. All of the risks were presented in graphic detail.

The only question left for us to ask was, should we get a second opinion? Intellectually it seemed like an obvious thing that we should do in case Dr. Ryder was mistaken. Yet, it just didn't feel right. These people had been so good to us and so accurate in all that they had done so far that it felt as if asking for a second opinion would be disloyal. It also felt like we would seek a second opinion as an academic exercise, because we are so confident that the first opinion is accurate. We chose not to seek a second opinion, which might be the wrong decision but we are happy with it.

I called the cancer centre and spoke with Carmen who answered my final couple of questions without problem and told me that she was already working on a date for my next surgery.

It seems that every little thing triggers a thought about selling the business. The lyrics in the coffee shop this morning were from "Sittin' on the Dock of the Bay" by Otis Redding and I went to bed with that happy song in my head. I kept thinking that if I sell the business I could get to that peaceful place that Otis was in where you can do whatever you want—even if that is just sitting on a dock all day—if I just find the courage to sell.

When I woke up early this afternoon I was plunged into the sale question immediately because there was a message on the machine asking me to join a teleconference with Dave from Ironside and Jennifer from the law firm at 3:30 p.m. I had a run scheduled with Anne at four o'clock, so I sent her an e-mail to tell her that I wouldn't be able to make it.

Anne sent me back this message: "No prob on the run—gives me an excuse to blow it off. Everything okay? It seemed like something was bugging you yesterday. Tell me what's wrong because you know that I will drag it out of you eventually. HaHa."

I typed back the lie that I was fine, but just had a bad sleep and didn't feel up to the run. She is pretty astute and I am sure she suspects that something is up.

Dave jumped right in and announced that he had been fielding calls from more people than he expected.

"Even when I filter out the tire kickers, I am left with six serious inquiries. I have sent books to each of them and have scheduled calls over the next few days. Jennifer has agreed to host the diligence from her office because I will need to get some of these guys up to Toronto very soon."

He assured me that there were serious buyers on the list and that many of these guys don't get involved unless they intend to play. Jennifer asked if Dave knew any of the companies personally and Dave, a bit sheepishly, said that three of them were previous clients and that they were the first ones that he had sent the book to. Over the phone line, I received Jennifer's telepathic message of "I told you so."

Dave said that the only negative feedback that he had received was around the possible price. Ironside had originally said that they felt that they could get over $15 million for SunRay, but Dave said that he was getting some initial feedback that the serious buyers may be angling closer to $10–$12 million, given that the business was limited to one Canadian city, which was not as attractive to some of the buyers as he may have originally thought. Dave assured me that they would of course push for the higher price, but he wanted to get my reaction if the best price was only $10 million.

I was about to tell him that $10 million was an unimaginably high number to me so I didn't really care about the extra, but I was interrupted by Jennifer.

"Dave, let's give Lee time to think that one over." Then Jennifer directed the conversation onto something else and ensured that we never returned to that topic.

As soon as our three-way call ended, Jennifer called me back. "Lee—we haven't had time to discuss this, but you need to be careful with Ironside."

I said, "Wait, Jennifer. You told me that Ironside was a great choice and now you doubt them?"

"That's not it. It isn't Ironside; it is anyone who works on a percentage fee. Look, remember when Dave said that this process is like residential real estate? Well, Ironside is like your real estate agent. If a real estate agent makes 3 percent on selling a house and they have an offer for $950,000, how hard do you think that they will work to get to your asking price of $1 million? They will boost their commission from $28,500 to $30,000 by fighting long and hard to get to the $1 million asking price. All that work for an extra $1,500 isn't worth it, so they are going to convince you to just take the $950,000."

"If Dave thinks that he can get a fast and easy deal at $10 million, he isn't going to fight hard to get you to $15 million or more. His incentive is severely diminished. Dave is on your side and will help you in a lot of ways, but you need to play against him a bit on this point. Pick a number and let him know that if you don't get at least that much, then you will just keep running the business. He needs to believe that you are serious, so be convincing and don't waiver."

It never occurred to me that I would have to play against people who are supposed to be on my team, but Jennifer made perfect sense. I guess that I can concoct a story about why I could not possibly be satisfied with a measly $10 million, but it may be hard to be convincing. The take-away message from the calls today is that there are buyers at the door.

I turned back to the e-mail and found Anne's note: "Tomorrow at 4—mandatory run—no wimping out —see you there."

No wimping out? Christ, if only she knew how right she was. This shit is getting real.

Grant

The coffee shop had another lyric that seemed like it was meant just for me this morning. The lyrics were from the terribly sad song, "Sittin' on the Dock of the Bay," which is about a guy that is so down on his luck that he doesn't know what to do. The poor guy sings about having nothing to live for but he doesn't know what to change so he decides to change nothing. That could be me in the song—I need to make changes, but I am doing nothing. Time for action.

If I am going to tackle the big issues of my marriage and my career, I need to set things in motion, so I started making calls this morning. I met a guy at a conference a year ago who thought that I would be a catch for his firm in Chicago. I can't call him up because this industry is too small and word would leak back to Jack Cash, so I did the next best thing and called an executive recruitment guy that I know in New York. He put me in touch with a fellow headhunter in his Chicago office and I talked to that guy for half an hour today.

Seems that Chicago is hot and that there would be a couple of great opportunities for me there. I was impressed that the recruiter was so insightful to identify my significant track record and leadership potential. He articulated my strengths perfectly and I think that he could represent me well in the market. I was quite non-committal and kept things casual, saying that I was only fishing and that once I had some time to think about it I would get back to him.

With Jack in town, it may be tough to go man on man with him in Toronto. Also, it makes sense to think about moving because if I leave Ellen it may be easier to be in a different city. Other than Ellen and the job, there is nothing tying me here and the thought of a fresh start is invigorating.

I could really start over in Chicago as a single man in a new firm. If I had a new firm, I could create a little different image for myself—maybe loosen up a bit and then people would say, "Not only is that guy super smart, but he is also super fun." I could definitely make friends quickly—it's easier in a new city. Everyone is nice to the new guy and you get introduced around a bit and you can be "out there" making friends. If I suddenly get "out there" in this city after all this time not being out there, then people will be suspicious.

Chicago is a great sports town: two baseball teams, a basketball team, a football team and the Blackhawks. I could cheer for the Blackhawks—at least until they meet the Leafs in the cup final.

Chicago seems like a man's city and to me, seems wonderfully void of a woman's touch. I imagine that all of the artsy stuff is there, but it doesn't seem like the focus of Chicago like it is in New York or Paris. Chicago is famous for the Cubs—not for its art galleries or opera houses, and it doesn't require you to see Broadway shows. It doesn't have a village for bohemians and jazz, or a big park demanding romantic walks around the reservoir. Chicago is a working man's town with sports bars, beer halls and diners. It's cold and tough and has blues clubs where people sing about how rough life is.

There would be women in Chicago. Not a woman—I don't need one woman—I don't need a wife. I need women—one-nighters, the thrill of conquest, the spirit of pursuit and the uncomplicated pleasure of two strangers having no-strings-attached sex.

Work hard all day, go to a game in the evening, hit the bar, pick someone up and get laid. Rinse and repeat.

Terry

I might have cancer but I don't feel sick, so while waiting for my next surgery I returned to work today. The staff seemed unsuspicious of the lies I told regarding my absence from the shop, so the day was not stressful. In fact, I would say that going to work lowered my stress level today.

Cory and I came up with a great game for the lyrics board that had the customers buzzing all day. We called it "A Day of Confession" and we gave a free cookie to anyone who would stand in the shop and sing song lyrics the way they misunderstood them before they learned the real lyrics. We all have made this mistake of blissfully singing aloud the wrong lyrics of a song to the great amusement of friends or family. These tiny humiliations in our past are almost always hilarious memories, so we thought we would try to tap into that and see if we could get the customers laughing via a musical confession of their error.

We had no idea that the game would strike a chord with so many or that we would have so many brave customers who had no fear of singing in public. By 10:30 a.m. I had to call in a rush order for more cookies because we were gladly giving so many away.

One of our first vocalists was a regular. Helen, a frumpy woman in her early sixties, said that her children never let her live down the day when she insisted that they turn off the radio and the vulgar song that was playing. Her children were perplexed as they were listening to what they thought was a harmless song. When her children pressed her to explain what was so bad with the song, she thought that they were just trying to embarrass her by making her say the offensive lyric out loud. She refused and tried to drop it, but the kids wouldn't let it go.

So finally, Helen blurted out, "I don't want to listen to you sing about how only the lonely get laid." Helen had thought that she heard the line, "It's like I told you, only the lonely get laid." The kids laughed uncontrollably and left Helen red-faced when they explained that the line is: "It's like I told you, only the lonely can play." I vaguely remember the song, but I had to look it up for Cory. It was a hit in 1982 by a very forgettable band called The Motels, but the song never sounded as good as when Helen sang the lyric in the middle of a busy Beanfest this morning.

Sometimes people struggle with understanding the lyrics of a song because the composer has taken liberty with language. Example? You will know these lyrics:

"Some people call me the space cowboy.

Yeah! Some call me the gangster of love.

Some people call me Maurice,

'Cause I speak of the pompatus of love."

You have probably sung along dozens of times to this classic Steve Miller Band song, "The Joker," but have you ever considered what the hell "the pompatus of love" is?

Grab your dictionary—it's not there. Steve made up the word—and we never noticed.

Some other great stuff that we heard throughout the day: The Who's line, "Eminence front, eminence front" was sung as "M&M's for lunch, M&M's for lunch." The Beatle's line, "She's got a ticket to ride" was sung as "She's got a chicken to hide."

We were surprised to hear the same mistake by two different customers just hours apart. They both misheard Jimi Hendrix singing, "'Scuse me while I kiss the sky" as "'Scuse me while I kiss this guy."

However, our unanimous favourite misquote of the day was sung loudly and proudly during the peak of the lunch-hour rush by Margaret, a regular who we adore from the accounting firm's administrative staff.

She belted out a Robert Plant line that should have been, "Might as well face it, you're addicted to love," with the hilariously butchered, "Might as well face it, you're a dick with a glove," to a rousing ovation from the entire shop.

What made that one especially funny was that Al laughed so hard that he couldn't stay in character and the customers saw the real Al laughing along with them. The customers loved that they had finally cracked the hard shell of the grumpy Soup Nazi. I know that Al will come back twice as grumpy tomorrow and that they will love stopping in to see that show as much as they enjoyed the laughs today.

Lee

On Saturday night, Gord and I were standing in line for popcorn at the theatre when I spotted my employee, Mrs. Chen, making her way back from the cash with an armload of popcorn and soda. I introduced her to Gord and the three of us talked for a while about what movie we were going to see and how cold it was for early October—completely unremarkable things. As soon as she was out of earshot, Gord said to me, sympathetically, that it must be difficult to get through a cleaning shift with only her to talk to.

"She seems nice, but there is not much going on upstairs— hard to have a real conversation with that."

I didn't want to have this discussion in the lobby of a movie theatre so I just shook my head and went into the theatre without saying a word back to Gord.

Mrs. Chen and her husband had successful positions within the Communist Party of China in Beijing and those positions gave them the money and status to send their only child to a Canadian University fifteen years ago. Her son stayed in Canada when he graduated and sponsored his mother's immigration when Mr. Chen died.

Mrs. Chen has incredible stories of their life in Beijing and how she and her husband succeeded within the Communist Party while privately never seeing any merit in communism.

She had a fantastic vantage point for life with Mao, life after Mao, the Tiananmen Square massacre, and the birth of the modern Chinese economy. And Gord thinks that she isn't interesting to talk to? Mrs. Chen is a living encyclopedia on classic literature and she has read every great book written in the last hundred years. She can't seem to do anything to reduce her accent, but her English vocabulary is much bigger than mine. Gord's comment was so wrong and it pissed me off. I sat and quietly steamed as we watched some mindless action flick that Gord had begged to see.

I know that Gord is not racist. He does not have a bit of hatred within him, but he makes the mistake that so many people make in that he takes someone's lack of proficiency in English and extrapolates that to a lack of intelligence. It is a dangerous mistake. If any of us were dropped into a situation in which we had to learn a new language and be employed and socialize in that language, our full intelligence would not be on display. That is the case with many of the women from SunRay. I know that many of them are extremely well-educated and those who are not have earned a level of intelligence beyond that which is taught in any educational institution that I have encountered. They may speak with an accent or use the wrong English word from time to time, but if you write them off as unintelligent, then you are missing out on an opportunity to learn from them.

I knew that Gord was not being hateful, so I didn't approach the issue with anger, but I felt that Mrs. Chen deserved to be defended. On the drive back to Gord's place, I calmly explained Mrs. Chen's background and described her intelligence to him. I wasn't argumentative, but maybe the action flick had put him in a feisty mood because he wanted to argue the point and wouldn't accept that Mrs. Chen was smart.

"Lee, she was straining to stay up in a conversation about a chick-flick and I couldn't understand most of what she said. If she is smart, why doesn't she learn to speak English?"

I tried to stay calm and made gentle counterpoints, but Gord was on the attack and stuck to his points. We volleyed back and forth in gradually spiraling volumes and it seemed that the argument would go on all night until we exchanged two final shots.

In exasperation and sensing that he was losing the argument, Gord blurted out words that he could never get back: "If she is so smart, why the fuck is she a cleaning woman?"

"Take me home, asshole."

Grant

I overheard the end of a conversation between two young staffers in the office tonight. I was working late and had gone in the back door of the company lunchroom to make myself some tea. The two guys were just outside the front door of the kitchen and obviously they thought that they were alone.

My ears perked up as I heard one say, "Woodyear is too uptight for that and Jack doesn't play on that team, so I guess she has nothing to worry about."

I heard his buddy reply, "She is definitely hot, but I hate the way that she pushes her tits up all the time. They are just too small."

I knew that they were talking about a new member of my team just from their two-line dialogue. Amy is a young girl that transferred into my department from the slumping high-tech group last week. She is not incredibly smart, but she is beautiful and charming and can probably get by on looks and personality. The young guys don't understand that I would never pursue a romantic interest in the office and so they say that I am uptight. That is just something that they say to sound cool in front of each other. I know that each of those guys privately aspires to become me. They said that Jack doesn't play on that team meaning that he isn't a lusting old pervert, but I wouldn't be so sure. I bet Jack is still attractive to these young girls and I am not so sure that he wouldn't take advantage of such an opportunity.

They are also wrong about her breasts. She has lovely small breasts and she displays them well. I may be her boss, but if you are going to put them on a platter, I assume that I should at least briefly look at them.

I like breasts—most men do. Some people say that men's fascination with breasts is a lingering holdover from the nursing experience. That's stupid. I don't know if I was breastfed and I certainly don't remember it if I was. I think that our interest is easier to understand and it is simply that breasts are a gateway to sex. Breasts are foreplay and if a woman is displaying her breasts, it is an indication that she is a sexual being. Young Amy is not signalling to the office that she wants to have cloakroom sex on the lunch break. She is simply saying, Yes, I am a professional woman, but I am also a young, attractive woman in my sexual prime so take a little peek at these. That's appropriate.

My interest in breast watching has been heightened over the years because of Ellen's stupid little insensitive pair. You see, during our courtship and early marriage I was in love with Ellen's small but stylish breasts. I would lavish my affection upon them during prolonged foreplay and it seemed that Ellen truly enjoyed the attention. However, one night after we had been married for a couple of years, Ellen stopped me mid-suck and asked if we could skip this part and move on.

What?! I was horny and hard so I just got on with things, but after we were finished (at least I was), I rewound back to her breast comment to ask what I was doing wrong. According to Ellen, I don't do anything wrong, it is just that she has little or no sexual sensation in her breasts. She says that she can feel my manipulations, but it doesn't give her any pleasure and, in fact, it usually frustrates her. She begins to lose interest in the eventual sex as she waits for me to finish up with her chest. It would be better for everyone if I just left her breasts out of my repertoire.

I was young and still enjoying that newlywed benefit of frequent sex. I was also filled with the sappy romantic notion that whatever made my spouse happy was just fine with me. So I accepted her request and her tits became a no-fly zone. Now, many years later, I am bitter about it. She knew that I loved breasts, and especially hers. It was a great source of pleasure for me and she ripped it (them) away from me in a purely selfish act. Why couldn't she fake some enthusiasm for my benefit? If breasts are a gateway to sex, then maybe I should be happy that Ellen removed the gate and left the path to sex wide open, but I really miss that part of my love life.

The result is that my breast fascination has heightened because, although I sleep next to a pair every night, I never touch any. I probably look more than I should. That might be part of it for many men—the attraction to something that they can see but can't touch.

Grant

A New York client left me a voicemail earlier this week asking if I could dial into a Friday meeting that he was having with an acquisition target because the deal had hit a few snags. I jumped at the chance for a weekend in Manhattan and sent the client a message saying that I would fly in and attend in person. My young staffers were surprised to hear that I was dropping everything to bail out the client, but I used that opportunity to give them a brief lecture about how you have to place client needs ahead of your own.

The truth is that I have been looking for an opportunity to test out what I learned in Miami, and New York is the perfect place. I have been on the Internet searching for the best places to go in New York. I want to stay away from the pulsating nightclubs that the twenty-year-olds will be at and find places that are going to attract an attractive, mature crowd. Not dull and stuffy—it has to be fun but for slightly older people. One place that is mentioned on several websites is Stone Rose in the Time Warner Center at Lincoln Circle, which is weird because I have been there for after-work drinks on a couple of occasions and never noticed anything unusual about it. Now, I am reading write-ups about young execs being lured away from the bar by vamping divorcees. One website suggests wearing a sign that says, "Not looking to get laid" for self-defence because otherwise you are fair game for the cougar hunt.

The weekend is off to a great start because I am getting credit for saving our client's deal. I guess that I did save the deal, but frankly my solution was so simple that it feels silly collecting praise. I introduced a milestone fee based on future performance to break an impasse that the two sides were having on the expected level of future performance. Cookie cutter stuff but the problem was simply that the two negotiating teams were mired in the mud of the deal and needed fresh eyes with some experience to point them toward the obvious. Everyone is happy and my team will earn a nice fee for some pretty basic advice.

The senior VP of my client and I left the details for the teams to complete and went for a martini. He was very happy and relieved to have the deal done and he shared with me that he thought that he might have gotten fired if the deal wasn't concluded. On the second martini, he shared that this deal might be the first positive thing that has happened to him in six months. It seems that he was having an affair and his wife found out and immediately started divorce proceedings. He was about to lose half of his money and had already lost most of his friends because it turns out that they were her friends, too. Most importantly, he lost the respect of his three adult children and none of them would speak to him.

"I have been screwing around with one-night stands on the road for years, but this was the only time I ever started a relationship with someone else in my hometown. One night turned into once every week for a year and a half, so it was only a matter of time before I got caught."

It was uncomfortable for me to hear about his troubles and I was happy to escape the bar when I reached the bottom of the second martini. It was, however, good for me to hear his story. He is paying a big price for his mistake and truly he deserves to pay. If he had just stuck to playing one-time road games, no one would have gotten hurt, but he got greedy and wanted action in his hometown and that was his mistake. As I get ready to head out tonight, I will keep his story in mind and keep all of the women that I meet off of the scent of my home life. I can't afford to make a mistake because, although I am probably going to divorce Ellen, I don't want our marriage to end because she catches me having an affair.

Terry

Carol and I just read and read and read. Every medical article remotely connected to my condition is on our must-read list. By engaging your brain so thoroughly, it leaves little room for emotion to creep in and that has helped me over the last few days.

Unfortunately, it seems that you can only defer the drama for so long because there is no way to run from the emotion of the disease. Ultimately, we made the choice to not hide the disease from those we love the most. So Carol and I sat, like a couple of screenplay writers, and decided what the right words would be when I talked to Ben, our closest friends and my staff.

It was early in the semester for Ben, so I didn't fear disrupting his finals or anything, but I didn't like the fact that I would have to tell him over the phone. I wanted to look him in the eyes and I wanted to put my arms around him. I called his cellphone and found him just getting ready to leave the library where he had been researching a paper. He called me back a few minutes later, as he was walking back to his dorm, and he was in an upbeat mood.

"Hey Pop, what are you crazy college kids doing? Need me to send money?"

"Ben, I am having a medical problem that I want you to know about."

As co-screen writers, Carol and I had decided that getting to the point was how this scene would be played. We also had decided that Ben deserved the truth and that he was mature enough to handle it. I explained what had happened and that I was heading toward another surgery. I explained all that we knew about the disease and the survival rates. I spoke for ten, uninterrupted minutes with my eyes closed, but all the while picturing eleven-year-old Ben sitting on the side of his bed listening intently to me. I imagined him looking up at me with soft wet eyes and trying to speak with a crackling pre-pubescent voice.

When I finished, the replying voice was not that of a meek eleven-year-old, but a man's voice, which simply asked, "Are you scared dad?"

I began to cry—definitely not in the script—but maybe not for the reason that you would think. I began to cry because in that short question from Ben I heard concern, comfort, support, maturity and I instantly knew that Ben was going to be fine no matter what happened to me.

"Yeah, I'm scared. Worried is more like it. There is just no way of knowing what will happen," I said while poorly hiding the fact that I was crying.

"It sounds like you have some great doctors and that they are on top of this thing," Ben offered, encouragingly and courageously. "How many lists has Mom made for you?"

We shared the laugh at Carol's expense and that eased my tension considerably. We spoke for a few more minutes and promised to talk tomorrow. With tough times ahead, I now see Ben not as someone that I have to support but someone that I will be able to lean upon.

Lee

With the possible sale transaction rolling along, I finally gathered up the courage to tell the SunRay management team what was happening. With lawyers and bankers around, it won't take long for the team to realize that something is up and although I haven't decided to sell, I feel that I have to be honest with them about the process that I am in and what the potential outcome could be. I started by calling Anne to see if we could get together for lunch. She was just on her way out to get some soup for lunch and suggested I just meet her at her favourite lunch counter.

It turns out that her soup place is my coffee shop. I had never been there after 7:00 a.m., so it was strange to see the place buzzing with a huge lunch crowd. I had only seen the staff in their laid-back morning mood and it seemed weird to watch the slightly frenzied pace that pushed customers through a soup line. I had an odd sense that I had caught them being unfaithful and had exposed the double life that they had hidden from me.

Anne was unusually pensive as we took seats at a little bistro table by the window. She leaned in and half whispered, "Just tell me what's wrong Lee and we can get through it together."

"Get through what?"

"Don't be brave Lee. You have been acting nervous around me for a couple of weeks, you haven't been running and you're here at noon when you should be asleep. Are you sick?"

I had no idea that I was sending out such worrisome signals to Anne and I quickly apologized for causing concern. I explained that I was completely fine but that I was contemplating a business change, which I needed to discuss with her. I just poured it out in full detail to her. How the opportunity presented itself and that a sale would give me all the time and money that I would ever need. I explained that I didn't have a buyer, but it seemed that they were out there if I didn't chicken out. I expect that whoever buys SunRay will keep all of the employees, but at this point it was too early to tell. I hope that she will not be affected, but she might be and I wanted her to know this up front.

Anne was relieved that I was not ill and confessed that she had mixed emotions about the possible sale. She was very happy for me to have this opportunity, but sad that she would not work with me in the future. She said that she would be happy to help with the sale process and would give the new owners time to see if they wanted to keep her and if she wanted to stay. I assured her that she was brilliant and any smart owner would want her. She was grateful for my respect, but she also surprised me by letting me know that she did not need my protection. "Lee, I love working for you, but I was earning a great living before SunRay and I can land another job in a minute. I love you sweetheart, but my career will be fine without you."

We talked about the possibility of her taking a year off work to travel if she didn't like the new owner and she seemed invigorated by the impending but unknown changes. We went back to the office and told the other administrative staff. They were very surprised and a bit sad, but the reaction was smaller than

I had anticipated. It was just business and although we are a tight-knit group, everyone knew that it would not last forever—maybe everyone but me. The team assured me of their cooperation and confidentiality.

I sought the team's advice on how best to communicate the news to all of the cleaning staff should I actually sell. It seemed that they didn't understand the question and they shared a collective blank stare back at me. I explained that all of these cleaning women trust me and now I am selling out on them, so I need to find a way to explain it to them so that they will not hate me. After more prolonged silence, Zhou finally spoke up. Zhou is the woman who screens and hires the cleaning women. She reminded me that none of the women actually know that I own the business, so a sale will not matter to them unless they will lose their job or their pay will be changed. "Lee, they will lose their manager, but we can find a good replacement for you so don't worry about them. They will be fine without you."

In much the same way as my role within the company was downplayed in the book used to drum up interested buyers, my staff was trying to comfort me by telling me that the business would be fine without me. I guess that this is healthy and positive, but shouldn't someone be terrified that the world will end if I leave?

Lee

Jackson has friends of every shape, size, and colour despite the fact that he has a very distinctive size, shape, and colour. Jackson is the tallest in his class, although he may weigh the least. He has obviously Asian facial features with the skin tone of his Indian sperm source. He looks different from all of his classmates, but in this multicultural school community, it has never seemed to matter. It certainly doesn't matter to him. It is a testament to our country that until last week Jackson had never been exposed to racism.

The racism event was not remarkable and showed no imagination on the part of the perpetrators, but it became a big deal for my little family. At recess, three boys from Jackson's grade followed him down the stairs towards the playground calling out to him, "Wait up, Zipperhead." Jackson turned to wait for them and cheerfully asked, "What's a Zipperhead?"

"You are, you stupid Zipperhead."

"Yeah—you're a dumb nine-iron."

"Slanty-eye Zipperhead."

Jackson had no idea what these terms meant, but he knew that he was being made fun of and he didn't like it. He ran outside, but because the other boys saw that their chants were having an effect, they chased him and continued.

For five minutes Jackson endured the harassment while two teachers stood gabbing less than twenty feet away. Jackson yelled for them to stop, but they didn't and the teachers never budged. Finally, Jackson snapped and pushed one boy in the chest and the boy fell onto his ass and got his pants dirty. That was enough of a crime for the teachers to awake and Jackson was grabbed by the arm and ushered to the principal's office.

Quick aside—I don't know what a Zipperhead is, but I know that the three boys heard the term from the lips of Clint Eastwood in the movie Gran Torino. The movie repulsively portrays a hard-core racist (who calls Asians Zipperheads and gooks) as a loveable, good-natured man who happens to have one minor character flaw. What's wrong with being a bigot if you seem like an otherwise nice old fella? Incredible! And why are ten-year-olds watching such crap without any parental supervision or interpretation?

Back to Jackson at the principal's office: The school staff called home to report the problem. My mother answered and decided not to wake me, so she went to the school. She learned of something called a zero-tolerance policy towards violence and was told that Jackson is suspended for the remainder of the day and the next full day. Mom asked no questions, apologized for Jackson causing trouble and quietly led Jackson from the school.

Jackson told her exactly what happened and Mom instantly took Jackson's side. She decided that since he had been so brave, they would use the next day and a half as time for fun, starting with the ice cream shop. She also decided that it was best if I didn't find out about this incident and she proceeded to enroll Jackson in her deception.

I found out about the deception on day two of their truancy. I was enjoying a sound sleep when the phone rang just after 1:00 p.m. It was Eddie from Fast Eddie's Pizza—we had been going to Eddie's or ordering delivery from Eddie for so long that he is almost family.

"Hi Lee, your mom and Jackson were just here for lunch and she left her purse behind. Can you let her know—oh, forget it—she's just coming back in. See you, Lee."

My mother refuses to carry the cellphone that I bought her, so when I called her cell number, I heard it ring in her bedroom. I thought of calling the school, but decided the problem couldn't be health related if they were eating pizza for lunch, so I just waited for the end of the school day. The criminal duo came giggling into the house together and were surprised to see me awake and sitting stone-faced at the kitchen table. My mother stumbled through another lie about how she was running errands and decided to pick up Jackson rather than make him ride the school bus. Jackson tried to skirt by me and into his room, but I fixed him to his spot with an icy stare.

All that I said was, "Did you have pizza or the calzone for lunch?" And the two battle-hardened felons melted into a couple of confessional songbirds. They competed to tell me the details of the playground, the principal's office and the pizza parlour.

So many things to sort out—Jackson's school behaviour, the school's reaction, Jackson's deception, my mother's deception.

I was so angry, but as I searched for words to fire at the two hoodlums, I inexplicably melted. Tears poured from my angry eyes and, as I sobbed uncontrollably, I pulled Jackson close and hugged him. He tentatively hugged me back as he looked toward his grandmother to help sort out his confusion.

When I regained my composure, I explained to Jackson that the only mistake that he had made was in lying to me. I was not angry about the push and promised to review that with him later. I reminded him that he and I have a special relationship— the most special—and that trust is a key component that he needs to hold on to. It was his turn to have a quiet cry and I let him offload the tension of the emotional run that he had been on.

As I turned to my mother, she knew what to expect and tried to change the game before it started. "This wouldn't happen if you would find a husband. Jackson needs a father. This is your fault..."

"Beautiful try, but I am not biting. This has nothing to do with men. I have told you that I need to be involved with big issues and big decisions, and this was big. You can't make these decisions for me."

We argued, deflected, attacked, counter-attacked, yelled and finally cried (again). I know that she was doing what she felt was right for Jackson and me. I also know that the issues that

Jackson will deal with over the years are going to get more complicated. I can't have my mother and her old-world ways advising Jackson on sex, drugs, alcohol, bullies and gangs. This incident was a wake-up call. My original emotional reaction arose because I knew that I was not available to solve this issue when it arose. I cried because I wasn't involved.

Now let me tell you what I did. Without an appointment, I was seated in the reception area of the principal's office the next morning when Principal Peters arrived for work. If I asked you to visualize what a fifty-five-year-old civil servant looks like, you would conjure Mr. Peters. He wore brown trousers with tennis shoes and a chequered, brown sports coat that I am certain is a daily staple of his look. He has a droopy face and eyes and carries an extra forty pounds, so he gives the impression that any activity leaves him completely exhausted.

I began the discussion by explaining that Jackson was not a violent boy and had no history of violence, so I would like to understand what led to him deciding to push the boy. Peters was uncomfortable and despite my calm and polite tone, he undoubtedly saw conflict brewing.

He chose to head off the conflict and ignore my question by offering, "There were two teachers who saw Jackson push the boy, so there is no doubt that he did it. Our school proudly supports the zero tolerance of violence policy and therefore Jackson had to be suspended. We had no choice."

I bit down hard on my lip as a reminder to stay calm. I think that I smiled when I replied, "I accept that Jackson pushed a boy. Guilty as charged. As a mother I am just trying to understand what happened to cause him to react that way."

"There was no violence from the other boy toward Jackson—that would not be tolerated—zero tolerance for violence." His face began to blotch with red patches as his discomfort grew.

I used my softest tone and tried to sound respectful, "Did you talk to the boys and the teachers on the playground to see what led to the push?"

"No matter what the cause, violence is not tolerated," chirped Peters the parrot.

"It would be helpful to understand why it..."

I was interrupted by more babbling, "Under the policy, there is no just violence. The cause is not relevant."

I changed tactics and dropped my fake smile. "Do you know what a Zipperhead is, Mr. Peters?"

"What, um, no I don't think that I do."

"Neither do I, but it can't be flattering. Neither is slant eyes, gook or nine iron."

"I don't know where this is going. This has nothing to do with the violent outburst."

"It has everything to do with the little push that you call a violent outburst. Jackson was teased, ridiculed and bullied while your teachers stood idly by. When no one else would stand up for him, he stood up for himself and for that he gets dragged away and suspended. No discussion of punishment for the three bullies, and their parents will never hear about it because you hide behind a policy. Zero tolerance doesn't mean that you can be blind and lazy. Punish Jackson—fine—but do some investigation and see who the bad apples are."

"The Board requires strict adherence to this policy and if you are unhappy with the policy, then you should discuss it with the Board of Education." His words trailed behind me as I had decided, mid-sentence, that this effort was futile.

By the time I made it to the parking lot, I was actually feeling a bit of sympathy for portly Peters. Like so many before him, he had traded his powers of reason, logic and fairness for a code-book that he could execute with minimal cerebral function.

Three days later, I wrote e-mails to the parents of the three boys who had harassed Jackson. I tried to sympathize with the challenges of being a parent in a world in which racism was continually demonstrated on TV and in the movies. I explained that I was not writing out of anger, but instead I simply wanted to identify the issue for them so that they could nip it in the bud.

I got back two e-mails thanking me for my comments and apologizing for their son's behaviour. The third e-mail simply said, "I don't need your advice. Hilarious that you used the word nip yourself." I guess that tells me who rented the Clint Eastwood movie for the kids.

Terry

I closed the store for fifteen minutes this afternoon so that I could tell the staff what was going on. I described the cancer and the procedures in detail and told them that it was extremely unlikely that this would be life threatening, but quite probable that I would be off work for a while. The team was great. Everyone was supportive and encouraging and the offers to take on extra chores while I am off were pouring in. Some expressed concern about the cancer, but no one was overly upset. I reopened the store and the afternoon staff went back to work.

I was relieved that the meeting had gone so well, so I decided to treat myself to a cup of tea in the sunshine in the courtyard outside the building. I was happily thinking that the meeting could not have gone better when I saw Al with his head in his hands on the far bench.

From twenty feet away I cheerfully called, "Hey, don't you have a school bus to drive old man?" Al lifted his head in surprise and tried unsuccessfully to hide the tears in his eyes.

I reached the bench and Al answered the question before I asked it. "Mary was the strongest person in the world and she was gone within two months. It was vicious and the doctors didn't know what to do. They just kept trying things on her, but they knew that she had no hope. They tell you that you can beat it, but you can't."

My news was forcing him to relive his heartbreak and he sat and cried on that park bench like he had just learned of his wife's death.

I asked him about her type of cancer and then patiently tried to explain the differences between the liver cancer that had killed his wife and the melanoma that I have. He looked back at me with sad eyes that seemed to say, you're just too young to understand, son. In complete role reversal, I offered every encouraging thought that I had to assure Al that I would be fine. He said all of the right things and apologized for misunderstanding and causing a scene.

"That's great, Terry. I am so happy that your type can be beaten. I am feeling so much better." As he walked away, I could see that he didn't believe his own words.

I have to say that the talk with Al took the wind out of my sails. Intellectually, I know that the big problem is that the single word "cancer" is used to describe dozens of conditions, each with unique symptoms, treatments and prognoses. Mary and I shouldn't be lumped (ha!) under a single disease heading. Emotionally, however, I found the negative message from the always-positive Al hard to digest. I sat alone in my quiet living room and just let the silence rest with me. I can't believe the emotional roller coaster I am on. I was feeling good after the staff meeting, but now I feel the depression pulling me down and, this time, not slowly—down like the roller coaster hill.

The doctors don't have all the answers, as Al said. The doctors don't know what caused my cancer and they are really just taking their best guess at what will rid me of it. There is no certainty. I hope that Al will be okay because it seemed like his heart was freshly broken by his wife's death this afternoon. Cancer grows beyond the confines of the patient's body and spreads into the lives of those around them. It punishes the bystanders emotionally in ways that may be more severe than anything that the patient feels. I need to call Ben. He was brave on our last call, but I need to see what he is really thinking. Carol and I have been talking all along, but we need to have the conversation that we have been avoiding: What happens if this gets worse?

I was feeling so good just hours ago. How did I get to this place?

Grant

The Rangers were playing a rare Friday-night game against the Blackhawks (my new team?) and I decided to take in the game on my own. I walked from my midtown hotel to Madison Square Garden and the half-hour walk served to shake the martinis out of my head. I bought a single ticket at the blue line from a scalper for $200 and took a seat next to four firemen from Chicago who were in New York for some conference. As I sat down, the firemen asked if I was a Rangers fan and, when I explained that I was from Canada and was just a hockey fan, they quickly adopted me as one of their own and offered me free beer to join the Hawks fraternity.

These guys were all huge, intimidating guys but they were constantly joking and laughing, and everyone around them, including the Rangers fans, enjoyed them. When I returned from the men's room during the first intermission, they had parted so that I was given the middle seat within the new group of five.

"We need to protect you Northern Hawk," my new nickname, "because these Ranger fans are going to get ugly when we take it to them in the second." The Hawks did take over in the second and cruised to a 5-1 final to the disappointment of everyone but five crazy guys in Section 122.

During the second intermission, a couple of the guys went to get more beers and I found myself telling the two remaining guys that I was seriously considering relocating to Chicago. That led to a flurry of recommendations on places to live, eat, drink and how best to get Hawks season tickets in their section. We exchanged e-mail addresses and I promised to connect with them all if I make the move. The game was a blast and the guys were great. They were heading out to a steakhouse after the game and asked me to join, but I declined with some lame excuse. Truthfully, I was excited about my plan for the cougar bars and I didn't want to waste my research effort. I had selected three bars that I found on various websites and the first was strategically located close to the arena. If I wanted to stay on schedule, I didn't have time for steak with my new pals.

I wish I had friends like those guys back home or that I could make friends like that if I do go to Chicago. Not those guys, obviously, but guys like them. If I could meet some good guys like that, that belonged to my social sphere, that would be great. Firefighters and investment banking executives don't mix well, and that's regrettable because I haven't had that much fun in years.

Lee

Gord doesn't read signals very well. The last thing that I said to him before this weekend was, "Take me home, asshole," but somehow he remembers that as, "I think that our relationship needs to go to the next level and perhaps we need to make a commitment if we are going to make this work, and I am not a young woman and I have a family to consider, and I need a man in my life and we should spend a weekend discussing it."

I attended Gord's cousin's wedding yesterday because I had made the commitment long ago. It was the first time we had been together since the theatre incident with Mrs. Chen and things were tense. Gord had tried to communicate for the two intervening weeks, but I avoided him completely. I was busy with work, the sale, the fucking school mess with Jackson, so I had plenty of good excuses. But, truthfully, I think that my interest in Gord has been sagging for a while.

He tried to break the ice by asking about Jackson and whether things at school had settled back to normal after his suspension. I hadn't talked to Gord, so how did he know about that? He squirmed a bit before he admitted that he had dropped by one night this week while I was working and had tea with my mother. He explained the visit as a sign of how much he cared about me and how worried he was when I wouldn't reply to his messages. I felt like it was an intrusion of my privacy. I also knew that my mother would have used the opportunity to push her marriage agenda.

Gord changed the subject and asked if any progress had been made on the business sale. He probably thought that this was safe territory and indeed he probably had no personal agenda when he asked it, but I tersely answered "No progress" while trying to stifle my real thought, which was, "Keep your hands off my money."

The wedding was very nice. At the exchange of vows, Gord squeezed my hand as some lame expression of love. He looked a little dewy-eyed and kissed me on the cheek as we stood to leave the church. It was a little pathetic. The dinner and reception were fine because the presence of others kept us away from anything other than light banter. I had a few drinks and danced to the terrible wedding band with all of the bridesmaids. As the evening wound down, Gord and I had our first and only slow dance of the evening, as the band butchered "At Last" by Etta James. Gord tried to offer something romantic into my ear, but I kept it informal.

"Did I ever tell you about the time that I saw Etta live? She was talking about how people always come up to her and tell her that this was their wedding song or that they are going to have it at their wedding. She said that in a few instances, people have stopped her in places like the grocery store and asked her if she would come to a wedding and sing it. Can you imagine? Asking Etta to come and sing at some stranger's wedding? Anyway, Etta always asked for the time, date and location and assured them that she would be there. Then she never went. She is a twisted and hilarious old bird." I was wishing that the story was longer, but then the music mercifully ended and we were able to leave the dance floor.

Back at the B&B, I quickly changed and got into bed. I good naturedly pecked Gord on the cheek, announced that I was tired, and rolled over. Gord wanted to talk. I tried to delay the inevitable until morning, but Gord was persistent, so I turned on the bedside lamp and sat up in bed and looked expectantly at him to begin. I was expecting a lecture about how unfair I had been for the last two weeks and how we have to communicate better.

Instead I got this: "Lee, I want more with you. I want to be a bigger part of your life. I want Jackson and your mother to be in my life. I want to live together. I would like to get married, but I don't want to put that pressure on you now. So I am not proposing marriage yet, but I am proposing that we take a big step towards it and live together."

He must have rehearsed his delivery all week. He had a small but confident smile when he finished, but I could smell his nervous uncertainty regarding my reply. We had been together for a long time, so I didn't blurt out an answer. I like Gord and I respect him. I thanked him for the offer and suggested that we talk about it in the morning when the wine had left my system and I had had a good night's sleep.

Over breakfast, I said that I thought it was astute of Gord to recognize that we had reached a fork in the road of our relationship. We needed to go to the next step or stop. "I choose stop," I told him. I said that I didn't think that we were compatible enough to be married and that probably neither of us really wanted to be in love and married anyway. I went on about how great our time together had been, and I was about to say more, but he had stopped listening the moment that I said, "I choose stop." As he raced his car back into the city, I could tell that he just wanted this humiliation to end and that nothing I could say would make it better, so I said nothing. Our relationship ended with ninety minutes of silent, high-speed driving and a "See ya" from Gord as I pulled my bag from the back seat.

Grant

My first stop was called The Ainsworth on 26th Street, which is just a few blocks from Madison Square. Although it doesn't look like much from the outside, the interior was very nice and looked like the kind of place that Ellen and I would enjoy for dinner. In fact, The Ainsworth is more of a restaurant than a bar and I initially thought that the Internet write-up that I read was wrong, but when I saw the clientele around the small but bustling bar I was reassured. This had a similar feel to The Rose

Room in Miami, with a predominantly female clientele, mostly in the thirty-five-plus category.

I took a beer at the bar and tried to look like a casual business guy at the end of a tough week, rather than the prowling pervert that I felt like. I overheard the conversation between the couple next to me as they prepared to leave and I learned that they were not a couple at all, but had actually just met and were heading back to his hotel. That should have given me confidence, but instead it panicked me a bit. I had two simultaneous thoughts: First, this plan may actually work and, second, I better hurry because all the hot ladies are already pairing up. The result of these thoughts was some misguided urgency as I clumsily raced over to a woman three seats away and stumbled over my words, making an ass of myself before she politely declined my drink offer and lied that she was waiting for a friend.

One piece of advice that I remembered from Miami was not to fear failure. Jerry had told me a story about Ricky Henderson who not only holds the major league baseball record for stolen bases, but also holds the record for most times caught stealing. No one remembers his numerous failures, just that he had more success than anyone else. If rejected, I should just move on and ask another one. I was playing that advice back to myself as a third consecutive woman rejected my free drink offer. I wasn't completely discouraged, but I was acutely aware of how small the bar was and couldn't help but feel that all the other women in The Ainsworth had watched me swing and miss on three straight pitches.

I finished my beer and left for planned destination number two. A change of venue was all that I needed, but as I rode in the taxi back up to midtown, I realized that I was hungry and I kicked myself for not going to the steakhouse with the firefighters.

Terry

I have been working a reduced schedule so Carol has been helping out with the administration of the shop. She is doing the banking, paying the bills and generally making sure that the employees are getting what they need. She came back today and said that Al had told her about the strange message that I put up on the lyrics board a while ago. The staff didn't know that I had cancer at the time, but that message worried them. Now that they know about the cancer, they are more worried. Thanks to them, now Carol is worried as well.

"What are the things that you need to fix?" She asked in an annoyed tone.

I explained that it wasn't a self-directed message, but instead a plea to others to reject a shitty status quo. It's cliché to say that facing death makes you appreciate life, but that was really what was behind the sign. And because I was frustrated that people were wasting their life, I wrote the message. I told her about the cleaning lady, about a woman who looked like she was abused, a regular who hated his wife and I told her about Fuck Stick.

Carol listened to each story and agreed that all of these people have serious challenges. She would not, however, accept that I could write such a message right after my diagnosis without having some deep-seated problem of my own. I told her how happy I was with our relationship, the coffee shop, Ben. I really think that everything—except the cancer—is awesome.

Carol sighed and rubbed her eyes as if she were trying to decide if she should deliver a hard message to me. "I was hoping that you would come to this realization on your own and in your own time, but isn't it possible that the message was about your mother?"

Carol and I have discussed my emotional impasse with my mother on a few occasions, but it has not been a major subject of conversation, nor was I aware that it had been bothering her.

"I wrote that stupid message on the board impulsively and in a short bit of frustration. I can honestly tell you that my mother was not in any way responsible for the sign. She lives five hours away and she is not a part of my daily life. My relationship with her sucks, but I don't care! I don't need to fix it!"

That came out a little louder than intended and I took Carol by surprise. She apologized for making an incorrect assumption and headed to the kitchen to make some tea. And now I am lying on the couch exasperated and wondering if I had or have some subconscious desire to repair the relationship with my mother because Carol has an annoying habit of being right even when she is mistaken.

I haven't told my mother or siblings about the cancer. Carol and Ben have agreed not to say anything despite the fact that both of them think that I am making a mistake. My sisters are just too dramatic and I can't imagine that telling Mom that I have cancer is the ideal icebreaker for our frigid relationship.

I wish that I had never written that stupid message on the board because now everyone is trying to decipher my hidden trouble that needs to be fixed. I didn't write it for me—I wrote it for others. I don't have anything to fix except for the damn cancer.

Lee

On Sunday night I sat alone in my bedroom and listened to Etta James sing "At Last." I needed to refresh my love for that song after the terrible wedding band version and I was happy to hear that Etta still sounds incredible. I lied to Gord this morning. I told him that I don't want to be in love, but nothing could be further from the truth. I thought about how much I wanted to fall in love as Etta mocked me, "At last...my love has come along. My lonely days are over and life is like a song."

The only real problem with Gord is that I don't love him. You can't will love to happen if it isn't there and it wasn't there for Gord and I. But I do want to be in love. Does that make me sound like a thirteen-year-old girl?

I am a serious person with serious issues to deal with. I am a boss. I am running a sizeable business and possibly selling it. I am a mother and dealing with increasingly messy issues and an unusual family dynamic. I can't spend my time dreaming about fluffy issues like love.

My mother has been pushing me to find a husband since Jackson was born, but her desires are practical and have to deal with providing for a child and having a father figure for a young boy. She doesn't see the hole in my life, but it burns in those rare moments when I can sit alone and listen to my music.

"For you are mine...at last."

Having Gord around was a pleasant way to distract me from the romantic void in my life. I was able to delude myself that, because I had someone to dine with or have sex with, I was fulfilling my needs. Good companionship impersonates love.

I have been thinking that the only thing I needed to fix in my life was to gain time. I could fix that by selling the business. Now I am chilled by the thought that the one thing I really want to fix in my life may not be within my control to fix. I want to be in love. How do I find that, do that, fix that?

Terry

I was in a rocky ebb and flow of shallow sleep and reached out for the comfort of Carol, only to find that she was not in bed. I drifted to consciousness and listened for sounds of the late-night television that Carol has retreated to on many of these nights when insomnia gets the better of her. There was no TV, but I could barely make out the sound of Carol in conversation. I checked the clock—12:25 a.m. Who could she be talking to?

I shuffled halfway down the stairs and from there I could see Carol at the kitchen table talking into her laptop. I realized that she was at her late night best in a Skype call with Ben. I didn't want to disturb them so I tiptoed back to bed without alerting Carol.

A couple of times a month Carol and Ben will connect in a late-night call. The calls are officially triggered by a number of things: Ben is stressed about school, Ben is having girl problems and, lately, I suspect Ben is worried about his dad's cancer. I think that the real trigger for these calls, however, is that there are times late at night when Ben simply misses his mom. Ben and Carol have developed these calls as the medicine to cure homesickness. Sometimes they have deep and meaningful conversations about real-world problems, but just as often they share a soft banter of no consequence, yet that is a comfort to both.

I went back to bed contented with the happy thought of the mother and son bond between Carol and Ben. That peaceful thought almost got me into the sleep that I was seeking, but just as I was drifting off I was struck with panic—what if Ben ever dropped Carol the way that I have dropped my mother? What a horrible thought. I found myself getting angry at Ben for committing some hypothetical act at some undetermined future time. That was illogical but allowed me to direct my anger outward for a few minutes before accepting that Ben wasn't the guilty party.

The relationship that I have had with my mother is not the same as what Carol and Ben have, but it was still a decent mother and son relationship. Seeing the Skype call tonight made me think about my failed relationship from the mother's perspective and I began to imagine how severe the pain would feel. I am punishing my mother and I am sure that I am hurting her.

It would be so simple for me to reach out to her and fix this, but it is not in my heart. In my head I wish that I could be kind toward her, but I tell you truthfully that I would be faking kindness—I just don't feel any love or kindness in my heart for her. Maybe I will get there soon, but I can't bring myself to do it yet.

Grant

I went to the Bridges Bar in the Hilton Hotel and The Monday Bar on 54th Street and finished the night at the Stone Rose in the Lincoln Center. I could walk you through every step of my night or you could just figure out what happened by noting that I made it back to my hotel—alone.

There were plenty of cougars out there, but I just couldn't snag one. They seemed so plentiful, but I felt like a thirsty man at the seaside: Water, water, everywhere but...

I was a rookie in a game with chiseled veterans. In hindsight, I can see my mistakes and it's frustrating that I wasn't better out there tonight. Many of the times I was over anxious, but the couple of times that I did play it slow and cool some other guy swept in and beat me to the girl.

I was able to engage a few women in conversation, but the most promising contacts from the night were part of female packs and I had no opportunity to cut one from the herd. I also wasted ten minutes and a $20 cocktail on a prostitute. Truthfully, she was the only one that truly seemed to be seriously interested in me. Maybe New York is different from Miami—it certainly seemed easier in Miami.

I decided to retreat to my hotel room after I took my only insulting rejection of the night. I approached a woman sitting alone at the end of the bar at the Stone Rose and introduced myself. She said, "Look, you're wearing a wedding ring, you smell like beer and you look like a child molester. Go home, jerk off and sleep it off."

I had no reply and actually thought that jerking off would be the best that I could do. I walked slowly and sadly through the southern edge of Central Park, despite the cool rain of an early fall evening. I was cold, wet and tired by the time that I made it back to the hotel. I was pissed off that the doorman stopped me and asked to see my room card before he let me proceed through the lobby, but when I saw my reflection in the elevator mirror I understood because indeed I did look like a child molester.

Terry

Cancer draws out a kind of depression that is beyond a side effect of any of the medication. It brings out pure, vanilla depression. I don't feel well physically, but I don't feel as bad as I am letting others believe. It seems easier to lie that I am physically unwell than to explain this unexplainable mental state that I am stuck in.

There is a heaviness upon me that I lack the energy or desire to lift. I don't want diversion, entertainment or companionship. I want to stay in bed and wallow. I am not thinking about hospitals or, for that matter, morgues, so this feeling is not some type of morbid fright. It's just a lack of...a lack of... anything—everything.

I am not scared. Nor am I upset about the cancer, the upcoming surgery or missing work. I don't seem to care about any of that right now and I am not teary. I am not worried—there is no anxiety within me at all. I have no idea what this is. One part of my brain makes an internal speech about the need to get off the couch and make something out of the day, but the rest of my brain tells the speechmaker to fuck off and so I stay on the couch. The voting majority of my brain wants to maintain some status quo that is just slightly above a comatose state.

I have been sad before and I always thought that depression was synonymous with sadness and that depressed people churned through boxes of Kleenex. I could never understand why depression persisted, as I always thought that these people should just have a good cry and get over it. Truthfully, I privately always saw depression as a character flaw. If what I am feeling now is depression and this is what others feel on a daily basis, then I feel guilty for ever thinking that this was a personality defect.

Sleeping is my only peace and that is hard to come by. My always-comfortable bed is suddenly made of lumpy rocks. I even lack the mind for mindless television. I tried to watch the three magi of daytime: Oprah, Ellen, and Dr. Phil, but I couldn't get into them today. I would have turned them off, but that would have required me to break my lethargic state, so I let their vacuous words drift over me.

If they have meds that will make this feeling end, then I wish to sign up for the big dose, please. To those who need Prozac, Paxil, or Zoloft to get them through their day, I apologize for the times I openly expressed, or privately thought, that the need for such happy pills made you weak and inferior.

Lee

We all have bad habits. One of mine is pretty nasty. Whenever one of my relationships ends, I have to have a one-night stand within a week of the breakup. Gord was my fourth meaningful breakup and he led me to my fourth meaningless one-nighter.

I hate to sound immodest, but I think that I am pretty good at one-night stands. I have a pattern—maybe rules—that I follow. I look for tall, healthy-looking men and I emit a signal to attract their attention. I don't want short men, or fat men or men of questionable hygiene. My intention on such nights is physical, so I apologize to all the great personality and character people that I have overlooked because they are short, fat and unshaven, but I am not looking for a soulmate at these times. Once an appropriate man is engaged, I will allow for appropriate social protocol—he buys me a drink while I take a few minutes to evaluate whether Mr. Right Now could be dangerous. If he is not dangerous, then he has passed my only test. I do not try to find out if he is interesting or intelligent—I don't care. In fact, the more conversation we have, the more likely it is that my man will say something stupid and ruin the opportunity.

I move things along quickly by suggesting that we leave the bar before I even finish my drink. Once we get to a hotel room, I initiate the festivities immediately—again, avoiding the risk of conversation. If the foreplay is good, I will go with the flow. When it is time for business I insist on two things: a condom and that I am on top. There can be no doubt that I am the hunter not the prey on these evenings, and I think that my self-esteem is better maintained if I have the view from above. Not to mention that if I have any hope of singing in the key of O, I need to be on top. No first timer is going to crack the code for me if he is fumbling away in missionary. I am responsible for my own pleasure, so he just needs to lay back and stay hard.

Last night, Mr. Right Now turned out to be Mr. Cumming Right Now and I felt his decent dick sag a minute before I was satisfied. I slid off, grabbed my clothes, went into the washroom and locked the door—then I finished myself off while I leaned against the vanity. I know that he would have enjoyed watching me, but why the fuck does he deserve that? I got dressed and said good night as I walked past him to the door. He protested and asked me to stay, but I was gone before he could find his tighty-whities.

Grant

On Saturday morning, I was reflecting on how hard it was to pick up someone that you don't know and how unrealistic I was about my prospects. Then it occurred to me that I actually know someone in New York who wanted to have sex with me. Kate—my almost affair—works in Manhattan and probably lives nearby.

Without taking any time to develop a plan, I dialled and immediately heard Kate's voice. It was initially hard to hear her, as she was in a restaurant or café. She told me to hold as she walked outside.

"Hi Grant, must be a big deal for you to call me on a Saturday morning."

I assured her happily that it wasn't a business call. I was in town and hoping to see her. Her reaction was shocking. She was angry and cursed me for interfering in her personal life.

"I am having brunch with my husband for Christ's sake. Did you think that you could make an 11:00 a.m. booty-call on a Saturday morning to a married woman? What the fuck is wrong with you?"

I tried to defend myself, saying that I simply wanted to let her know that I was in town and available and that I was not being presumptuous. She fired back with a barrage of foul-mouthed bullets. She made it clear that she regretted her actions with me and even called me a creepy stalker.

That seemed harsh.

Again, I can now clearly see my mistake in hindsight. I should have thought this through before I just jumped into a call. I was unprepared—I didn't have my lines down. Perhaps I should have started with a text or an e-mail—build up some anticipation for the call and obviously avoid the stress of her being with her husband. Another rookie mistake.

That probably ruined my one sure thing in New York, so I am back to playing long odds. That summarizes my problem from last night—my expectations were too high. It takes practice and patience to become a player. To be honest, this may take longer for me to get the hang of it than the average guy. I was never a great ladies man in my youth and I am not great at small talk. Add that to the fact that I have been out of the game for decades and I can see why this is going to take a while. I am determined to make this work, but I will need to find a way to handle rejection better because I fear that I may encounter a bunch of it for a while.

Terry

Not every event that we try at Beanfest is a success. Leftover Pizza Breakfast was a total flop. Wine Tasting Luncheon was a disaster. We tried our own version of Fear Factor—you know, the show where people are confronted with their fears, most notably eating bugs of various kinds. In hindsight, that was an obviously bad idea for a place that sells food.

It seems that our identity is tied to music, so when we run events or games connected to music our success rate is higher. Sometimes we put the games on hold and just find an excuse to share good music.

We occasionally take a departure from our "guess the lyrics" game so that we can share some great lyrics that are too hard to guess but too good to leave off of the board. Once, every couple of months, Cory will take control of the morning sign and under the title "Great Lyrics from Songs that You Have Never Heard," he will profile four or five songs that he feels people should run out and download. The kid really has a great ear for music and he finds bands that only our younger customers know, but that all music lovers can come to appreciate. We often have customers come back and thank us for introducing them to some new band.

Yesterday Cory kindly sent me a couple sets of such lyrics that he posted while I was away in hopes that I would head to iTunes and download the songs, which I did. Cory sent me: "We were certainly uncertain, at least I'm pretty sure I am," Modest Mouse, "Missed The Boat;" "Moats and boats and waterfalls, alleyways and pay phone calls," Edward Sharpe and the Magnetic Zeros, "Home."

I returned the favour by sending him the lyric "Everyday's like Christmas Day without you...it's cold and there's nothing to do," from "Come On Home" by Everything But The Girl.

Then Cory finished off the exchange with, "A man needs something he can hold onto—a nine-pound hammer or a woman like you," Ray Lamontagne, "Jolene."

I vaguely remembered hearing Ray Lamontagne before, but I couldn't place him so I quickly downloaded the song and was treated to a brilliant tune. When I hear people of my generation say that they don't make great music anymore, I just cringe because there is great new music all around us—it just isn't played on your classic rock station or the teenage pop station. If people are unsure where to find it, they should stop by Beanfest for a coffee.

Grant

The lyrics on the board at the coffee shop this morning were: "And the man in the back said everyone attack..." Too easy—that's "Ballroom Blitz." I couldn't help myself and I actually sang out the next line of the song to the complete shock of the kid behind the counter. He just stood, open-mouthed, looking at me and I said, "Sorry, but my band covered that tune."

"You are in a band?" He said without changing his dumbfounded stare.

I really didn't want to have a conversation and I regret bursting out, but I was annoyed that this guy couldn't see me as a band member so I explained, "Not now, but when I was in school I was the bass player for Fried Eggs and we covered that Sweet song and a bunch of other 70s bands."

The kid asked some more questions about the band and our type of music, but I got out quickly with my cappuccino and headed to the office. It's funny how people are so quick to make everyone so one-dimensional. A guy in a nice suit is a businessman and nothing else. He can't be a sports fan or play in a band.

What is surprising is how much of a lift I got from thinking about running the bass line for "Ballroom Blitz." I was starting to shake off my bad mood by the time that I got to the office.

I had been really feeling like a bit of a loser after my failures in the New York bars, but when I returned to work today I was treated like a returning hero for saving the deal in New York on Friday afternoon. There was a real buzz in the office as a number of staff members were busy completing the paperwork on the deal. I received an e-mail from Jack saying that he was away on vacation with his partner this week but he had heard about the deal and wanted to pass on congratulations.

Jack is awesome to work with, but he can be a bit annoying at times. First, he is always offering upbeat comments to me as if I need positive reinforcement for my actions. I could have had his job, so I don't really need reassurance. Second, he is very proper in everything that he says. For example, he says "partner" to describe his girlfriend. Maybe "common-law spouse" is too awkward and maybe "girlfriend" is too casual, but "partner" just sounds weird. At least he doesn't say "life partner"— that sounds so bohemian that it drives me crazy. Ellen's sister has a "life partner" and they are two of the oddest people that I know—they are both vegan nudists.

After lunch I stopped into one of the meeting rooms where three young guys from my team were working on the New York deal. These young guys would be part of my fan club, if executives had fan clubs, so I know that they are always a bit nervous around me. Today, however, they seemed more casual and I soon learned why.

Zach—the one with the friggin' earring—asked, "Is it true that you were a Fried Egg?" As the two others tried to hide their nervous laughter.

I didn't mind finishing the story that the kid from the coffee shop had obviously started for them, as I am sure that this story only helped to build my reputation with the younger staff. They already have a great deal of respect for my intellect, my experience, my BMW—why not let them see that I also have a wild side? It is good for them to know that they can grow into a successful executive and still be cool.

The coffee shop had another game going on with their lyrics board this morning. They wanted customers to write down the name of the love song that they share with their one true love. The game had obviously started the day before because the board was littered with song titles and decorated with big red lips and cardboard hearts.

The song on the bottom of the board was, "I Can't Fight This Feeling" by REO Speedwagon and I felt myself blush as I read the title. Blushing was a silly and unnecessary reaction today, but it was a throwback to how I would have reacted in 1985.

In 1985, my handful of friends and I were the outsiders at school and we took great pride in opposing anything mainstream. We didn't listen to top-forty music and we didn't watch *Family Ties*. Our music was original and edgy and not anywhere close to the music that the cheerleaders listened to. We listened to The Beat, The Cure, The Talking Heads, and Tom Waits. Finding obscure, import albums was a badge of honour for anyone in my crowd. I didn't really appreciate how good our musical taste was until years later, and at the time all I cared about was balking at the popular stuff. The dirty little secret that I hid throughout that era was my unreasonable love for REO Speedwagon. REO was everything that I was supposed to rage against. They were the kind of white bread, AM radio, power-ballad band that we detested. Except that I loved them and especially "I Can't Fight This Feeling." That was the song that I would perform in front of my bedroom mirror (door locked of course) as if I were in my own music video. My friends would have banished me if they ever found the album hidden somewhere between Kate Bush and Depeche Mode. I know that it wasn't a great song back in 1985 and truly the years have not been kind to it, as it sounds pretty lame now: "It's time to bring this ship into the shore and throw away the oars forever..."

However, if I ever find a true love, I think that this will be our song.

Even if I wanted to play the coffee shop game today, I couldn't have because I have never shared a song with a true love. I have never been in any relationship that contained "our song" and I can sadly say that I have never had a true love. My recent relationship with Gord is about as deep as I ever seem to get—serious like, with a bit of lust. I barely miss him and I guess that confirms that I was a long way from love.

I don't think that I have ever fully invested myself in a relationship and taken the risk that being in love implies. Maybe that's what I need to fix. Sell the business, have more time, put myself on the line, fall in love, sing REO Speedwagon songs together.

Terry

As I prepare for the second surgery, I have been working a little from home to help with the administration but I haven't worked a regular shift in the shop for quite a while. This morning I woke up early and in a good mood so I decided to put in a full day at the shop. I was hoping that I could have a normal day and not have to discuss cancer or treatment, but all of our regular customers know why I have been away so there was no avoiding it.

It began when customer number one. The usually exhausted and quiet cleaning lady started by saying, "I had a hunch that you were sick when you wrote that message on the lyric board a few months ago." As I was explaining to her that the message was not for me, we were interrupted by customer number two.

Grant, a.k.a. Fuck Stick, jumped in with, "I remember that sign—that was really weird. Did you write that because you knew you were dying?"

Cory, unnecessarily, sprang to my defense, "He isn't dying so—"

But I cut him off to maintain some peace.

I tried in vain to explain that the sign didn't pertain to me, but neither customer seemed convinced. Thankfully, the conversation turned to the nature of my treatment and what my next steps were, but as the two customers left I could hear them discussing the sign together.

The rest of the morning was terrible, as well. I came to work for a break from cancer. I willed myself to ignore my depression and get off the couch in search of something better. I thought that the distraction of work would allow my brain a short respite from the tumour-riddled thoughts that dominate my daily life. It didn't happen.

Everyone has been touched by cancer and everyone has a cancer story. When people hear that I have cancer, they immediately reach for another cancer story that they feel I should hear. These stories never have any relevance for my situation and are rarely positive, as most of the central characters are now dead.

"Oh, you know that my father had cancer. Prostate. He fought bravely for almost two years." Some storytellers catch themselves talking about dead relatives and try to cover up. "But Dad died fifteen years ago. They have made great advances since then, you know." Others are not even that aware and will blather on about the end stage of the disease and the funeral details.

I am not talking about a small percentage of self-absorbed assholes that are so insensitive that they tell cancer death stories to a cancer patient; I am talking about almost everyone, including many of the nicest people that I know. Our level of self absorption is just that high. Perhaps I should be more kind and allow that it is difficult to react properly when confronted with shocking news. People want to say something and perhaps they are trying to offer some weird kind of comfort by making cancer seem familiar, but it doesn't work.

Respectfully, those of us with cancer do not want to hear any of your stories.

The signboard in the coffee shop has some kind of spooky connection to the cosmos that is centreed on the day when the message urged people to fix their lives.

As I suspected, the shop owner has a problem. He has cancer and the message on the board was a cry for help. His staff had told the customers and posted a giant "get well soon" card for everyone to sign, so I knew about his condition. Today was his first day back from some treatments or something and I tried to simply welcome him back, but somehow found myself telling him that I knew that he was sick because of his "fix them today" sign. Why do I have to do these fuckin' things? Do I really need everyone to acknowledge how perceptive I am?

Anyway, it seems like his cancer might be fairly minor so the message may have been a bit of a freak out to the initial diagnosis. When I spoke with him today, he seemed pretty grounded and pretty calm. He is still in denial about the sign, but it sounds like he will return to full health.

The cosmic connection went even deeper because, while I was talking about the sign to the shop owner, my old hotshot ECON 101 classmate walked in and joined the conversation. It seems that the "fix your life" message was significant to him too and he said that it had stuck with him ever since the day he read it.

The two of us talked about the message for several minutes outside the coffee shop. It was odd because I know exactly who he is dating back to classes in Ottawa, but he has no idea who I am. I was interested in his views on the sign and asked if he felt compelled to act. He dismissed my question in a manner that suggested that his life was far too perfect to require repair.

While he spoke, I had this vague and strange sense that I was standing in a singles bar. I think that guys like him only have one way to address women and it is rooted in some predatory instinct. It was just after sunrise and I was filthy from a night's work, but I still had the sense that I was being hit on. It wasn't his words—he didn't say anything unusual—but I got a vibe that he saw me as another potential conquest in a very long line of extra-marital affairs.

I have found myself thinking about that freaky sign all day. I haven't really done much to fix the issues that steal my happiness and I was reminded today that the message board had urgency in its message—fix them today. It is a solid reminder that it is time for action.

Grant

The guy that owns the coffee shop has some kind of incurable cancer. Too bad because he seemed like a decent guy. I learned about it a few weeks ago when the café staff was talking about it and then I saw the guy today and briefly talked to him.

I was headed into the office early and stopped for a coffee and there was the owner talking to some hot Asian woman. The amazing thing is that they were actually talking about that weird sign that was in the shop a while ago—the one about fixing your problems today—so I jumped in to tell him how weird I thought the sign was. The Japanese lady said that she knew that he had a big problem when she saw the sign and I asked if it was because he had cancer.

The guy is still in denial because he said that the sign wasn't about him, but was meant for others with problems. No way, pal. If you write that while you are dying, it is for yourself. The guy looks pretty good, so he probably hasn't started treatment yet—the drugs hit you as hard as the disease. He really should be off enjoying his last healthy days before treatment, but instead here he is serving up coffee. That just tells me how bad his finances must be that he needs to sell every muffin he can before he packs it in.

I spoke with the hot woman for a while outside the coffee shop. When I say hot, I mean in a kinky way, not in a beauty queen way. This woman has smaller tits than Ellen and is almost shapeless, but she is an immigrant from a mysterious place and that is intriguing. She was dressed shabbily—I think that she may be coming from a workout before she showers and heads to the office. Anyway, she was very interesting. Her perception of the sign on the lyrics board was perfectly accurate. She saw it as a cry for help from a sick guy.

She said, "I remember thinking that only a person in big trouble would issue a directive to fix your life." I remember thinking that as well and reminded her of the other unrealistic part which was, "fix them today" and told her that most problems were too hard to fix in a day. Isn't it interesting that we had the same reaction to the sign?

I have been thinking about that Asian woman today. If I go to Chicago, I bet that I could hook up with someone like that. The sex would be exotic. These women come from distant lands and she would probably teach me fantastic and mysterious techniques. The conversation would be great, as well. She seems like a highly-educated professional and we would find many shared interests. She also doesn't have her head in the clouds—I could tell just by the way that she understood how messed up that lyric board message was. There was an obvious connection.

Terry

The Beanfest crew has been incredibly supportive since learning about my cancer and now that I am back in hospital for the second surgery, they felt like they needed to do something special so yesterday they organized a cancer fundraiser in the shop. Working with the Canadian Cancer Society, the team arranged to sell the signature yellow plastic daffodil pin of the Society together with real yellow daffodils from a local florist. All of this was done with another giant get well soon card for me, which dozens of customers signed during the day.

It was a very kind and caring thing for them all to do. Cory, Al and Carol dropped the giant card off while visiting me in hospital last night and I expressed how very appreciative of the effort I was and how they made me feel so much better. I completely hid all cynical thoughts that I had about the event from everyone, including Carol. Especially Carol.

My true thought—never to be revealed—is that such fun-draisers are horrid. I don't want to be monstrous about this, but does anyone really feel that we have weakened the power of cancer by raising $238 for cancer research? I understand the concept that "every dollar helps," but in cancer research that rings hollow. The pharmaceutical and biotechnology industries spend billions on research annually. Governments, universities and non-profit organizations spend billions more. Is someone really supposed to believe that buying a $5 daffodil will move the needle?

Maybe it's nerves or sleep deprivation, but this morning, I am still irrationally bitter about the giant card and the dozens of other cards that litter my hospital room. Why do people send these get-well messages? When did this start? When did the evil minds at Hallmark figure out this scam?

No need for unsolved mysteries when you have an iPad and Wikipedia. Nothing is left to wonder these days—within min-utes I knew that greeting cards dated back to ancient China and Egypt and that they were being exchanged in Europe in the 1500s and mass produced by the mid-1800s. I had assumed that greeting cards were the creation of an evil corporation, but it seems that they had a long and positive history. Obviously peo-ple like them or we wouldn't have aisles full of them in the drug stores. So maybe it's just me—I hate them. They are a waste of money and so trite and overly simplistic that they annoy me more than comfort me. Sorry about your cancer, but here is a picture of a puppy so that should even out your karma.

I thought that I could still validate my hatred by digging up a little dirt on Hallmark. I was hoping to find that they operate a conglomerate that includes greeting cards, cigarette manufac-turing and the sale of baby seal pelts. No luck—Hallmark has been a family business for a hundred years and they seem like wonderful corporate citizens. Disappointing.

Do you ever find that there are parts of your own personality that you wish were different? I wish that I didn't need to see the futility in an act of kindness. My mother used to tell me that "It's the thought that counts," but even as a young child I remember thinking that her comment was bullshit.

My parents immigrated to Canada when they were 23 years old in 1963. My father was a skilled draftsman and was drawn to Canada by a family friend who was already an employed draftsman here and helped to secure my father a job before he left China. The immigration went perfectly—no border problem, the job was waiting for Dad, and they found an apartment on their second day in the city. My mother now tells the story of them coming to Canada like we tell stories of how we popped down to Vegas for the weekend—no big deal. But can you imagine how terrifying that must have been for a couple of kids who spoke limited English and only knew Chinese life?

My mom (and dad, when he was alive) is the most grateful and patriotic Canadian you will ever meet, but let's not pretend for a minute that Canada welcomed (welcomes?) immigrants with smiles and open arms. The history of Chinese immigration to Canada is not pretty.

Let's skip the 1800s when Chinese immigrants were brought into Canada with no rights and were sent to work under extreme and deadly conditions in mines or building railways. Start with the early 1900s when the notion of industrious, sober and inexpensive Chinese workers was perceived as a threat to the fat and lazy white worker.

The government fuelled this fear—Chinese are "unfit for full citizenship" reported a 1902 Royal Commission on Chinese and Japanese Immigration. "They are so nearly allied to a servile class that they are obnoxious to a free community and dangerous to the state."

The result of that commission was to increase the head tax charged to Chinese immigrants from $50 to $500, which almost shut off the tap of Chinese immigration, as $500 may have been a million for a Chinese worker. China was the only country subject to a head tax by the Canadian government during that period.

Things changed in 1923—for the worse. That was the year

that the federal government passed the Chinese Immigration Act, which was a law that virtually suspended Chinese immigration, including banning men from bringing their immediate families to Canada. The act also required that Chinese people living in Canada had to register with the government or face deportation. Chinese Canadians still refer to the day that the law passed in 1923 as Humiliation Day. Canadian citizens often followed their government's racist lead and the level of discrimination, harassment and abuse that Chinese Canadians experienced in that era left a permanent smear on our history.

The act persisted until the discriminatory legislation was repealed in 1947—partly in recognition of the Chinese Canadian effort in World War II. Immigration opened up somewhat after 1947, but was never properly developed until Canada completed an immigration strategy initiative in 1967. My parents arrived in 1963 when things were still very complicated and the racism, though not officially endorsed, was also not very far below the surface.

My father wouldn't talk about the abuses that he endured in his early years in Canada, but Mom has told me what Dad went through and it is disgusting and makes you question human intelligence. Some of his hardest days came during the Vietnam War when his coworkers equated my father with the Viet Cong and hurled abuse at him on a daily basis. Somehow, my father kept his blood pressure in check and his head down and just did his work. He did his work well, but of course without recognition or advancement while he watched lesser talents get promoted. I guess that whatever he left in China was worse, but please don't think that he arrived in Canada and experienced Eden.

My father never returned to China, neither has my mother and she says that she has no desire to go back. My brothers and I have all offered to take her, but she refuses. I would assume that she would want to visit her sister, but even the opportunity to reunite with a sister who is only one year younger is not enough incentive.

I know that she misses her sister terribly—their love is deep and strong. What they have is nothing short of a love story.

Beginning in 1963, my mother has written two letters per week to her sister. In return, she has received two letters per week back and neither of them has ever missed a turn. My rough math says that they have exchanged about ten thousand letters—long, heartfelt, soul exposing letters. I have watched my mother cry with elation and sob with despair as she read page after page from her one connection back to her childhood home and family. Very occasionally, we are able to reach my aunt by phone, but when my mother speaks to her sister the conversation is formal and trivial as if they suspect that their calls are being monitored. Somehow the magic is in the letters and it seems that modern technology cannot find a place in their sacred connection.

I will never fully understand and appreciate the life that my parents have led. It has been hard and it has been painful, but my parents only saw the rewards of their work and pain. It is humbling.

Lee

I spent the entire day today with three guys from CleanPro, a prospective buyer of SunRay. Ironside has been on the case for weeks, narrowing down the list of buyers, and CleanPro seems like an obvious choice. They are one of the biggest in the industry, are very profitable, have lots of cash and are expanding aggressively. Last year, they made five acquisitions and they seem intent on beating that number this year.

They make no apologies about the rigid process that they follow in analyzing target companies or the integration process that they use to fold in their acquisitions. Their method is to swallow up these small companies and to immediately install the CleanPro approach to running the business. It seems to me that they are buying the customers and the staff, but they are certainly not interested in anything to do with management. They believe that they have a successful management formula and they invite targets to take it or leave it. It is extremely inflexible. The people that they sent to represent them in this transaction are smart guys, but no one would accuse them of modesty. They have a big company swagger and although they are tactful enough to show respect for the way that we have managed the business, there is an obvious sense that they will change everything once they take over.

Their process certainly is efficient. They will complete all of their assessments on SunRay within three weeks. They allow one week for negotiation on deal terms and then close the transaction three weeks later. One of the junior staff members on my legal team pushed back on the process, saying that the timetable seems overly optimistic. CleanPro assured him that all of the sellers in their last eight transactions managed that timeline and actually seemed grateful to move so fast because the lawyers had less time to rack up big bills. He said it with a smile but he cut the junior lawyer off at the knees and, I admit, I kind of liked it.

"Lee, one reason that we finish these deals so fast is that we believe everything that you tell us. All of the revenue and profit assumptions that we put into our acquisition price are based on your numbers. I mean, we do some digging to make sure that the numbers are fairly reasonable, but we would need several more weeks to assess the final 10 percent of accuracy so we just skip that part."

"My records are very accurate, but I can't believe that you just take my word for it."

"We do because we hold 40 percent of the purchase price back for fifteen months as an indemnification against any errors or misrepresentations. You get 60 percent up front and the remainder in fifteen months when we have enough experience to see if your numbers were right. I wanted you to know this up front, Lee, because we never waver on this arrangement and if you won't agree to it, we can stop now and save each other a bunch of time."

My advisors from Ironside must have known about this provision and should have told me about it before they brought Clean-Pro in to meet me, but I am beginning to learn that their objective is to get a deal done, not to help me. They may be on my side of the table, but they are fighting for the deal itself. All that I said back to CleanPro was, "I understand," which I intended to be a vague way of saying that I am not completely opposed.

CleanPro continued with their pre-packaged list of deal breakers: "We will also need you to agree to a three-year, non-competition agreement—a three-year agreement not to solicit any employees and a three-month transition contract in which you will continue to work in a full-time capacity."

I felt that I should have prepared my own deal breaker list, but I couldn't think of anything. I didn't like the rhythm: Clean-Pro asks, I agree; CleanPro asks, I agree.

I racked my brain and finally came up with something that I felt certain would become a point of give and take in the upcoming negotiation. "And from my side, I will insist that CleanPro take on every cleaning staff employee that I have, no matter their language skills," I asserted with a badly acted seriousness.

"Lee, those employees are your greatest asset, we can completely assure you that we will take on every one of them," was the quick CleanPro reply. I was beginning to feel like the quaint, little, naïve Canadian shopkeeper that the CleanPro guys undoubtedly saw me as.

There is nothing really wrong with CleanPro, but there is no chance that they get what SunRay is about or that they could run it properly. I understand that the CleanPro approach is successful, but I can't imagine how I could sell to them. I created SunRay and I have carefully nurtured it to have its own identity and its own culture. It is a friendly little company run by people who make time for the unique issues of any staff member or customer. It is intentionally not a cold and calculating business—it is the corporate equivalent of my '80s counter culture, musical taste. It's a free-thinking and independent organism. CleanPro is the polar opposite—it is manufactured pop music with no soul.

I just can't shake this image of CleanPro as the Borg from Star Trek. The Borg assimilated all other life forms into their own pseudo life form in an attempt to perfect the race. The Borg was a collective that operated solely for the benefit of the collective with no individualism permitted. Individuals were considered imperfect and the Borg sought to eliminate imperfections by combining individuals into a massive single being that would, over time, eliminate imperfections and become an all-knowing, perfect being.

There are two lines from the Borg that echoed in my head during the CleanPro meeting. The first is the line, "Your culture will adapt to service us." The second line has transcended science fiction and is now part of our everyday language, "Resistance is futile."

Terry

I had been waiting for a few days for the hospital to call to book a results appointment and they finally called Wednesday. I was napping and Carol took the message that we had an appointment scheduled for Friday to learn the results.

When she told me I almost freaked out, "Friday. Oh, my God. What time?"

"Why do you care what time?"

"Just tell me!"

"Your appointment is at noon; you are acting crazy."

"Noon! What the hell does that mean? I have read that doctors never want to give bad news on Friday afternoon—it depresses them for their weekend. Doctors give bad news on Friday mornings and good news on Friday afternoons. Noon is too hard to call—it could go either way."

Everything hinges on this set of results and the range of possible outcomes is huge. I could be declared cancer free in this meeting or I could be pushed to stage four, which makes survival a mathematical long shot. Now we are sitting in the doctor's waiting room and I feel like I may die of a heart attack, so the cancer news may not be relevant.

We stopped by Beanfest on the way over here to pick up coffee for our cancer treatment team. I made the ridiculous comment to Carol this morning that maybe if we brought coffee for the team it would improve the results, so I think that we should stop by the coffee shop. Carol happily accepted my insanity without so much as a raised eyebrow and agreed that taking in coffee was a good idea. Things at the shop were shockingly normal. On this ultimate Day of Judgment, people still wanted decaf lattes and blueberry scones. The staff was bright and cheerful and the music was upbeat—Sharon Jones and the Dap Kings—as if this were just another Friday morning. I guess for the rest of the world it is just another Friday morning.

An older couple just left the doctor's office with obvious tears and the strain of bad news. The doctor is ahead of schedule and we are the only ones left in the lobby—it is only ten minutes to twelve—clearly we are on the "before" side of noon and the only prayer offering that I have for the doctor is cold coffee.

Grant

My Dad called last night as he does every Tuesday night. He does all the talking—usually about his RRSP or his mutual fund performance or some fantastic answer that came to him to unlock his crossword puzzle. I was half listening when he caught my attention by saying that he ran into Alan Weir at the grocery store.

Alan was my best friend in high school and my bandmate in Fried Eggs. I haven't talked to him in years. Dad said that Alan wanted to know if I was coming back to Ottawa for the reunion because they were thinking about getting the band back together to play one or two songs. I told Dad that I would send an e-mail to Alan and that I was not going to go back for the reunion.

I have no desire to reconnect with the high school crowd and the thought of a reunion seems so cliché. I didn't have many friends back then and I have no desire to strike up adult friendships with people who can recall how uncool I was as a teenager.

The thought of a Fried Eggs reunion, however—that's interesting. I don't even own a guitar, but I could pick one up and probably relearn a couple of songs in no time. Not sure how the vocals would hold up, but the music would be great. It would be such a rush to be back on stage—even if it is only for a group of drunken reunion guests—just to feel the energy from a hard-driving band. I could bring Ellen and she might finally understand that I am a rocker and that I have a wild side bottled up. We could always do "Ballroom Blitz" or maybe "Smoke on the Water." Shit, we could even learn something that we have never played before.

If only I could do it. I wish that I could just set my success and status aside for a while and go back to being a rock star. The world expects me to act in a certain way and I can't fight that. I have an image to uphold and as a serious and senior person, I cannot take on another personality. Word would make it back home that I had lost my mind and my image would be damaged. Even worse, I could end up on YouTube for all of my staff and clients to see. I find it so frustrating that the world keeps me in a tight little box when I would really enjoy the opportunity to smash down the walls and rock out a bit.

Part Four

*Time may change me,
but I can't trace time....*

Terry

Dr. Ryder and Carmen were waiting behind a large desk when we were ushered into the office. As Carol strained to pass the coffee across the desk with visibly shaking hands, Carmen ended the suspense by quickly taking the tray from Carol and saying, "Relax, we have good news."

Dr. Ryder jumped in: "Pathology from the surgery shows no signs of melanoma in the nodes at all. We could not have asked for a better result. At this stage, we believe you are cancer-free."

Carol hugged me hard and I could feel her chest heave as she openly wept. I didn't cry and I don't know that I even smiled. My relief came out physically not emotionally. I remember feeling an exhausted relief, like I had just proudly finished a marathon. My breathing was heavy and didn't have the energy to talk. I accepted hearty handshakes from Dr. Ryder and Carmen, who had clearly decided that they could deliver good news before noon on Friday.

I dropped into a chair and put my head down between my knees and tried to catch my breath, "Can I have some water?"

I barely got those words out before I quickly grabbed the trashcan and vomited. Cold cloths, cups of water, mouthwash and more were expertly administered, and ten minutes later I was composed and sitting through the detailed discussion that Dr. Ryder said we still needed to have.

She explained, "While this result is fantastic, there is no assurance that this is over. There is a not insignificant chance that this can recur and that there are some cancerous cells lingering around. I would like to consider an additional treatment step, and I would like to recommend a one year treatment regime of Interferon."

Dr. Ryder had just saved my life, so if she had recommended that I needed to wrestle an alligator once a day for a year, I would have agreed. Carol, however, was prepared and engaged in a discussion of the relative risks and benefits of further treatment. Carol was given a few articles to read and she promised to let Dr. Ryder know our decision by next week. I will do whatever she tells me to.

I still don't feel any joy. I just feel like I want to sleep and perhaps, with this good news in hand, I can finally have that long, restful sleep that has been so hard to find recently. My body is sore and weak, and I feel old. The news invigorated Carol and she seems to have ten times her usual level of energy. She is so outwardly happy and excited that I am embarrassed by my contrasting mood. I should be taking her out for a celebratory lunch and singing from the rooftops. Maybe tomorrow. Right now, I just want a big cup of tea and a blanket on the couch.

CleanPro spent three days in town and by the time they left I felt like I had endured a three-day physical exam of continual poking and prodding. On their last day, we had a meeting without the advisors present—just the two CleanPro guys and me. I was expecting them to run down SunRay as an attempt to beat down the price, but they didn't do that at all. They were extremely complimentary and congratulated me on building a great business. They indicated that they feel that the business has significant value and that they will definitely be putting forward an offer to me. It was a surprisingly nice ending to three mostly unpleasant days.

Today I met with Jennifer who is the advisor that I trust the most. I was telling her how nice it was to hear some recognition from CleanPro and that I almost fell for the seductive approach that the CleanPro guys had used to try to suck me in. I shared my comparison of the CleanPro to the Borg with Jennifer as justification for why I could never agree to work for CleanPro and why the deal would probably never happen.

"I can't be assimilated, Jennifer. I built myself up from nothing and I can't allow myself to become part of some soulless collective."

Jennifer nodded along as I spoke and then simply said, "You're right—it is not time to sell—you are not ready yet."

I objected, "I didn't say I won't sell—I just can't sell to CleanPro. I want to sell to someone who will preserve what I have built and maintain our culture."

"The culture can only stay if you stay, so if that is the most important thing, then you shouldn't sell. Things are going to change no matter who the buyer is. I am not lobbying for CleanPro; I am just telling you that anyone that buys will make big changes."

With some passion in my voice I said, "Jennifer, I do not want to be assimilated. I don't want to be part of the Borg. I have worked too hard to let that happen to me."

Jennifer calmly replied, "They don't want to assimilate you; they want to assimilate SunRay. You will be home counting your money." Jennifer is such a pro. She wouldn't allow me to analyze the possible transaction on a purely emotional level. "When we started this process, you told me that your goals were to gain time and money and so the team has been working to fulfill those goals. If you want to add another goal to the list then we can adapt, but we need a logical approach. Is preserving the culture of SunRay a requirement that needs to be fulfilled before you will accept a deal?"

It sounds silly when you say it out loud, but maybe that is what I want.

"Do you think that I can find a deal that would hit all three goals?" I asked optimistically.

"I doubt it, and I don't think that Ironside would stay involved if you made that a requirement. Lee, this is the deal that you asked everyone to find for you. The deal is not the problem and the buyer is not the problem. Maybe it just isn't time to sell."

Grant

Ellen and I had dinner at Medici's tonight. It is one of our favorites. We have been going there for years so the staff know us well and always sit us at the same table and bring our cocktails without asking. Ellen and I haven't seen each other much, as both us have been travelling for work. I have been away a lot during the week and she has been away the last three weekends so our schedules have not overlapped.

Once we got together things seemed unusually tense. I tried not to act differently, knowing that I am about to sleep around and probably leave her, but I was feeling very self-conscience. I was also strangely aware of her minor annoying habits. For example, despite the fact that we had been going to Medici's for years and have never had a bad meal or seen a speck of dirt in the restaurant, Ellen always meticulously cleans each piece of cutlery with her napkin. It is embarrassing, as I know that the Medici family must see this as an insult.

I have always said that one of the keys to a successful marriage is "don't sweat the small stuff," but now I've found that everything that she does is a cause of perspiration. It is not a one-way street either. Ellen was illogically critical of me tonight, which just reinforced my sense that I have been acting differently despite trying to hide my intentions.

Ellen mocked my selection of Medici fettuccine as unimaginative because I have it most nights we dine at Medici's. I had no counterargument except that it is great fettuccine. Once dinner was served, she ripped into me for tucking my napkin into my shirt collar. Apparently this drives her crazy, although she has never once before mentioned it. I explained to her that this is not considered bad manners and, indeed, it is how Italians eat pasta all the time.

In seeming exasperation, she said, "Will you just not do it this one time?"

Obviously, I wasn't going to remove the napkin and patiently explained to her that, perhaps if I were having the steak or the fish I would abide by her request, but that it was irrational to stain a very expensive shirt when a napkin was at hand.

These are the things that are making it harder to stay with Ellen. From the cutlery polishing to the irrational criticism, I now find so many of the little foibles that I have long accepted to be agonizing. I hope that I can maintain my patience. I am not ready to pull the plug on Ellen yet, but the day is coming soon.

Terry

Carol and I finally had our celebratory post-results lunch today. I told her that I was taking her out for lunch for her birthday, but she countered with the idea that she would take me to lunch because I was finally getting off the couch and ready to celebrate. In the end, we agreed that we would go to lunch together and she promised not to talk about cancer if I agreed not to tell the restaurant staff that it was her birthday.

Carol quietly turned forty-nine yesterday. She would not permit any celebration—not even a funny hat while the waiters sing happy birthday—and she admonished me for buying her a gift. She is not one of those women who lie about her age or go to outrageous extremes to fight aging. No cosmetic surgery or Botox, but I know that she also doesn't want to shine a light on her age.

She is totally realistic about the inevitability of aging, but she battles valiantly to hold age at bay in her own subtle ways. Carol works out almost every day and is strong and fit. She eats well—not fanatical trendy diets, just sensible stuff with allowances for the odd dessert or cheeseburger. She always pretends to be just throwing on any old thing as she dresses, but everything she wears is worn with planning and purpose. She dresses casually and well. No sweat pants, no ball caps. She knows how a cool forty-nine-year-old should dress and doesn't wear things intended for sexy twenty-year-olds.

She wears very little make-up, but you seldom see her without any. She colours her hair, but not dramatically—I suspect that she is hiding grey but I have never inquired. It seems to me that she has figured all of this out—battle aging but don't deny it.

In the end, we did talk about cancer over lunch. Carol explained the pros and cons of Dr. Ryder's recommendation to take a year of treatment. I listened and asked a handful of questions. My final question was, "Am I going to have the treatment Carol?"

"Yes you are. Top up my wine, please," she smiled back to me.

I will have the treatment—this doesn't seem like the time to disagree with my doctor (or wife).

We finished a bottle of wine over lunch and we were both feeling drunk, so we cabbed home. There was a day when I could have a few drinks at lunch and have a productive afternoon, but those days are gone. One drink at lunch and my day is done. I once read a biography of Winston Churchill and remember marveling not only at his political and literary achievements, but also about he lived such an incredibly productive life while being almost permanently drunk. It seems that throughout his most prolific eras, he had a daily drinking routine that included a bottle of wine with breakfast, champagne and wine with lunch, champagne and wine with dinner and, of course, nine of his signature scotch and cigar combinations throughout the day. Can you imagine achieving anything on that diet?

By 2:30 p.m. Carol and I were sleeping lazily on the couch as the afternoon drifted by. That was a nice day. Goodbye cancer; happy birthday Carol.

My mother is officially panicked now that I have dumped Gord. She had a soft spot for him and I now know that the two of them had been conspiring behind my back for a while. I am sure that she feels that the time that she invested in Gord was wasted.

Mom has always complained about my single status, but her rhetoric has always seemed somewhat playful as I think that she always felt that I would find a husband eventually. Now that Gord is gone, I think that her concern about my pending slide into old maid status is reaching frantic levels.

Yesterday she actually said, "You will dry up as you get older, so you have to find a husband before you dry up." I don't know that she actually meant vaginal dryness, but that's where my mind went and I was too freaked out to ask her to clarify.

She has enlisted some help and today I received a rare call from my eldest brother. He takes his traditional responsibility as the eldest male (even if he is younger than me) far too seriously, so I wasn't surprised to receive a lecture from him on the importance of marriage. His marriage and family are cardboard cutouts of a perfect suburban family and he is constantly updating me on his marital status: "Sixteen years of marriage and I love her more today than ever before."

Of course my brother loves his wife—she is a throwback wife who makes June Cleaver look like a renegade. She treats my brother like a king and he treats her like his servant. She is small and thin—in appearance and personality—which is just what he wants. If that works for him that's fine, but I can't imagine how he would think that I want what his wife has.

I didn't take the bait for argument today and instead simply thanked him for his concern. I assured him that I would let Mom know that he called, which was enough for him to decide that his mission was complete and he signed off.

I have actually had a few first dates over the last month, but no second dates. I really don't think that I have the bar set too high, but no one has come close to crossing the bar.

I hate to say that all the good ones are gone or that the pool isn't very deep at this age, because I am still in the pool and I don't want to be labeled as one of the sorry leftovers. Everyone who is dating at my age feels that they are one of the few good catches left and they are just hoping that they can find just one other rare, good leftover.

Single people in their forties generally have baggage. Many, if not most, are divorced—maybe more than once. That isn't a deal breaker for me—I can accept that matches aren't always what they seem and that people change, so I don't rule out divorced guys. However, maybe telling me long stories about your ex and your divorce isn't a great first date idea. Two of my recent first dates gave me detailed accounts of why their divorce was not their fault. What am I, a family court judge?

Another first date was a life-long single, like myself, but I found myself working like a detective to find the fatal flaw that kept him single—convenient of me not to hold up a mirror. It actually wasn't hard to find this guy's flaw. We met for coffee and early on he asked if I liked mixed martial art fighting. I told him that I had seen it on TV a couple of times, but didn't like it at all. I thought that I had given him a nice signal to move the conversation on to something else, but he instead gave me an education on the sport while working in as many other overtly macho things that he could think of to impress me. I don't remember him asking about my interests at all. He was too busy selling himself to listen. So, no sale.

I have no qualifications to give dating advice, but I think that I could help people on first dates by letting them know to relax and just be yourself. We are all going to see the real you sooner or later, so if you pretend to be someone else on date one, I can only assume that you are not interested in an honest relationship. I also don't want an elaborate first date in which a guy tries to impress me by spending big money and trying to show me how much fun he can be. At my age, I am really just looking for someone whose company I will enjoy on the sofa on Tuesday nights for the rest of my life. So, maybe, let's just sit and talk on our first date.

I am just not sure how and where I will meet the man of my dreams. I feel like I have exhausted all of my personal contacts and I think that my friends are tired of setting me up as none of their efforts have succeeded—and I am sure that they think that I am to blame. I have dabbled on the online dating sites, but I am not a believer. I am trying to stay positive, but lonely and positive are words that just don't go well together.

Grant

Jack and I did promotional work for the firm in New York earlier this week. We flew in to Newark and visited two pharma companies in New Jersey before heading into Manhattan for a late afternoon meeting with Pfizer. Jack ran the show and is a great front man for the firm in general and me in particular. I find it very hard to brag about my own expertise and experience so it is much better to have Jack explain my attributes to prospective customers to save me from appearing arrogant. The one-two punch of Jack and me working together is impossible to top and our business chemistry is perfect. At least, it has been perfect but it is possible that our business relationship could change after learning what I learned that evening.

Let me back up. At the end of the day, Jack and I went for a drink. It was his selection, but ironically we ended up at The Stone Rose in the Lincoln Center—the scene of my recent failure. We were enjoying a beer and talking about more promotional visits that we could do together when we were interrupted by two fairly attractive women who asked quite directly if they could join us for a drink.

I was about to reach for chairs for them when Jack spoke up: "No thank you ladies. My friend here is happily married and I am gay so I think that we will pass."

Just like that. "I am gay," he says, then returns back to our conversation without acknowledging his shocking comment. It seemed impolite to return to his comment so I let it go and a few minutes later, Jack noticed the time and while apologizing for sticking me with the bar bill, ran off to a dinner engagement.

My world was spinning. I ordered another beer and made a couple of calls to colleagues who confirmed that Jack has been openly gay for as long as they have known him. It seems that his status was known to everyone but me. I wasn't sure how I could have missed it, but after a second solo beer, it began to come clear for me. I have always respected the work that Jack does and his deal-making skills. He is a highly skilled professional. That level of respect blurred my vision. I didn't see what are now some pretty obvious homo traits because I wasn't looking for them. I was thinking about him strictly in business terms and not based on his sexual preference. I will be able to fix that from now on and, with this improved vision, I will be able to assess whether it is appropriate to keep working for Jack. I have never had a gay boss before and I don't know how that will affect me. Will clients see me as gay by association? Perhaps I will need to have a stronger hand in managing the team to compensate for Jack's limp wrist.

Ellen, of all people, was really insightful on the issue of Jack's gayness. I explained what I learned in New York to her and she said that while she had never heard that Jack was gay, she had always assumed that he was. It's unbelievable that she would never have shared that belief with me, but that's Ellen.

Anyway, Ellen asked me a series of questions about my office relationship with Jack and it was obvious that our working relationship is great. She asked if I could go for post-work cocktails with Jack or dine with him and I feel confident that I can. When I said that my fear was that he may hit on me or that I may get drawn into an uncomfortably gay scenario, she assured that Jack would never let that happen. Jack has had plenty of chances to make advances towards me and never has. He has never invited me to any of his non-work social events nor introduced me to gay friends. It just occurred to me that he has a "partner"—I remember him saying that—so I guess he has a steady relationship. He probably will not change his behaviour because, as Ellen pointed out, Jack has assumed that I always knew his disgusting secret.

I can probably make this work for now. Having a gay boss is just one more reason to consider making the big fixes that I have been considering. It may be time to take another look at Chicago and that move would let me dump Ellen, my gay boss and the Leafs in one motion.

Lee

I spent Saturday afternoon in Jennifer's office reviewing the offer that had arrived from CleanPro on Friday night. The offer was good—$14 million. It was strangely gratifying to see a big dollar figure placed on my creation. I imagine that artists must feel this way about their paintings—they are too artsy to admit that the money is important, but even if you don't want the money it is the truest measure of how much your work is appreciated. Art critics and the gallery crowds can lavish praise at an artist, but when someone is willing to back up their praise with a cheque—now that's a fan.

Other than the dollar figure, there was nothing to like about the CleanPro offer. The language was harshly one-sided and gave them rights of indemnification and other protections should my business be anything less than what I claimed it was. It was obvious that this was a standard document used by CleanPro for all of their acquisitions and that they would probably not accept many, if any, changes to the text. I shouldn't have expected anything different from the Borg.

We spent a couple of hours reviewing the document together—not so much to make modifications, but mostly so that Jennifer was convinced that I fully understood everything that the offer contained. We focused on the details and the language subtleties and never acknowledged the elephant in the room because we never discussed whether I should accept or not. As we broke for the day, I told Jennifer that I was heading home to do a little soul searching that I would accompany with a nice bottle of red.

Jennifer insisted that instead of spending the night alone that I join her and a group of her women friends who were attending a charity dinner that evening. I truly was dreading the pending decision point, so I thought that a girls' night out was a great diversion.

The dinner was a stuffy fundraiser for some disease that I didn't care about, so I was only too happy to follow Jennifer's sign to escape before the dessert was served. Four of us from the dinner group ended up at the hotel wine bar and Jennifer ensured that our wine glasses never emptied. Over dinner, I had mentioned that I was contemplating selling my business and that brief reference was enough to cue these women that this would be our discussion topic for the evening. Our chatty foursome included Cheryl, who is a partner in a big accounting firm, and Martha, who owns a rapidly expanding chain of retail stores—soap and creams and such—and they are both long-time friends of Jennifer.

I was extremely comfortable with these women—the wine probably helped—and so, surprisingly, I found myself reading off the pros and cons list that I had been carrying around in my head. Jennifer found herself defending CleanPro when the others jumped on board with my attempt to demonize them by reminding the group that this was a sale and not a merger.

"Lee has to help them for a few months after the deal, but that's it—she will never have to think of them again."

The accountant was moved on behalf of my staff and felt that I was their great protector and had a duty to stay with these women. "They can't succeed inside a big company Lee. You need a buyer that will protect them."

Martha took the argument to a higher level by questioning my motivation to sell. "Lee, this is the wrong time to get out. You have too much momentum. You should buy companies, expand, dominate. We need women entrepreneurs like you to become role models. If you sell now, you will never have that chance and you may feel unfulfilled at home."

We were well into our second bottle and the messages from Cheryl and Martha were coming in loud and clear. Jennifer stayed neutral and had been quiet for a long time. I told the other two that I thought that they made a lot of good points, but to be fair, Jennifer made a lot of good points in favour of why I should sell to CleanPro and I needed to fully consider the advice from all of my friends.

Jennifer saw an opportunity to leave her neutral position. "All of the advice that I have given you has been as a legal advisor, not as a friend. As your advisor, I have told you that CleanPro has made a good offer and that no buyer is going to run the business the way that you have. If you want to sell, this is a good deal. Now—as your friend—in an off-the-record conversation, I do not think that you should sell. SunRay is a special company and it is in your heart and it is so much of who you are that you shouldn't sell. SunRay will die without you—not financially, but spiritually—and that would be a sad thing."

Jennifer looked relieved to have unburdened her personal view on the transaction. As the moment of silence after her soliloquy grew, she became a little embarrassed by her minor sermon. I thanked her and the others for their advice and changed the subject. Looking back on the night, I am thankful for the opportunity to open up to three smart women and listen to their views. They raised a number of points that I simply had not considered and armed me with more criteria to help make the decision. However, I am still feeling a certain kind of loneliness and the pressure of having to be the one that makes the ultimate decision.

Grant

I am not gay, but last night I hugged a gay man. I hugged Jack after a night out in San Francisco. I hugged a gay man in San Francisco!

Jack and I spent Thursday and Friday on a marketing tour of the biotechs in San Francisco and we have really hit our stride as a promo team. We finished in South San Francisco at noon and headed to the airport for our 2:00 p.m. Air Canada flight. After three hours of delay, during which the incompetent AC staff told us nothing, they finally announced that the flight was cancelled.

It was too late to make any other flights that would get us back east, so we were stuck. Rather than spend the night at an airport hotel, Jack insisted we head into the city and make a night of it. Did we ever! We took rooms at the Hilton in the financial district, which was close to our dinner spot. Jack selected the Slanted Door in the Ferry Building. They don't take reservations, so we were three martinis deep before we sat for dinner. Dinner was great. Jack ordered for both of us—stuff that I would never select, but everything was amazing.

We talked about work for the first couple of hours together, but the more we drank the more personal the conversation became. As I recall the conversation, I am astounded by what we shared with each other. Jack told me that the driving force behind his relocation was that his partner had taken a new job and given Jack the ultimatum to move with him or end their relationship. Jack didn't want to move, but he is in love and wants to stay with his partner, although now he is beginning to resent the pressure that his partner put on him and is feeling weak for caving in. I remember at one point slurring out a bit too loudly, "Fuck this guy, Jack. You can do better."

I told Jack all about Ellen—how cold she is, how annoying she has become and how insensitive her breasts are. I told him that I planned to end my monogamy and to eventually leave my wife. Jack said that I reminded him of a couple of friends who talk bravely about big changes but never pull the trigger. He astutely identified that I had been contemplating these changes for quite a while without doing a single fucking thing. He questioned whether I had the balls to make changes—a gay guy challenged my manhood!

With the sobriety of morning, I am struck by how right Jack was. It has been months since I identified my problems but I really haven't done anything about them. You could call it analysis paralysis, but I am afraid to take the first step that leads me away from my wife or job. I will find the courage soon.

Terry

I had been easing my way back into Beanfest over the last few weeks by working half days, but I was physically ready for more so I intended to start back full-time this week. I was really looking forward to the normalcy of a routine workweek. It never happened.

My mother died yesterday—a massive heart attack in the grocery store parking lot. All she bought was two jars of marmalade. I imagine that she was the last living marmalade customer, so that industry probably died along with her. When my sister called, she was completely distraught, so I just jumped in the car and sped down the 401 back to Ottawa. During the drive, I replayed the conversation with my sister several times and decided that I had only imagined a snide undertone telling me that I had been warned that Mom would die before we reconciled.

The day was a struggle. My sisters and their families were overcome with emotion and poured it out as if I were there to absorb it all. I was able to offer comfort and help stabilize the chaos because I truly wasn't feeling any great sadness. My relationship with Mom ended when Dad died a few years ago, so her death initially seemed like some inevitable event—almost like an expected final step. For over forty years we enjoyed a loving relationship, but somehow I was unmoved by her death. Outwardly, I think that I conveyed an appropriate amount of grief, although I have never been able to cry on command. I felt like an actor in a movie and when I finally turned out the lights in my sister's guest room for the night, I was half expecting to hear a director call out "….and cut."

If yesterday was a struggle, today was pure hell. I had lunch with both sisters so that we could discuss funeral arrangements and such. But, inevitably, the conversation turned to my strained relationship with Mom. My sister Pam surprised me by saying that the fact that I saw Dad's suicide as an act of bravery was isolating me from Mom and my sisters.

"What? We all saw it as a dignified and brave way to go, didn't we?"

Angie, my little sister, simply said, "No. Just you did."

I reminded them that during the period after Dad died all that Mom talked about was how noble it was of Dad to go out on his own terms and how admirable it was that he saved them all from watching him waste away. "She even went on about it during her speech at the funeral."

Pam countered, "She might have believed that in the midst of grief or maybe she just said what she thought that people wanted to hear. But she was angry. We were all angry. Maybe we still are a bit. Dad got to decide how he would leave us and what our final moment with him would be, but what did we get? Nothing. We didn't know that he was going to leave. He said goodbye to us, but we didn't say goodbye to him. We didn't get to say we love you, we didn't get to ask for some final fatherly guidance, we didn't get a hug. He should have told us."

"Mom felt betrayed and she stayed angry for a long time. You kept Dad up on a pedestal and Mom just couldn't tell you how she felt and made us promise not to tell you how we felt. It was hard to keep that promise, but we always thought that you would figure it out. When you were cold to her, she always assumed that you knew how angry she was at Dad and that you resented her for it. She tried to explain it to you many times but you just wouldn't listen."

I had no idea that any of them felt this way. Maybe Mom did try to explain it to me, but I certainly didn't hear it. If I had heard her view, I am certain that we could have talked it over without anger. Maybe I was even feeling a little of what they were feeling—Lord knows, I wish I had a little more time with him and that I had an opportunity to say goodbye. Mom and my sisters thought that he should have shared his plans before he killed himself, but I don't know if that was possible. Telling someone that you are planning suicide sounds like a cry for help, not a respectful goodbye.

There are a lot of possible reasons for the way that I felt towards Mom after Dad died. Maybe it was an odd part of the grieving process, maybe I blamed his decision to commit suicide on her and maybe I was misdirecting anger at my father towards her. It no longer matters. What matters is that I lacked the will and courage to confront the issue and instead just accepted it as a failed relationship. I feel so foolish for stubbornly not investigating my feelings. Why didn't I fix this when I had the chance?

My mother is dead and I missed the last few years with her because I was too confused to realize that I didn't have any reason for shutting her out. Worse than that, she died thinking that I was angry with her and that I didn't love her. All the grief that I faked yesterday is a chest-crushing reality today. I am stunned—maybe in some kind of state of shock. I feel like the blood has drained out of my body—I am pale and weak and nauseous. I can't seem to put together sentences and I certainly can't think straight. Among all the feelings of grief and loss I also have to deal with simply feeling foolish.

I wish that my mother had died slowly. Not a slow, painful death—just a slow death. Maybe a prolonged illness would have been the impetus for me to thaw our relationship.

My mother and I never said I love you to each other and we never had deep emotional conversations. We never talked about her hopes and dreams and the things that she gave up on. We never talked about religion, her beliefs or her thoughts on death. We never talked about what made her happy or why it always seemed that just beneath the surface she was a little sad. If she had died slowly, we would have talked about all of that. Maybe we would have talked about Dad. Maybe not.

Maybe we would have just talked about the weather and movies. Either way, we would have talked. Damn.

Track 36

Terry

I stayed in town for a couple of days after the funeral. Ben flew in for the service, but needed to get straight back to school. Carol drove down and she and I stayed at my sister's for a few extra nights. We took care of all the practical things during the daytime—met with the lawyer, engaged an agent to sell the house, sold Mom's car, and filed death certificates with all of the appropriate authorities. Evenings were reserved for heartfelt conversations and crying.

We retraced the days between Dad's suicide and Mom's heart attack and my foolishness felt like a knife twisting in my stomach. The greatest pain comes from knowing that I can never repair my mistake. My sisters offered comfort, but I can tell that a little frustration still exists because they had been trying to tell me for a long time before mom died. Carol raised the question about the blasted "fix your life" sign and wondered aloud if, on some level, I knew that this issue with Mom was the problem. The sign was certainly not written because I had cancer, and I know that I wasn't thinking about my mother when I wrote the sign, but maybe on some subconscious level there was a connection between the sign and my mother. I clearly missed an opportunity to fix a problem that lingered for a long time. For a guy who was bold enough to chastise his customers about their troubled lives, it is painful to admit that I needed to repair parts of my own life. Now the opportunity is gone.

My sisters and I shared recent events in our own lives, including my cancer and recent surgeries. I think that I made another mistake by not sharing with them while I was in the middle of treatment. Sure they are overly dramatic, but they really do love me and would have been incredibly supportive. I, again, feel foolish about that one.

On the last night together, we sat at the dinner table for hours and drank wine and cried. We were in a downward spiral that was going to reach a depressing crash as we focused our conversation on our mistakes and regrets with Mom and Dad. It would have ended badly if not for my brother-in-law Phil.

Maybe Phil was less drunk than the rest of us, but he somehow sensed that we needed to change focus and he quietly slipped away from the table. Shortly after, we heard the sounds of three children singing, "Hey, hey, we're the Monkees" coming from the next room. Conversation froze and we ran to the living room to see the Super 8 film that Phil had set up—my sisters and me, ages six to eleven, singing the Monkees theme on a backyard stage that Dad had built. Mom and Dad danced crazily at the front of the stage, while Uncle Richard tried to hold the camera steady through his laughter. That grainy black-and-white film was great medicine for all of us. We watched two more film rolls and talked into the night about all of the great times we had as kids and how lucky we were to have the parents we had. It was a great finish to the hardest few weeks of my life.

Lee

Now that I am single, I find that all of my battles are in my head. At least when Gord was around I had a lover and a foe. Without him, I am left with masturbation and silently debating both sides of every issue with myself.

I keep looking for my guy, but I am worried that I won't find him. I do believe that there is someone for each of us, but what if I was late for the random meeting that the cosmic power pre-ordained in a not-at-all random manner? What if I am always an aisle away from him in the supermarket or wherever it is that we are destined to meet? I feel like the more that I want this to happen the less likely it is to happen. From minute to minute I switch from, "Relax, don't force the issue, love will find you" to

"Holy shit, I'm forty-three-years-old, go find him, hurry!" My anxiety is probably obvious to anyone that I meet, so there is a decent chance that I will terrify my one true love before he gets to know me.

Want evidence of my anxiety and perhaps a sign of the impending apocalypse? I agreed to go on a date that was set up by my mother.

My mother heard about a friend of a friend who has a nephew who recently moved into town. He is forty, single and Chinese—and therefore perfect in my mother's eyes. I think that I shocked her when I agreed to meet the guy, but really I had nothing to lose. Geez!

I have never dated a Chinese guy or anyone who looks remotely like me. When I was young, I think that I avoided Chinese guys to spite my parents. As an adult, I don't think that I went out of my way to date or not date Chinese guys, it just never happened.

I agreed to meet Edward for dinner on Saturday night at a new restaurant that I have been hoping to test out. He was already seated at the table when I arrived, but rose to meet me, as I was escorted to the table. I was surprised to find a muscular man of at least six-foot-two. He has a strong jaw, bright but soft eyes and was dressed impeccably in a bold pink shirt and a black sports coat. He had the look of a sophisticated financial executive and, as I sat, I was expecting to hear about his recent transfer from Wall Street.

Instead, I learned about his recent move from Beijing through slow and heavily accented English. My mother conveniently neglected to tell me that Edward wasn't just new to town—he was new to the Western Hemisphere. Despite the linguistic challenge, the conversation was really interesting. Edward is an engineer and worked inside the Chinese government for a short time, but spent the last ten years working for a large engineering firm in Beijing. He was recruited by a Canadian firm and he accepted the position with the expectation that his firm and/or country would deny his emigration. When no one objected, he found himself on a plane and, only six weeks later, having dinner with me.

He explained that the Canadian company has continually

flattered him regarding his engineering skills, but that he under-stands that the reason that he was hired was to help win Chi-nese contracts for his new Canadian employer. He said that he was happy to play the game and help win contracts because it was his ticket to get into Canada. Impressive insight for some-one who was supposedly locked up in communist darkness in Beijing.

We talked for a long time about politics and business, and the dessert had arrived before we had a chance to talk about family, friends, plans and dreams. We will have to save that for the sec-ond dinner. We shook hands at the restaurant door and I entered my taxi. I had a nice night, but I could feel a headache coming on and couldn't decide if the cause was straining to understand Edward's English, the wine or maybe some rare emotion that I was feeling. It could be a fantastic journey to fall in love with a man with such different perspectives and experiences—there would be so much to learn about each other. I went to bed won-dering if I had just experienced love at first sight and whether there was a special spark between Edward and me.

This morning, I woke with a clear head and now feel a little silly about my juvenile feelings at the end of last night's date. I had dinner with a handsome, intelligent and interesting man. That's nice, but that's all that it is. Edward is a project. He was raised in communist China, speaks broken English and will take a very long time to adapt to our culture. I don't need a project. I am smarter than that and need to rely on my brain, not suc-cumb to my childish impulsive heart that wants to find love.

There will be no second date and I will let my mother know that he is a nice man but not my type.

Grant

I have had a couple more attempts to pick up women, but they have all ended unsuccessfully. In hindsight, these events were not completely unproductive because I've learned a great deal and have now had a chance to analyze my game.

An objective assessment of myself in comparison to the other guys in the bars has been revealing. It hurts to admit it, but

physically I am below average. I am not fat and ugly, nor am I fit
and handsome. I am ordinary looking at best, so that isn't going
to draw women to me. I am also not the life of the party and I
know that small talk is not my thing. I have tried to outplay the
other guys at their game by dressing in a cool and casual way
and trying to nail the great opening lines—without any success.

Now I have finally analyzed this challenge like a business
case and identified my strengths and weaknesses. I accept
that I will not win on looks, sense of humour, or small talk.
More importantly, however, now I recognize that I have areas
of competitive advantage over these bar guys: I am successful,
powerful and wealthy—I have my career. Some women will be
attracted to that, so I have to get that info to women early if I
am going to use it as an effective lure. Obviously, not all women
are going to be attracted to my assets and even fewer are going
to be willing to jump into bed with me, but I only need one (per
night) and I am certain that I can find her sitting on a bar stool
in most places.

I just spent $3,000 on a new Armani suit, shirt and tie, and I
feel powerful just putting the new clothes on. I have meetings in
Chicago tomorrow and tomorrow night I will see if there is any
magic in this suit. My plan is to set up at the bar, order the most
expensive scotch available and maybe make a few fake phone
calls so that all eavesdroppers can get a sense of my importance.
Then, I will simply wait for the ladies to come to me. The role
of a big businessman is in my repertoire and should come to me
more easily than the smooth-talking fun guy that I have tried to
play. I am finally going to be in my comfort zone and using my
strengths. I am totally excited to have a plan that could work.
I have been looking for something to get me out of the analysis paralysis and I think that this plan is the little push that I
needed. Once the plan is in motion, all the dominos will fall.

Track 37

Terry

While packing up Mom's belongings, we came across a small notebook that belonged to Dad. It contained a series of famous quotes that Dad had seemingly collected over the years and written out in long hand. It was not something that I would have expected of my father, but it was interesting to review the quotations that he found striking.

There were two quotes that he had highlighted in yellow with a note in tiny script beside each of them that read, "Love this one." The first was a phrase that I had heard him say before and I love it as well: "Whether you think that you can or you can't...you're right."

The second one was attributed to Fulton Oursler, which was a name that I didn't recognize. According to Google, he was an editor and author and perhaps Dad knew of him because he wrote some of the pulp fiction detective stories that Dad liked. Anyway, the quote is: "We crucify ourselves between two thieves: regret for yesterday and fear of tomorrow."

It seems like my father is still trying to teach me a few things years after his death. I copied out the quote in my own long hand version and it is now folded neatly into my wallet where I hope that it will serve as a reminder of how I want to live my life.

I recognize the mistakes that I made with my mother and family, but I cannot change them or fix the past. I am not brushing the mistakes under the carpet, but I am letting go of the guilt because it will just eat away at me if I don't forgive myself.

Similarly, I have lived for several months in fear of the future and I again see no benefit from that and will try to let go of the fear, as well. I know that cancer is scary, but worrying about things that I cannot control is fruitless, so I will try to ignore the fear of the big C. I will not fear the future.

Introspection can become unhealthy. I am not suggesting that I will live a shallow life or that I will not recognize the consequences of my actions. I simply think that there is too much self-inflicted anxiety in my life, so I will try to eliminate the crucifixion.

No regret and no fear. I don't know that it is realistic to shed regret and fear completely, but I love the objective.

My mother clings to the notion that listening to CBC Radio is part of her responsibilities as a good Canadian. As a result of mom's devotion, I often catch the second-hand smoke of the burning CBC corpse. The local drive-time shows are so horribly underfunded that the producers are thrilled to devote ten-minute segments to the upcoming hospital bake sale or the raging controversy of kids playing street hockey. I feel bad for the people associated with these shows because they just don't have the resources to be better. My big complaint is saved for the national shows like *Definitely Not the Opera*, *The Vinyl Cafe* and *The Debaters* that are not interesting, not funny, and so patently nerdy that I am certain that CBC has not earned a single new listener in a decade. They should simply stick to being a news service or maybe a "news plus" service because *As It Happens* is worth keeping.

In the car late this afternoon, my mother insisted on listening to CBC because Rex Murphy's show was starting. Mom sees Rex as a wise elder who has the pulse of all Canadian issues. I see Rex as an elder as well, but one who pines for the past and is frustrated by all the changes that have happened to his beloved country. During today's show, Rex seemed ever so subtly surprised by how clearly spoken and articulate a caller was who had recently emigrated from India and was contributing to his show. He didn't say anything and maybe I imagined the slight pause and the "well I'll be darned" tone of his reply, but I think that it was there. When Obama was elected last year, many thought that his presidency would signal the end of racism, but instead his election is one of the most common sources of subtle racism that I hear. I often hear comments about how well-spoken he is or how calm and respectful he is—and you know that the unspoken second half of that sentence is "for a black guy."

In fairness to Rex, that soft and subtle polite racism is everywhere. I am not even sure that racism is the right word because it connotes hatred, which is not what I mean. I just think that there is an expectation that people have based on someone's ethnicity, colour, orientation, and more, and when the expectation is foiled, it creates surprise. I see it on strangers' faces on a daily basis—mostly because I speak without an accent, but also because I can be loud, foul-mouthed and decidedly not worthy of the Chinese stereotype.

It must be worse in other countries where the immigrant population is a smaller percentage of the population, but even in Canada we struggle with this issue. You would think that we would be past this by now based on how many immigrants we have. Do you know that over 20 percent of Canadians were not born here? That is a big number—way bigger than that of any other G8 country. In the big cities, it is even higher and Toronto sits at almost 50 percent foreign-born citizens. What astonishes me, however, is that people like Rex seem to think that this is a new phenomenon and that Canada only recently opened its gates to immigrants. The truth is that the highest level of foreign-born Canadians that we have ever had occurred in 1931, so immigrants have been essential to the Canadian story to date and will be critical for our future success.

The bright future that immigration supports for Canada is in strong contrast to homogeneous countries like Japan, which have well under 2 percent of their population as foreign-born. Japan has a big problem ahead of them based on their demographics. A friend sent me an article about the declining Japanese population. It is forecast to drop from the current 127 million to 87 million by 2060. There are two factors contributing to the problem: the first is that the Japanese don't fuck enough and have one of the lowest fertility rates on the planet; and the second is that they don't take in many immigrants. When they reach that forecast of 87 million people, 40 percent of them are forecast to be over sixty-five years old, which leaves a very small group to drive the economy and care for their elders.

So you see, we are in a better position because of our relatively open door. Now, let's begin to squash the stereotypes and prejudice. We have made progress on violent racism, we have made progress on hate-based racism and now it is time for us to begin working on the polite racism that is still too common.

Track 38

Lee

One of my earliest memories is from a family summer vacation when I was probably four or five years old. I don't recall the specific location, but my father and I were walking along a beach at a lake. The sun was bright but low in the sky and the reflection in the water was shimmering bright as we walked hand in hand.

My father stopped and told me that he had proof that I was the most special person in the world.

"Do you see how the sunray shines in a straight line right at you? It's like a bridge across the water for you. It means that you are the sun's favourite."

He urged me to run down the beach a bit to see what would happen and when I did, I was in complete wonder that the bridge of light was repositioned to end on my tiny feet. Wherever I ran the sun followed.

"Look down the beach. Is the sunray pointing at the people way down the beach?"

It wasn't—it missed them by a few hundred yards. And I knew that the only way that they could see the sun bridge would be to stand next to me. I marvelled at the sun's special recognition of me.

My father thought that I was special—most fathers feel that way—but my father gave me proof. Long after my father died, I kept this memory with me as a strange source of confidence and drew on the memory to name my company. I still feel a tingle whenever I see a sunray glistening off the water and reflecting up directly at me. I had a special connection to the sun and to my father, and to be favoured by both of them gave me an inspiring sense of purpose and a certainty in my direction. Maybe this connection is why I never felt the need to fit in—I was always comfortable doing things my way and I have always been unconventional. Maybe this connection is why I will listen to advice, but not necessarily follow it.

Maybe this connection is why I sold SunRay to CleanPro this afternoon.

I think that I made my decision to sell the other night when Jennifer said that SunRay is so much of who I am. She meant that to be a point against selling, but it struck a chord with me. I had been mingling my identity and the identity of SunRay throughout this process. I am not going to be assimilated into the Borg. SunRay might be, but, truly, once I cash the cheque I have no say in what happens to the business. Most of my employees will not notice the change of ownership, especially since they didn't know that I ever owned it! They probably always thought that the owner was some big, faceless company like CleanPro. The employees don't need my protection—in some ways, I actually wish they needed me more than they do, but at this moment it is beneficial that they are not dependent.

If you arbitrarily hate all big companies, then you would hate CleanPro. They probably started out as a quaint little company like SunRay, but you can't become their size without standardization and structure. The guys that represented CleanPro today may not be the most entrepreneurial guys that I have ever met, but they really know what they are doing and what they are looking for in acquisition targets.

They are confident guys—bordering on cocky—but they are not evil. They are just big and have a standardized process. Truthfully, I kind of like these guys and I think that if I were a big company buying up small ones, I would have the same kind of process that they have. They are smart and I think that they are smart enough to see that treating staff and customers well is critical to success.

After weeks of internal struggle, I have no reservations about my decision and I am positive that I have made the right call.

Not everyone would have taken this path, but I have always had a unique self confidence that started on that day with my dad on the beach. As I pulled out of the parking lot, I instinctively turned up the volume on the stereo and smiled as Michael Franti's music poured over me. Franti was singing the incredibly happy "The Sound of Sunshine" and it made me smile and sing along as I turned for home confident in my decision and feeling the warmth of my father, the music and the sunshine.

Grant

I was on the very edge of the abyss. One more step and my life would have changed forever. My new bar plan was good. It seems that women are attracted to wealth and power—at least some women. Fortunately, my night in Chicago was an awakening and resulted in the first bit of clear thinking that I have had in months.

I followed the plan—I was wearing my new power suit and went to the bar and ordered an expensive scotch. Then, as I ended my first fake phone call, a woman immediately sat next to me and introduced herself. Her name was Deidre and although she was somewhat attractive, she strangely reminded me of expired milk. Although her jewellery was a bit tawdry, she was dressed well so it wasn't her appearance that gave me the sense that there was something past ripe about her. I politely bought her a drink and as we talked she put her hand on my upper thigh. It was clear that I was minutes away from the one-night stand that I was seeking—victory was within my grasp.

Except that for some reason I didn't want it—or her. When I explained to her that I was here on business and married, she was gone before I finished my sentence.

A second woman moved in five minutes later and although this one was prettier, she was sloppily drunk. The alcohol had removed any inhibitions that this woman had and she immediately told me that she had no intention of going home alone. Her version of playing hard to get was to tell me that she hadn't yet decided if I was the one that she would take to her bed. I got rid of the second—and then a third woman—and went to my room alone.

I went to the bar as a character—a wealthy, successful, powerful businessman. Over the course of the night, I realized that this is not an act—it is who I am. I also realized that as a man of such significance, I could not stoop to a level that is beneath me. I cannot have one-night stands with dirty and defiled women—it is beneath me; it is not dignified.

I almost lost my way for a while. The short-term lure of leaving my wife, changing jobs and moving to a new city were all shiny thoughts that distracted my attention momentarily. Men are weak and we can get pulled into a course that is initially thrilling but not sustainable.

Life isn't a movie. You don't party all the time, have your dream job and surround yourself with friends. That kind of happiness is fleeting—a couple of good months, but then things bust up and you have bad years after that. Then a couple more good months and more bad years. In that Hollywood life, the highs are too high and the lows are too low. What I have is level.

Lou Gehrig is remembered as one of the greatest baseball players of all time. He was called the Iron Horse and he held the record for most consecutive games played. He was a constant presence for the Yankees and showed up for work every day for 2,130 consecutive games. He played in an era with Babe Ruth when players smoked and drank heavily and kept women in every city. But Lou never went in for any of that wildness. He was a serious and stoic all-star. He was on an even keel and he achieved greatness through consistency.

The lesson that Lou gave for the rest of us was that you can never take a day off. You can't create a code for living and then decide to violate your own code once in a while. You can't be a good man but cheat on your wife occasionally, or steal a little from your boss. To be a good person you have to uphold a standard as an everyday commitment—just like Lou.

Lou's record was broken decades later by Cal Ripken. In Cal's generation, baseball players were rock stars with limos and bling. Cal was a serious and stoic all-star. While other stars endorsed shoe companies and energy drinks, Cal did commercials for milk—white milk.

Get your heads out of the clouds and accept life for the long journey that it is. I don't have love like some romance novel because it doesn't exist. I have Ellen and that is good enough. I have a job that I am good at and, like Gehrig and Ripken, I never miss a day. It isn't my dream job, but it is good enough.

When the coffee shop guy wrote the sign that said "fix them today," he was imploring people to get on this road that I am already on. He wanted people to find this even rhythm that I have. I wasted a lot of timing thinking about what I should change in my life when it turns out there was nothing for me to change after all. I am already a serious and stoic all-star.

Terry

There is an old song by Glen Campbell called "Gentle on My Mind." That's Carol. That's the best explanation of why I love her. That is probably too boring and underwhelming to ever say to her, but I think that it is the highest compliment that I could offer. My heart doesn't race when I see her and my breathing doesn't shorten—the opposite happens—I relax, I feel comfort, my mind eases. Isn't that wonderful? It is a gift that she constantly gives me and I am grateful.

And before you knock me for a Glen Campbell song, you should go back and listen to the brilliant lyrics. It's too bad that a great song like this gets buried under the stinky stigma of "Rhinestone Cowboy" and other horrible songs that Campbell recorded.

Anyway, Carol is not here tonight and therefore my mind is not at ease. I am edgy and crabby and restless. Carol is on a three-day shopping trip in New York with her sister. I can't be upset that she is away because it was my idea. I thought that she would enjoy herself and the opportunity to get away from our emotion-packed life.

I also suggested that she time the trip to occur while I was in treatment. These treatment days are medically simple, but I hate them and I am not pleasant to be around during them. The treatments are not physically painful, but I find them mentally taxing. The procedures are a harsh reminder that although I may feel well, I am still a cancer patient. I have to go to the cancer centre, meet with cancer nurses and doctors and sit around with other cancer patients. I want to move on from cancer, but it is impossible to move on if you have to hang around a cancer ward.

When I was between treatments today my nurse sent me back to the waiting area and offered this chipper advice: "Many of the people in the waiting room are at earlier stages of their disease than you and they would probably really appreciate hearing from you about how successful your treatment has been."

She's probably right, but screw them and their stupid cancer—I am sick of talking about cancer and I don't want to become part of the cancer cheerleading squad. I just don't want to be that guy who is upbeat and smiles a little too much while he assures everyone that they will be fine. Most of them won't be fine.

Told you that I was in a crabby mood.

I will return for more treatment tomorrow and I offer no promise of improved demeanour.

I miss Carol.

Part Five

*Life goes on, long after
the thrill of living is gone.*

Track
39

Lee

Parenting can be so frustrating. Jackson and I had a great weekend together. As we drove home from a movie on Sunday night, I told him how pleasant it was to spend time with him and that it was great that we could enjoy adult activities together. He has really become a mature young man and he is usually pretty self-sufficient and respectful.

Then, just as I was starting to feel good about him, he regressed. This afternoon I came in around five o'clock to find Jackson playing video games on the couch with a friend. That's his first crime. He didn't ask to have a friend over and told me that he was going to go straight home from school to study for a test tomorrow. My blood pressure rose when I saw the slice of pizza resting on the sofa and the grape juice spill on the carpet. When I asked Jackson to explain, he said that he didn't know how to clean it up so he decided to wait until I got home. Then for toppers—and to impress his buddy—he said, "I don't know why you are making such a big deal. Just relax." Strike three!

I lost it—absolutely lost it. Jackson's friend left quickly and Jackson received some clear and loud instruction on how to clean the mess. While he cleaned, I packed up the video games into a box that he may never see again. He was then lectured at length about how he may speak to his mother before being sent to his room. Once he got to his room, I burst in and gave him a repeat performance of my angry lecture. When Mom came home a few minutes later, she found me screaming at Jackson as he sat in stunned silence on his bed. Mom led me away, calmly made me some tea and began to make dinner.

It wasn't my best moment. He made me mad and he deserved to be punished, but I shouldn't have snapped.

It has been a tough day. I am still working off my time with CleanPro and when I came home this morning, I just couldn't fall asleep, so I am certainly sleep deprived. Then, this afternoon I went to a funeral and although I did not know the deceased very well, it was an emotional service that drained me further. I was down to my final frayed nerve by the time I encountered Jackson, but I need to be a more consistent parent no matter how bad my day has been. Now I need to grab a quick bite and get ready to go to work, which I can already tell is going to be a struggle.

When I finished my shift this morning, I went to grab my cappuccino but the shop was closed. I read the notice on the door announcing that the proprietor, Terry North, had died from complications with his cancer treatment and that the funeral was this afternoon. I don't know why I decided to go—I didn't really know Terry, but I felt an incredibly strong need to go to the funeral.

The service was so emotional and I sat in a packed room full of strangers and cried. If this funeral were for a close friend or family member, I would have tried not to cry. Why do we do that? You are clearly upset, so let it out! But when we are in the midst of people who know us best, we have to hide who we are and fight back tears. Today, in a room full of strangers, I had no identity to hide and no loved ones to hide it from, so I quietly but openly cried and cried and cried.

Terry's wife appeared to be in shock. I sensed that she felt that an error had been made—some kind of miscalculation—and her eyes scanned the room as if looking for a supervisor to plead her case with or with whom she could file her complaint. The son was stoic. He never let go of his mother's hand, he never shed a tear and he accepted condolences with quiet dignity.

The young kid, Cory, who I see every morning was crushed. His devastation was palpable and his broken heart was visible. I wanted to hold him and tell him everything would be okay, but

I don't know him well enough to hold him and I certainly don't know if everything will be okay.

It seemed that Terry had the cancer behind him, but he was apparently undergoing some follow up treatment when he experienced a complication that quickly led to a heart attack, and he died immediately. It was supposed to be routine stuff, but I guess that none of this stuff is truly routine, and today I learned that chemo is very hard on your heart. His wife was on a shopping junket in New York and apparently got the news in a call from the doctor while she was sitting in a Starbucks in Times Square. I can't even imagine.

From my early-morning brief encounters with Terry, I sensed a kind soul. What I learned from his friends who spoke during the service was that this was a man who knew and liked who he was and recognized that he was living a blessed life. One of his friends said that Terry died with no regrets and that he knows that Terry wouldn't change a thing if he had his life to live again. The reference to change reminded me of that strange sign that Terry posted in the coffee shop about fixing your life. When I heard that he had cancer, I felt that the sign was a cry of help for himself, but after hearing about Terry today, I wonder if he was really just imploring others to seek what he knew that he had.

I think that he wrote that message during a moment of frustration, but ultimately from a privileged place. He was trying to provide some inspiration to his little corner of the world and I think that he succeeded. It is remarkable how often I thought of that hastily scrawled plea on a coffee shop message board while contemplating the biggest decisions of this past tumultuous year.

His timing was impeccable for me—I hope that it helped others as well.

Grant

This is the third straight day that the coffee shop has been closed. It's not really a big deal because the Starbucks is only a couple of blocks away, but I just really like the cappuccino at

Beanfest, not to mention that the staff at Starbucks are clueless. They can never get my order right and they are always trying to upsell me things that I don't want. I remember when Starbucks first opened, it was like some kind of odd commune that just happened to sell coffee. Now, you can really feel the corporate presence—you feel like you are on their assembly line when you step in. While that efficiency would normally appeal to me, it strangely doesn't work for coffee shops and I prefer the hippy style of Beanfest.

I just wish that Beanfest had a bit more business sense because then they would be open today. Apparently the owner died a few days ago and they have been closed since. I understand showing respect and closing for the day of the funeral, but three days? Come on. And it's not like the guy got hit by a bus—he has had cancer for a while. So if they didn't plan for this eventuality, then they really are the fruitcakes that I suspected they were.

I remember seeing the owner in the shop not so long ago and it pains me that a guy who knew that his days were numbered had to spend those days schlepping coffee. On the other hand, maybe he was one of those crazy optimists that thought that he could outrun cancer—cancer is a speed demon and can never be outrun.

Every business, no matter how big or small, needs to have a succession plan and it seems that the coffee shop didn't. This is basic stuff—business 101—and yet I always see businesses that can't get it right. I hope that they make the right choice when they pick the next guy to run the place. They need to keep the same process and bean supplier, or whatever the secret is to making great cappuccino. This is a weird thing to go on about, but I just really love a great coffee and it would be terrible for me if this guy's death forced me back to Starbucks permanently.

Lee

My mother is never shy to tell me when she disagrees with my parenting decisions, which is why we started this very happy evening with an argument. I asked Jackson and my mother to join me for a drive out to the airport to pick up a friend who was coming in from Vancouver for the weekend. The flight wasn't scheduled to land until 10:00 p.m. and tomorrow is Friday (a school day), so my mother was incredulous that I was letting Jackson stay up so late and that I was taking the night off work. I just put my foot down and insisted that Jackson was coming, so she finally backed down and sulked into the passenger seat.

I explained to Mom that we were picking up Cathy Avery, who was a friend from high school who now lives out in Vancouver. Cathy was the girl who introduced me to Pink Floyd and weed—not surprisingly, at the same time. My mother never trusted her and felt that she was a bad influence, so I had to reassure Mom that as a grown woman and mother of three, Cathy was not going to lead to my damnation.

Jackson wasn't any happier in the back seat. If he was going to be allowed to stay up late, he wanted it to be for extra TV or video game time, not to meet one of mom's lame friends. I bought him ice cream at the airport and that seemed to even the scales.

Sometimes people can be linked at the heart or maybe the soul even if they don't see each other for years or decades. There is a bond in these relationships that is impervious to time or distance and when time and distance are removed, the reunion is visceral.

I nudged and budged Mom and Jackson to the front of the crowd waiting near the terminal exit doors. I could barely control my excitement. Jackson and Mom were agitated and annoyed by my enthusiasm and by the jostling of the crowd around us. We waited as wave after wave of passengers exited, met their loved ones and headed home. Where was she?

The crowd was down to a handful of expectant greeters when the doors opened one more time and a little old Chinese lady tentatively stepped forward. My mother gasped and my aunt set down her suitcase and smiled. Five seconds passed with my mother standing frozen beside me and my aunt smiling brightly ten feet in front of us.

Jackson cracked the freeze frame: "That lady looks just like you, Gran." And with that, my mom embraced the sister that she hadn't seen since 1963, as tears streamed down their cheeks and mine.

Although they have been apart for most of their lives, the connection between them is magical. Perhaps exchanging ten thousand letters has something to do with that, but their unity is at a cosmic level. When they eased their embrace, they instinctively moved their heads beside each other and softly and quickly spoke mouth to ear to each other for several minutes. I later learned that this is how they whispered to each other every night during their childhood. Two elderly women holding each other and whispering their love to each other was one of the most beautiful things that I have ever seen.

I don't know if this was too much for Jackson to take in, but someday he will be able to reflect on this moment and hopefully appreciate the significance of family.

I am heading to bed now, but the two sisters are curled up together on the sofa talking and laughing and crying. It took months of planning and deception to get my aunt here without my mother knowing about it, but it was worth it—this is truly one of the happiest moments of my life.

Grant

I think that I have explained my feelings about Ellen clearly. There have never been violins or fireworks in our relationship, but she has been an adequate wife. Over the last year, I have strongly considered leaving her, so obviously I am not dependent on this relationship. If I am honest with myself, I have stayed with Ellen because it seemed like the right thing to do and because leaving her would be undignified. Staying married is on my path of least resistance. I guess that I was just never able to pull the trigger that would end our marriage.

Ellen, on the other hand, shot our marriage right between the eyes.

It seems that she has been seeing this guy in her west-coast office for months. Most of her weekend trips for work had nothing to do with work and were, instead, just part of her deception—so that she could be with this asshole. It is all very unseemly and I am disappointed in her. She didn't have the decency to tell me before she started something and she had the audacity to continue screwing around for months while staying married. She was still having sex with me on occasion while she was stealing away for weekend romps with the other guy. The little whore just wanted to get laid at home and on the road. I am just disappointed that Ellen lacked the class to do this the right way. Rather than coming to me to say that things aren't working, she runs around like a filthy slut and has an affair.

The truth is that Ellen isn't perfect—not even close. To be honest, the real reason that I married her was to have kids and then once we were married we learned that she couldn't have kids. The one thing that women were made for and she couldn't even do that. I tried to accept it; I did accept it. But why? She is a failure as a woman and I should have recognized that and moved on. Physically, she has no shape, uneven eyes and insensitive nipples; emotionally, she is closed; and intellectually, she is not able to keep pace with me.

Ellen has left me, but it is really not a big deal and I am not even slightly upset about it. In fact, it is probably the best thing that could have happened to me as my decision to stay with her or not has been made for me. Look, this is what I really wanted, so no one should feel bad for me. I am now an eligible bachelor and whether I volunteered for the role or was forced into it doesn't change the fact that I will now be happy and single. Without the repellant wedding-ring factor, I will now be able to find success with women and play the field for a while. Yes, this is definitely a good thing.

Grant

I've got a meeting with Tim and Bobby at eight o'clock, so I left the house early to give me time to stop for breakfast on the way in, but the traffic is brutal so I'll be lucky to have time to grab a coffee before the meeting. Tim Baker, Robert Stewart and I are now the trio that runs the entire operation. Tim and Bobby have been in their role for years, but I joined them a week ago after Jack Cash left to join JP Morgan in San Francisco. Tim and Bobby seem very pleased with the stabilizing presence that I bring to this role and we are busy planning out the macro direction for the firm, which is why we have these twice-weekly meetings.

The official story regarding Jack is that he wanted to take our life sciences practice into a new direction with greater emphasis on emerging technologies, including green tech. Jack said that he couldn't find common ground with Tim and Bobby on this direction, so he thought that it was best to move on. I am certain that the real rationale has more to do with Jack splitting from his partner—from a personal stand point, why would he stay here when he could take a great job in the queerest city on Earth?

In the end, Jack was a minor blip for the firm, but now they have it right and I am in charge, as it should have been from the start. This is the job that I have always wanted and that I have worked for my whole life.

Ellen is staying in a hotel for another couple of weeks until her transfer is complete and then she will move west. All that she has taken so far are some clothes, so it still feels more like she is away than really gone. Maybe when the moving van hauls away all the furniture, it will feel permanent. Her attitude is hard to explain. She is cross and short with me as if it were my fault that she had an affair. A decent person would be embarrassed and apologetic, but she is neither. I have made several attempts to make things easier for her. I offered that she could stay in the guest room instead of a hotel until the transfer—rejected. I offered to write our own separation agreement so that we could save legal fees—rejected. I even offered that I could service her sexually until she transferred—violently rejected.

With the new role at the firm, I have really been too busy for any deep self-assessment, but I actually think that I am fine. It's time to get on with my new plan. I finally have the power at work and the freedom at home. This combination should allow me to live the life that I have always wanted. I intend to work hard and play harder.

I had worked two of the three months that I agreed to for Clean-Pro, but other than cleaning, there was nothing for me to do. I think that the CleanPro guys felt a little awkward about having a multi-millionaire cleaner on staff, so they called me on Tuesday to say that I didn't need to continue cleaning and that they considered my contractual obligations fulfilled.

We agreed that I would take the opportunity on Thursday night to roam from building to building so that I could say thank you and good bye to all of my—I guess that I should say their—staff.

What I didn't know was that the CleanPro team had decided that it was time to blow my cover as friendly manager Lee and instead reveal to all SunRay employees that I was the company founder. On Wednesday evening, every employee received a beautiful little storybook printed in both English and Mandarin called Lee's Story. The booklet told a beautiful story of how a single mother of immigrant parents had the courage to start her own business. It went on to describe my vision to hire fantastic people who would make the customers happy. They described the protection that I offered to the employees who may otherwise find it difficult to find good jobs in an English world and they talked about my self-taught business skills. The booklet was full of pictures of me and various staff members and had a beautiful picture of Jackson and I on the final page together with a pledge from CleanPro to uphold all of the values that were critical to Lee. There may be some exaggeration regarding my skills and smarts, but it was a touching and humbling gesture.

The booklet distribution on Wednesday turned my Thursday into a magical night. I had no idea that the cleaning crews knew that I was leaving or that I was the owner, so imagine my surprise when I walked into the first office and was gang-hugged by a crew of five. There were cheers and tears and heartfelt thanks were given and received. There were so many small gifts given to me that I had to drop them off at my car before heading to the next building. I repeated this scene dozens of times throughout the night and each stop got better and better.

I didn't start this business with the goal of creating safe and decent jobs for immigrant women. I just needed the fuckin' money and this was the best way to get it at the time. The rest of the story evolved—it was never designed, but I wasn't going to let the truth interrupt the gratitude that the ladies showed me in such a magnificent way.

The sweetest recognition that I received was from the final immigrant lady that I saw before ending my day. My mother had cooked up all my favorite breakfast foods and was just setting them onto the kitchen table as I came home. She had placed a copy of Lee's Story in the centre of the table and a simple, homemade card that said, "I am proud of everything that you have become —Love Mom."

Grant

I must admit that being single requires some adjustments. On a practical level, I need to manage the house, which I have never done. Ellen had been gone for a month or so when I came home one night and flipped on the Leafs game, only to find that I had no cable service. When I called to complain, I learned that Ellen had historically paid the cable bill via online banking, but had recently removed her bank account from the cable company records and, voilà—no Leafs game for me. The same was true for utilities, phone, property taxes, and everything else. I spent an entire Saturday setting up accounts and waiting on hold for customer service.

After a few weeks, it occurred to me that our house cleaner wasn't coming anymore. A couple of weeks later, I realized that the gardener was AWOL as well. I thought that I would never say this, but I am sick of pizza. I haven't had time to shop or cook, so I have been living a take-out or delivery diet for weeks. If I don't order mushrooms or pineapple on my pizza, I would never have any fruit or vegetables. None of this stuff is hard, but en masse there is a lot to do to keep this place running.

I guess I can admit that I am a bit lonely, as well. I don't miss Ellen, but I also don't like a constantly empty house. This house is very quiet, but in all of that quiet I must also say that this house makes some very disturbing noises from time to time. It can get a little creepy to be here alone, night after night. Some-how, I never noticed this on the nights when Ellen was just away on a trip, but it is really eerie now.

I will find a new rhythm soon. I need to get on top of my

diet, exercise and, most importantly, find the time to get out and meet new people. There is a lot of positive change coming my way, but I am just not quite ready for it. I am going to join a gym soon, but I need to do some exercise at home and run a little before I start because I really don't want to begin as the worst guy in the gym. Same goes for dating. Once I get a handle on my new role at the firm, I will have the time and energy for a social life. In the meantime, I am going to work harder than ever before and enjoy the freedom to do whatever I want in my personal time.

I have been in my new role for a few months, but I have to admit that this job is killing me. The timing for me to take over could not have been worse, as the biotech portion of the business is in its biggest slump ever. The west-coast firms, including Jack's group at JP Morgan, seem to be reeling in new deals, but we can't land anything. We are ice cold. I have been doing my part. I have been pitching for business in every city that we have ever sourced work from, but the business is just not coming in. I am getting heat from Tim and Bobby, but I think they know that this is beyond my control and that we just have to ride this out until the tide turns. They called an off-site breakfast meeting for the three of us tomorrow morning, which is very unusual. In this organization we usually reserve such off-site meetings for opportunities to fire people in a place where they will not cause a scene. Obviously I am not getting fired, but they must have some big news for me if they are going to such lengths to get away from the office.

The job stress has left me little time to open up my new social life. Ellen is gone and so is 90 percent of my furniture, but she left me the big-screen TV and a recliner, so I don't need much else. Although I am officially single, I still don't find sufficient dignity in the bar scene, so I have stayed away. A colleague set me up on a date once he heard about my single status, but it didn't go anywhere. My date was a single mother of three and her life sounded so burdensome that I wanted nothing to do with it. I will start dating others soon, but there is no rush.

I am glad that I survived the drama of the last year and I guess that all things happen for a reason. God only gives you what you can handle.

I lived through my own near infidelity, Ellen's real infidelity, a brief period with a gay boss, and serious contemplation of a move to Chicago. In the end, I righted the ship and it feels good.

I did take one more step toward being happy. This morning I was in the coffee shop and they were playing "Smoke on the Water" and it got me thinking about Fried Eggs, so when I got to the office I sent an e-mail to my old band mate Alan to see if he wanted to get together to jam. I am going to stop by a music store on the weekend and buy a new guitar.

Funny how that coffee shop always gets me thinking. I must admit that I was surprised to see it reopen after the old owner died. It really didn't change much and the music is still as prevalent (I figured out the lyrics clue this morning, which was pretty cool). The dead guy's widow now runs it in partnership with this cute little Korean lady. Both ladies and the other staff members now know me well and always say "Good morning, Fancy Shirt" or "Good morning, FS" whenever I come in. I admit that I like that familiar touch.

After years of finishing work as the sun rises, I now begin my workday in those same pre-dawn hours. I have maintained the connection between my father and the sun, as I am now a half partner in a thriving little coffee shop called SunRay coffee.

I never said that I wouldn't run another business, but even I have to admit that I never thought that it would be so soon after selling the cleaning company. When an opportunity feels so right, however, you have to listen to your heart and this was a perfect situation for me.

Terry North's widow reopened Beanfest shortly after Terry died, but a combination of grief and inexperience was not helping the business. My dear friend and former colleague, Anne, had a heart-to-heart with new widow, Carol, one afternoon when Anne was in for a late-lunch bowl of soup. The ever-thinking Anne immediately saw a mutually beneficial arrangement for Carol and me.

Carol is still grieving, but now she has a business partner and is slowly beginning to heal. Putting together a deal to buy half of the business from her and work out an operating schedule was really easy. We both work mornings and we alternate the lunch service. It is a perfect part-time role for me in my "retirement." During our discussions, I raised the issue that I feared would be the stickiest and said, "Carol—would you be open to changing the name of the shop?" She surprised me by laughing and said that the biggest argument that she and Terry ever had was over the name because she absolutely hated Beanfest. She loved my suggestion of SunRay and said she was certain that Terry would have loved it as well. That's a nice thought.

My life has changed in so many ways this year: I sold the business that dominated my life; I split with a long-time boyfriend; I added my aunt to my happy household; and I became a partner in a coffee shop. I have no man in my life, but I have this very positive feeling that he will come into my life soon. I have fixed most of the things that needed repair and I think that my happiness will be visible to the man of my dreams once I meet him.

I love that we have maintained most of the coffee shop traditions and this morning I had my first opportunity to select the lyrics that went up on the board for our little contest. I recently learned that this dilapidated message board with the terribly faded CHEZ 106 logo had been Terry's prize possession. I needed to uphold the significance of the board and honour the man with my first selection and I think that I found lyrics that would have pleased Terry and that were truly important to me. I wrote the simple words "No dress rehearsal ...."

I had just finished writing out the line when my old ECON classmate—a.k.a. Mr. Fuck Stick—walked in and came straight to the message board. He read the line and smiled in a sadly soft way and said "What is it with this board? I signed my divorce papers last week and yesterday I got fired from the only job that I will ever be good at, and somehow this message board knows what I need to hear. Time for me to fix things."

There really seems to be some magic left in the message board and throughout the day I had several customers comment on how meaningful those Tragically Hip lyrics are to them—no dress rehearsal, this is our life.

Acknowledgements

It turns out that I love writing as much as I love reading. Let me begin by thanking my reading partner of twenty-five years, Grace Newman, who was an early reader of this manuscript, for her encouragement and friendship.

Jackie Lefebvre began as my editor but quickly became my writing coach and friend. I appreciate her wit, guidance and patience in correcting my many embarrassing mistakes.

Sincere gratitude goes to Ron Corbett and Ottawa Press and Publishing for continuing to believe in the importance of supporting local writers. Thank you for the dozens of suggestions that significantly improved this work and for the crash course in publishing.

Thank you to the Tragically Hip for years of wonderful music and for the lyric that inspired the book title.

In thirty years of marriage, I have lost count of how many completely crazy ideas I have had that immediately earned the support of my wife, Christine. Her enthusiastic reaction to my idea of writing propelled this project idea into reality. My sons, Mathieu and Nicholas, are inspiring and continue to challenge me to break out of my comfort zone. I simply couldn't have a better family.

Finally, thank you for investing your time to read No Dress Rehearsal. In the writing world, reviews by readers are extremely important so I would be grateful if you would invest just a little more time and submit a brief review to a web site such as Amazon.com or Goodreads.com.

Thank you.

About the Author

Ken Newport joins the literary community with his debut novel *No Dress Rehearsal*. A successful entrepreneur who has co-founded several life sciences and biotechnology companies, Ken is a family man and avid traveller who draws upon these experiences in his writing. As a life-long fan of bands from The Beatles to Arcade Fire, Ken is also a music enthusiast and terrible guitar player. He understands the importance of music and how it brings people together and it is no surprise his debut novel draws on his love of music.

Ken and his wife Christine have two adult sons, Matt and Nick, and half a dog, Stella. They live in Ottawa except for those cold months when they can be found hiking in warmer climates.